Detective Chandler's expression never changed.

But Bailey wasn't surprised that his pupils had dilated when he finally lifted his head. They stared at each other, and she thought, *Don't let him want me.* It would be incredibly unrewarding for him. Men...well...she didn't do men. Not anymore.

When she looked at him again, his crooked smile sent a jolt through her.

"It's a pleasure to meet you, Hope Lawson," he said.

"Just...don't call me that."

"All right." There was that astonishing gentleness again. "Bailey it is. Unless you prefer Ms. Smith?"

"Either is fine." She retreated to her side of the table. "Thank you, Detective."

"If you're going to be Bailey, I'll be Seth."

The flutter in her belly wouldn't let her respond to that. *We're not friends,* she wanted to say, but she didn't want to alienate him, either.

This desire to cling to him was completely unfamiliar to her.

Dear Reader,

You see the articles about girls or women rescued after being held captive for months or years. There'll be occasional follow-ups that include photos in which she is now stylish and remarkably poised.

Studying them, you'd never guess what she endured. But on the inside, I doubt she is anywhere near as together as she appears. I can imagine many excellent reasons for her to develop a facade to hide the damage she still feels.

But as I contemplated this story idea, I started thinking about an adoptive sister who was always aware her role was to substitute for the "real" daughter who had been abducted and was still mourned by their mutual parents. And what about Hope Lawson, who finds her way home after twenty-three years to discover her parents replaced her with another little girl, whom she is now supposed to call sister?

What a cauldron of family conflict on top of deep emotional scarring!

The heroes? Not hard to figure out for each of these sisters what man would both draw and threaten her on an emotional level.

Minor confession: sometimes I'm a little ashamed of myself, being intrigued by such painful experiences. I mean—romance writer here.

But I tell myself a love story isn't really about the romantic stuff, it's about the terror of making an awful mistake, about being hurt and healed and ultimately believing in another person.

I hope you find Hope aka Bailey's miraculous homecoming moving, and will be on board for Eve's story in my October Superromance, *In Hope's Shadow*.

Janice

USA TODAY Bestselling Author

JANICE KAY JOHNSON

Yesterday's Gone

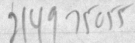

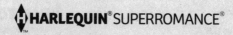
HARLEQUIN® SUPERROMANCE®

Recycling programs
for this product may
not exist in your area.

ISBN-13: 978-0-373-60920-8

Yesterday's Gone

Printed in U.S.A.

An author of more than eighty books for children and adults, *USA TODAY* bestselling author **Janice Kay Johnson** is especially well-known for her Harlequin Superromance novels about love and family, about the way generations connect and the power our earliest experiences have on us throughout life. Her 2007 novel *Snowbound* won a RITA® Award from Romance Writers of America for Best Contemporary Series Romance. A former librarian, Janice raised two daughters in a small rural town north of Seattle, Washington. She loves to read and is an active volunteer and board member for Purrfect Pals, a no-kill cat shelter. Visit her online at janicekayjohnson.com.

Books by Janice Kay Johnson

HARLEQUIN SUPERROMANCE

The Baby Agenda
Bone Deep
Finding Her Dad
All That Remains
Making Her Way Home
No Matter What
A Hometown Boy
Anything for Her
Where It May Lead
From This Day On
One Frosty Night
More Than Neighbors
To Love a Cop

The Mysteries of Angel Butte

Bringing Maddie Home
Everywhere She Goes
All a Man Is
Cop by Her Side
This Good Man

A Brother's Word

Between Love and Duty
From Father to Son
The Call of Bravery

SIGNATURE SELECT SAGA

Dead Wrong

Visit the Author Profile page
at Harlequin.com for more titles.

Other titles by this author available in ebook format.

CHAPTER ONE

DETECTIVE SETH CHANDLER tugged his tie loose and undid the top button of his white shirt as he settled into his chair. Testifying in court that morning had demanded his best getup.

Unfortunately, the detective bull pen was upstairs in the aging building that housed the county sheriff's department. In winter, they appreciated the scientific fact that heat rises. A heat wave right before the Fourth of July weekend meant today they sweated, as they would off and on all summer. A couple of window air-conditioning units rattled away inadequately. Doing the job meant tuning out physical discomfort along with the noise of too many conversations around him.

No surprise to find that, in his absence, over a hundred new emails had arrived. He was being inundated with "tips" right now. That's the way it was when you got word out there. Most were worthless, but once in a while, he found wheat among the chaff.

Within moments, he was engrossed. He skimmed, deleted, opened the next.

I saw this feature online about missing kids and how you can draw pictures so everyone can see what they look like once they grow up. One of them looks EXACTLY like this girl I knew in high school.

His phone rang. He gave it an irritated glance and saw the call was internal, which meant he couldn't ignore it.

Attention still on the open email, he snatched up the phone. "Chandler."

I bet she is the one you're looking for. Her name wasn't Hope, but I'm totally positive. Except you've got her hair wrong in the picture, and her nose, too.

"A Mrs. Lawson is here to see you," said the desk sergeant. Seth heard a murmur in the background. "Karen Lawson," the sergeant amended.

"Buzz her in."

Most police departments across the nation had grown cautious. Locked doors kept visitors from barging in to confront an officer.

Seth rose to his feet a minute later when the door opened and a slender, middle-aged woman, who reminded him a little too much of his mother, appeared. It wasn't the general physical similarities that had him making the comparison, but rather the sorrow that clung inescapably to both women.

Clutching her purse, Mrs. Lawson cast a shy look at the men and women too engrossed in phone calls and computers to so much as notice her presence. She wound her way between desks, her expression apologetic when she reached him, even though this wasn't her first visit and wouldn't be her last. He made a real effort to call and let the Lawsons know what he was doing, but she'd obviously read advice to families of missing children that told her to be persistent. Never let them give up, the advocates often advised.

Ironic, in this instance, when he was the one who had taken the initiative to revisit a case so cold, he'd had to defrost it.

She rushed into speech. "I know I shouldn't be bothering you, Detective, but Kirk asked last night if I'd heard from you and since I happened to be downtown I thought you might not mind…"

He interrupted. "Of course I don't mind. Please, sit down."

She perched on the straight-backed chair next to his desk, her blue eyes fixed anxiously on him. Damn it, he was disturbed every time he saw her by the resemblance the age-progressed drawing of her long-missing daughter had to her. There was a reason for that, of course; part of the art of age progression was using photographs of the parents as children and adults. And there was no denying that daughters did sometimes grow up to look like their mothers.

"I'm getting a lot of calls and emails," he said gently, "but nothing has jumped out at me yet. I *can* tell you that the photo of Hope at six years old and the artist's best guess at what she'd look like now have been getting wide currency. It's prompted some newspapers to run features on the fate of missing children like her, but I'm especially hopeful because those pictures are appearing everywhere on the internet. People are intrigued." It was the pretty young white woman syndrome, of course, but he'd use anything that worked. "Given her age now—" assuming Hope Lawson had lived to grow up, of course, which they both knew to be unlikely in the extreme "—odds are she and her friends spend a lot of time on social media sites. If she's alive, I'm optimistic that, sooner or later, someone will recognize her."

God, he hoped he wasn't giving this woman false hope. He suppressed his natural wince at his choice of word, as he too often had to these days. What a name for a kid who'd been abducted!

"Thank you," she murmured, and he knew damn well she hadn't even heard the "if she's alive" part. He'd been deluding himself that they both knew her daughter was likely dead.

From the beginning, he'd made it clear that he was fighting the odds here. Hope Lawson had vanished without a trace twenty-three years ago.

The 99.9 percent likelihood: she was dead. He'd set out to take advantage of improved police and medical examiner cooperation to find a match with an unclaimed body. Elizabeth Smart and Jaycee Dugard were the rarities, not the norm. But despite all his warnings, Karen Lawson wanted to believe that by some miracle he'd bring her daughter home alive and well.

A sheriff's department in a rural county like this one didn't have anything like a cold case squad. He was allowed to indulge his interest as time allowed, however. He'd found closure for a few people, mostly by giving them a chance to put a headstone on a loved one's grave. Not a happy ending, but better than suffering through a lifetime of wondering, as Karen and Kirk Lawson had.

Her gaze left him to fall on his bulletin board, where he'd tacked copies of the last school picture taken of little Hope Lawson and of the recent rendering. Other photos shared the space: a sweetly pretty wife and mother who had either suffered a terrible fate or fled from her husband and preschool-age children two years before; a toddler who'd disappeared from a picnic ground the previous summer; an elderly man with the beginnings of dementia who had gone for a walk and never come home.

If only to himself, Seth would admit that his gaze was most often drawn to Hope Lawson's face. As a child, huge blue eyes had dominated a thin face with high, sharp cheekbones. A few pale freckles dusted a small nose. Moonlight-pale bangs cut straight across her forehead. Her grin revealed a missing tooth.

The artist had seen the promise of beauty in her, or something very like. The cheekbones were distinctive. More than anything, they gave him hope that she would be recognized.

Hope. Damn.

"Eve mentioned that she hasn't seen you recently," Mrs. Lawson remarked.

Another wince he didn't let show. The Lawsons' adopted daughter was responsible for his current cold case project. They'd been on several dates when she told him something of her family's history. Intrigued, he'd done his research, gone to talk to her parents and made the decision to do his damnedest to find out what had happened to the little girl who disappeared sometime between getting out of the community pool after a summer swimming lesson and her mother arriving to pick her up.

He'd quickly got the idea Eve wished she'd never told him about Hope. She wouldn't talk about the missing "sister" she'd never met, much less how she felt about her adoptive parents' renewed yearning for their biological daughter. Any conflicted feelings she might have were understandable. Seth didn't see any chance of the relationship going anywhere long-term, but she was an attractive woman and he liked her. No one else had caught his eye recently. Why not call and find out if she'd like to have dinner this weekend?

"I've been working long hours," he told her mother, feeling guilty even though it was the truth. Among other things, he'd been working a murder/suicide perplexing enough to draw nation-wide attention. There was no one to arrest after that bloodbath, but everyone would feel better if he could come up with some answers to explain the unexplainable.

In fact, he'd barely had time to keep up with the influx of emails he was receiving in response to his multiple postings of Hope Lawson's story.

"Then I won't keep you," Mrs. Lawson said with dignity, rising to her feet. "I really shouldn't have come by. I know if there was any news, you'd have called."

"I would," he said gently, standing, as well. "But I don't mind you stopping by, either."

She searched his face, then gave a small nod. "Good day, Detective Chandler."

He stayed where he was and watched until she let herself out into the hall and was gone.

"You'll never get rid of that one," observed the detective whose desk was right behind Seth's.

He grunted. "Am I doing her any favors? Hell, face it. It's an intellectual exercise for me. For her…"

"It's a heartbreaker."

He turned to scowl at Ben Kemper, near his age, light-haired to his dark, a man Seth suspected was on a mission of his own, although Seth had no idea what it was. "Thanks. Just what I needed to hear."

Kemper grinned. "An intellectual exercise, huh? That's all it was?"

"Damn it, no! But I don't have the same stake that woman does, either." He scrubbed a hand over his head. "Shit. My best hope was a match in NamUs." The National Missing and Unidentified Persons System hadn't existed when Hope Lawson disappeared. A body found in one jurisdiction had in the past rarely been matched to a listing for a missing person even a few counties away. Now medical examiners, cops, even families could input information. A body found in a shallow grave in Florida could be linked to a woman snatched in Montana. As time allowed, some medical examiners' offices were inputting old information. Or the improvements in DNA technology meant they were taking another try at finding a name for a body long since buried but never identified.

"Nothing, huh?" Kemper leaned back in his chair, his expression sympathetic.

"No." He didn't kid himself that meant Hope Lawson had grown up and was living out there somewhere under another name.

Kemper was the one to grunt this time. "You get a call back from Cassie Sparks's school counselor?"

He and Kemper, often paired on the job, were working the murder/suicide together. Along with her mother, eleven-year-old Cassie had been shot to death by her father, who had then swallowed the gun. The fact he'd killed a kid—his own kid—had made the scene a difficult one, even for seasoned cops.

"Hell. No." Seth frowned. "I'll finish going through these emails, then head out to the school. I should still be able to catch her before they let out." They were trying to find out every detail of the lives of all three members of the Sparks family. Unfortunately, Cassie's very basic Facebook page had been unrevealing. Friends were denying any knowledge of problems with her dad. "You talk to the father's boss again?" he asked.

"Sure. Best employee ever. Great attitude. We have to be wrong. Dale would never do anything like this."

They'd been getting a lot of that. Too much, in Seth's no-doubt cynical viewpoint, one shared by his fellow detective. No one who'd known the Sparks family wanted to admit they'd seen any crack in the perfect facade. It sucked to face the reality that you might have knowingly blinded yourself. Or to realize you weren't nearly as perceptive as you'd imagined yourself to be.

"I hear a few of his coworkers have a favorite bar," Ben continued. "I figure I'll stop by tonight, see what they have to say after a couple of beers."

Seth nodded. "Good." He turned back to his monitor and skimmed down to where he'd left off on that last email.

Except you've got her hair wrong in the picture, and her nose, too. And her chin is kind of square, not pointy like that.

Uh-huh, he thought. But she was totally positive they had a match.

Delete.

Twenty minutes later, he logged out and pushed his chair back. "I'm off."

Ben had a phone tucked between his ear and shoulder as he tapped away on his keyboard. He glanced up. "You coming back?"

"Probably not. I need to knock on some more doors in the Garcias' neighborhood." Raul and Maria had come home after a hard day's work to find their brand-new Sony fifty-five-inch LED HDTV missing, along with the Dell Inspiron laptop the grandparents had bought the granddaughter just last week to take with her to college. Seth had little doubt the thief knew one of the Garcias. He had to have heard about one or both of those very nice purchases—the TV had a two-thousand-dollar-plus price tag. Otherwise, why had their house been hit when none of the others in their modest neighborhood had been?

Yesterday, people had been at work. He figured by the time he got there now, everyone would be reaching home. A kid might have said something to a parent about the guy she saw knocking on the Garcias' door, then going around back. You never knew.

With a last look at the bulletin board, he thought, *Too much to do, not enough time to do it.*

And then, *Damn, I've got to call Eve.*

BAILEY SMITH PAUSED by one of her tables. "How's your meal? Can I get you anything else?"

The guy, hot in an I-know-I-am way, was so engrossed in something on his smartphone, he didn't even look up. The girl did, even though her phone sat next to her plate, too.

Canosa was a high-end Italian restaurant only a few blocks from the Pantages Theatre in Hollywood. This couple's dinner along with their drinks and the bottle of wine would run them a couple hundred dollars. What Bailey couldn't figure out was why they hadn't eaten at home or hit the drive-through at McDonald's if they didn't intend to so much as look at each other or have a conversation over the meal.

But, hey. As long as they tipped generously, why should she care?

"It was awesome," the girl said in a bored tone. "Actually, we're probably ready for our check."

Bailey smiled. "I'll get it for you."

She paused at one other table, then went to the computer station tucked into an alcove by the kitchen and ran off the bill for table six. She glanced over it for accuracy, then smilingly placed it on the table midway between the two. The guy reached for it.

The girl said, "You know, I keep thinking you look familiar."

"Well, if you've eaten here before…"

"No, friends told us it was good. You don't work at Warner Brothers, do you?"

Um, no, she wanted to say. *I work at Canosa.* But really that wasn't fair. Living expenses were high in Southern California. She knew people who worked a part-time job or even two on top of a full-time one just to pay the rent.

"Afraid not," she said cheerfully. If the girl had looked even faintly familiar to her, she might have mentioned being a student at the University of Southern California, but, honestly, she didn't care if they might have crossed paths before.

The guy handed her an American Express card. She took it with another smile.

When she returned to the table, it was to find them both staring at her.

"I figured it out," said the girl, a stylish brunette whose handbag was either a genuine Fendi or an amazing knockoff. She sounded excited. "I saw your picture on, I don't remember, Facebook or Tumblr or someplace like that."

"Couldn't have been me," Bailey assured her. "I'm not a celebrity in disguise here."

"No, it was amazing! Everybody has been passing it around. It was about this little girl who disappeared and an artist drew what she'd look like now. And…wow. I'd swear it's you."

The darkness inside Bailey rose, dimming her vision for a minute. But she didn't let her expression change. "Really? That's weird. Pretty sure I've never disappeared."

"Yes, but you ought to look at it. It's totally uncanny."

She managed a laugh. "Okay. What's my name?"

The young woman frowned. "Hope something." And then her face brightened. "Lawson. Hope Lawson."

Oh God, oh God. Could any of this be true?

"I'll look," Bailey promised. "Gotta see my doppelgänger."

They were still looking over their shoulders at her on their way out. She was so engaged in holding herself together, she didn't even check to see what kind of tip they'd left. She had another hour before she could leave.

Part of the act of maintaining was convincing herself she wasn't going to bother to look at the *totally uncanny* picture that supposedly looked like her. It probably really didn't. And if it did? Why would she care? Nothing would ever make her Hope Lawson, even if by some bizarre chance that had been her name. *Hope.* She almost snorted. How sweet.

Long after she collected her tips for the shift, as well as her paycheck, and went out to her car, dying to take off her very high heels even if it mean driving home with bare feet, she stayed in the mode that could be summed up as No Way. There'd been a time she would have given anything to be found, to have it turn out she had a perfect family somewhere who would welcome her back with cries of joy and who'd kept her bedroom exactly the way it was when she disappeared. Then, she'd imagined it as very pink, with a canopy bed. Every so often, she made alterations in what that perfect little girl's bedroom would look like, but the canopy bed always stayed.

By the time she was thirteen or fourteen, though, she realized she didn't belong in that bedroom, and the family wouldn't want the girl she was now back anyway. Not long after that, she quit believing they even existed.

Now—was she really supposed to open herself to the possibility they actually did? That they were still looking for her? The idea would be ludicrous, except she'd occasionally, just out of curiosity, scanned websites focused on missing persons and seen the kind of age-progressed pictures the girl tonight had talked about. She'd read a little about how it was done, combining knowledge of how a face normally changed with age—what thickened or sagged or whatever—along with details of how that child's parents' faces had changed as they grew up, to achieve an approximation that was sometimes astonishingly accurate.

As she turned onto West Sunset Boulevard, she thought, *it might be interesting to take a look*. And then she could dismiss the whole silly idea, instead of leaving it to fester. Which it would. She knew herself that well.

Besides, if anyone else mentioned it, she could say, *Saw it—definitely not me*.

She hated that her apartment house didn't have gated parking, but that was one of those things you had to pay for. And she did, at least, have an assigned spot underneath the aging, three-story apartment house, so she didn't have to hike a block or more when she got in late. Even so, she had to put her heels back on, because she knew all too well what she might step in—yuck. She took her usual careful look around when she got out and locked her car. Her handbag was heavy enough to qualify as a weapon, and she held it at the ready as she hustled for the door that let in to the shabby lobby and single, slow-moving elevator.

Safely inside, she ignored the guy who was getting mail from his box. He had a key to it, so he must actually live here, too. He didn't make any effort to get in the elevator with her, which she appreciated.

There were only four apartments on each floor. She let herself into hers, turned both locks and put the chain on, then groaned and kicked off her shoes again. It sucked to have a job that required torturing herself like this, but sexy paid when it came to tips.

Her laptop sat open on her desk where she'd left it. She didn't let herself so much as glance at it, instead shedding clothes on her way to the bathroom, where she changed into the knit pj shorts and thin tank top she slept in at this time of year. Then she used cold cream to remove her makeup, brushed her teeth and stared at herself in the mirror. The light in here was merciless. She leaned in closer, the counter edge digging into her hip bones, and made a variety of faces at herself. It wasn't as if she was so distinctive looking.

But she knew that was a lie. She kind of was. Her cheekbones were prominent, almost like wings, her chin pointed, her forehead high enough she had her hair cut with feathered bangs to partly conceal it. Without makeup, her face was ridiculously colorless, given that her eyebrows weren't much darker than her ash-blond hair, and her eyes were a sort of slate blue. She looked young like this, more like the girl she didn't want to remember being. The one who had been invisible when she desperately wished someone would *see* her.

"Fine," she said aloud. "Just do it. Then you'll know."

While her laptop booted, she turned on the air-conditioning unit even though she tried not to use it any more than she could, but today had been *hot*.

Then she perched on her cheap rolling desk chair, went online and, in the search field, typed *Hope Lawson*.

A MONTH LATER, Seth admitted, if only to himself, that he'd done everything he could think of to do to bring resolution to the Lawsons.

He had interviewed witnesses afresh, at least those who could still be found. He'd talked to the first responding officer and the investigator who'd pursued the case thereafter. He had tracked down neighbors of the Lawsons', even those who had since moved. Hope's teacher that year. He'd studied investigations and arrests made anywhere around the time of Hope's disappearance, looking for parallels no one else had noticed. He'd read every scrap of paper in the box he recovered from the storage room in the basement.

Meantime, he'd made sure her DNA and a copy of her dental X-ray were entered in every available database, along with the two photos. He'd worked social media sites to the best of his ability.

The result? Something like a thousand emails, not one of which pinged. His best guess was that

Hope had been raped and killed within hours of her abduction, and her bones were buried somewhere in the wooded, mountainous area bordering Puget Sound in northwest Washington state. Maybe those bones would be found someday, but given the vast stretches of National Forest and National Park as well as floodplain that would never be farmed, it was entirely possible no one would ever stumble on them.

Sitting at his desk, he grimaced. He owed the Lawsons a phone call. If he didn't get on it, Karen Lawson would pop up, sure as hell, apologizing but still expecting an explanation of what he'd done *this* week to find her missing daughter.

And, if he was honest, he'd have to say, *Nothing. I've done everything I can. I'm sorry.*

If he was blunt, would she accept his failure and go away?

"Nope," Kemper said behind him. "Not happening."

"What?" He swiveled in his chair.

"You were talking to yourself. You asked—I answered."

He swore. Good to know he'd taken to speaking his every thought aloud. Was he talking in his sleep, too? Wouldn't be a surprise. He'd been having a lot of nightmares lately, too many populated by Hope. In the latest unnerving incarnation, she was a ghost. Sometimes a little girl, sometimes a woman, always translucent. Either way, he couldn't touch her, couldn't escape her no matter what he did.

The idea had apparently sparked his unconscious imagination—hey, pun! and not in a good way—because Cassie Sparks's ghost had joined Hope last night. She'd seemed kind of protective of little Hope.

Hard to imagine, considering her dark path, which had turned out to be even uglier than they had known when they found her body along with her parents'. He and Ben had discovered what precipitated that hideous final scene, and part of him wished they hadn't.

Shifting his thoughts back to Mrs. Lawson, he said gloomily, "She brought me cookies last week."

Ben's mouth quirked. "And they were good. Peanut butter cookies are my favorite."

"She brings pictures, too." He yanked open his center desk drawer and brandished the small pile. The one on top, the most recent, was a baby picture. *First smile*, someone had written on the back.

Radiant, open, delighted, it was unbearable to look at when he knew that baby's fate. He'd shoved it into the drawer the minute Mrs. Lawson walked away. Angry at her unsubtle emotional manipulation, he wanted to throw them in the trash. Because he saw her pain, week in and week out, he didn't.

His phone rang and he turned back around, reaching for it.

"Someone here to see you," the desk sergeant said, his tone odd. "Her name is, uh, Bailey Smith."

"Never heard of her. She say what she want?"

"To talk about Hope Lawson."

Seth sighed. *She looks EXACTLY like this girl I know, except...well, for her nose, chin, cheeks and eyes.*

"Conference room empty?" he asked.

"Yes, Detective."

"I'll be right down."

Ben had gone back to whatever he was doing, and no one else paid any attention as Seth walked out and took the stairs.

He emerged through the heavy, bulletproof door that led to the desk sergeant's domain behind the counter, beyond which was the waiting room. As usual, half a dozen people slumped in seats, some sullen, some anxious. One woman stood, her back to him—and a very nice back it was. Interested, he enjoyed taking a good look. She was midheight, slender, with a tight, perfect ass and fine legs. Chinos cut off just below her knees bared smooth calves. One foot tapped, either from nerves or impatience. *Nice foot, too*, he thought idly; since she wore rubber flip-flops, he could see toenails painted grass green with some tiny decoration he couldn't make out centered on each nail.

He lifted his gaze to her hair, bundled up and clipped on the back of her head. It was so pale a blond, at first sight he thought dyed, except it had some natural-looking striations of color in it.

Something inside him went still.

"Detective," the desk sergeant said in an urgent undertone.

As if hearing his low voice, the woman turned to face the two men, pointed chin held defiantly.

Stunned, Seth couldn't move, couldn't speak.

Couldn't breathe.

She was alive. And…damn. How could the artist possibly have got it so right?

CHAPTER TWO

THE MAN STARING at her in open shock was not quite what Bailey had expected, although she didn't know why that was. She'd looked him up online and even found a newspaper photo of him taken as he left the scene of a recent, really horrible crime.

The coloring was the same—dark hair, worn a little longer than she thought cops usually did. Brown eyes. Broad-shouldered, solid build. She had been reassured by a hint of bleakness the photographer had captured on that hard face. *He must be human*, she had thought, although, really, she knew it wasn't as if *he* mattered at all. If it turned out she really was this Hope person, he'd introduce her to her supposed parents, hold a press conference and bask in his victory as he sailed off to meet new challenges, while she was left to grapple with what, if anything, this meant.

Now, seeing the expression on his face, she felt like a fish in a very small glass bowl. She suddenly, desperately wanted not to be here. It was too much. He cared too much, she thought in panic. Why?

She slid one foot back, then the other. The door wasn't that far. If she took off, what were they going to do? Arrest her?

Seemingly galvanized into motion, he pushed through the waist-high, swinging door. "Ms. Lars— Smith," he corrected himself. "Please. You've come this far. I'd really like to talk to you."

Only a few feet away from her now, he was even more intimidating. Something in him seemed to reach out and grab her. Her feet refused to keep edging backward. It was as if they were stuck in some gluey substance.

"I shouldn't have come," she blurted.

He shook his head. "You need answers, don't you?" he told her more than asked, in a deep, soothing voice.

Maybe. Yes. She did want answers, just not the complications that would come with them. She didn't relate well to people on any but a superficial level. Whatever it was she saw boiling inside him scared her.

She did some deep breathing, not taking her gaze from him, feeling him as a threat on some level she didn't understand. Stupid.

"Yes. All right. I'll talk to you. That's why I'm here."

"Good." He produced a smile gentler than she would have imagined him capable of. "There's a small conference room back here. We can talk there." He stepped back and gestured toward the swinging door that led behind the long counter.

She studied it warily, then the police officer behind the counter who had also been watching her. Finally she pretended a confidence she didn't feel and walked forward.

Although Detective Chandler followed, he kept a certain distance between them she appreciated. She was afraid she'd given away her irrational panic, and *that* scared her. If she had one skill in life, it was an ability to hide all the craziness she carried inside.

She hesitated until he waved her toward a hallway, and then she stepped back while he opened the first door, glass-paned to allow passersby to look in.

"Please, have a seat," he said.

She took the first chair, the closest to the door. It also offered the advantage that nobody going by could see her face.

He circled the table and sat across from her, then did nothing but look at her for long enough to have her fidgeting. Finally, he gave his head a faint, incredulous shake.

"I assume you're here because you saw the picture," he said.

"Yes."

"Just out of curiosity, where did you come across it? Were you searching for information about your background?"

"No," Bailey said flatly. "A total stranger thought she knew me, then remembered a story she'd seen online about this little girl who was abducted. She said someone had come up with a picture of what that little girl would look like now, and I was right on."

He winced.

She raised her eyebrows. "What?"

"You have no idea how many times I've read or heard that these past several months. Except usually they say we got the nose or the chin or the eyes wrong." The shock in his eyes was back. "We didn't."

Much as she'd like to, she couldn't deny that.

"So, you went online to see if this total stranger was right," he prompted.

"I did."

"And made the decision to come to Stimson."

"Actually," she said coolly, "that was a month ago. In fact, I made the decision to pretend I'd never seen it. It's been a very long time since I've had any interest in finding out where I came from."

Instead of appearing shocked or disapproving, he studied her with interest. "You didn't believe anyone out there cared."

"No, I didn't." Her usual breezy persona was failing her. She was coming across as hard. No, brittle. Probably unlikable. *Yeah, so what? I am unlikable.* "Let's be honest, Detective. Even if you run a DNA test and it's a match to Hope Lawson, I am not her." She leaned forward, her gaze boring into his, her voice rising despite herself. "Do you understand? I can't *be* her. I don't intend even to try."

He raised dark eyebrows. "And yet you're here."

And there was the conundrum.

"I suppose, in the end, curiosity got to me. Also…" She frowned. This was the part she didn't understand. She thought of herself as utterly self-centered. Life hadn't taught her to be anything else.

"Also?" he prodded, that deep voice now easygoing, undemanding. He was going out of his way not to put pressure on her, because he'd read her with unerring accuracy.

"I suppose I thought it might mean something to these people. I mean, if they're still searching for—" Oops. She'd almost said *me*. "Hope," she substituted.

"Never knowing what happened to someone you love is incredibly hard." That sounded personal, as if he had lost a loved one. "Worse than seeing her murdered. Worse than burying her. Actually seeing you, knowing you are alive and well, will mean everything to the Lawsons."

"You're assuming I *am* Hope." She made it a challenge.

"We'll definitely run a DNA test, if you're willing." He waited for her nod. "Unfortunately, dental records won't be helpful. At the time of your disappearance, you were only beginning to get your first adult teeth. However, Hope did have a birthmark."

Bailey flinched. She hadn't seen mention of that.

"It's a small detail held back after your disappearance. DNA matching was then in its infancy."

She nodded. He waited. Finally she sighed. "I have one on my left hip. It's…sort of heart shaped."

"May I see it?"

"Here?"

"Why not?"

He was right. She certainly wasn't a shrinking virgin. After a moment, she stood, went around the table, unbuttoned and unzipped her chinos, and pushed them down enough to reveal the waistband of her panties—and the tiny, dark heart that always intrigued guys and disturbed her. She used to wonder if it was a brand *he* had put on her.

Detective Chandler looked for a moment that stretched and had her heart beating hard and fast. His expression never changed—but she also wasn't surprised to see that his pupils had dilated when he finally lifted his head. They stared at each other, and she thought, *Don't let him want me*. Because she was tempted? No, no, no. Because it would be incredibly unrewarding for him. Men…well, she didn't do men. Not anymore.

She fumbled hastily to fasten her chinos. When she looked at him again, his crooked smile sent a jolt through her.

"It's a pleasure to meet you, Hope Lawson," he said.

"Just...don't call me that."

"All right." There was that astonishing gentleness again. "Bailey it is. Unless you prefer Ms. Smith?"

"Either is fine." She retreated to her side of the table. "Thank you, Detective."

"If you're going to be Bailey, I'll be Seth."

The flutter in her belly wouldn't let her respond to that. *We're not friends*, she wanted to say, but she didn't want to alienate him, either. This desire to cling to him was completely unfamiliar to her.

"Can you tell me what you remember?" he asked.

She had known he would ask but had hoped for a reprieve. Still, maybe it was better to get this over with.

"If you mean about this town or the Lawsons or..." She stopped. "Nothing. I think *he* punished me if I asked questions or said anything about... about home. So I forgot. He made me call him Daddy."

Seth Chandler's face hardened. "He's the one who snatched you."

"I think so." She'd blocked out so much. "He

might have gotten me from someone else. I'm not positive."

"But he kept you, this man."

"For a while. I don't know how old I was for sure, but I think about eleven when he ditched me."

"Ditched you?"

"We moved a lot." She did remember that. "Stayed in crummy places. Sometimes he'd get an apartment, sometimes it was those motels that rent rooms by the week. You know."

He nodded. She saw that much, although she could no longer meet his eyes. The police and then social workers had dragged some of this out of her back then, but she hadn't told them everything, out of fear or loyalty, she didn't know which.

"It was a really scuzzy motel that time. In, um, Bakersfield. California," she added, in case he didn't know. "It was night. He said he was going out. He did that a lot." And she'd been relieved. Maybe he wouldn't wake her up when he came in. "Only this time, he never came back. When he wasn't there in the morning, I realized he had taken my stuff into the room but not his. He meant to leave me."

A shudder passed through Seth—no, Detective Chandler. His hand that rested on the table knotted into a fist so tight, his knuckles showed white. Bailey eyed that fist, knowing it should frighten her and wondering why it didn't.

What was truly remarkable, considering the rage vibrating in him, was the kindness in his voice. "What did you do?"

"I waited. I don't know, two or three days, I think. If he came back and I was gone, he'd have been furious. I sneaked out a few times and stole some food. There was a Burger King a couple of blocks away. If you sort of lurk in a place like that, people throw food away, or they just leave it on the table. Eventually, the motel manager let himself into the room because *he* hadn't paid. That's when the police came."

"Did they try to find out who you were?"

"I don't know," she said uncertainly. "I said he was my daddy, and I think they believed that. I know they looked for him, but he was gone. So I went into foster care." She shrugged. Habit. A way of saying, *No biggie, that's the way it was.*

"Why do you think he left you then?"

She looked down at her hands. "I think because my body was changing. He didn't like that."

"He used you sexually." Detective Chandler sounded almost calm.

Bailey flashed a dark, scathing look at him. "What do you think?"

He closed his eyes. Tendons stood out in his neck and a nerve pulsed in his jaw. She waited while he fought for control.

Finally he looked at her with eyes that were almost black. "I'd like to get my hands on him."

Surprised, she said, "That was a very long time ago. You didn't know me."

"I feel like I did. I've immersed myself in your life. In that day. What everyone did, said, thought. The child you were is very real to me."

"I'm glad she is to one of us," Bailey joked.

His eyes narrowed a flicker, as if she'd startled or even shocked him.

"That girl is a complete stranger to me," she explained. "It's why I wasn't sure I wanted to make this pilgrimage." Her word choice caught her by surprise. Was that how she saw this?

"I understand, although it's going to be hard on the Lawsons."

"I can't help that."

He nodded. "Are you ready to meet them?"

She had a feeling he'd been about to say "your parents," and appreciated the fact that he didn't. *Parents*... Well, there was an unreal concept.

Hoping her panic wasn't visible, she asked, "Would they be home at this time of day?"

He glanced at his watch. "I don't know, but we can find out."

Bailey almost begged him to give her time. *Maybe this evening*, she could say. Or tomorrow. Tomorrow sounded even better. But she guessed he wouldn't let her out of his sight if he could help it. He suspected her of wanting to bolt, she knew.

And, oh, he had no idea how much she did want to.

"You're so sure?"

His eyebrows rose again. "That you're Hope? Yeah, I am. They had a photo of you naked in one of those little kid pools. You were maybe two. Investigators had it blown up because the birthmark was visible."

After a moment, she nodded.

"I'll remind the Lawsons that DNA confirmation is still a good idea, but that could take weeks. It would be cruel to leave them in the dark. They've been waiting for this moment for a very long time."

She nodded, wringing her hands beneath the table where he couldn't see. "First, will you tell me something about them?"

"Of course I will. I'm sorry. I should have thought of that. Kirk owns an auto body shop and tow truck. He's a quiet man. I don't know how much of that has to do with what happened to you, or if he always was. Your mother—Karen—was a schoolteacher. She quit to devote herself full-time to hunting for you. Eventually, she started working part-time, but out of the home. She couldn't work with children, she said. She does machine-quilting."

Bailey blinked. "That's a big cut in pay."

"I get the impression she stays as busy as she wants to." He hesitated. "Three years after your abduction, they took in a foster daughter and eventually adopted her. Eve is a year younger than you, I believe."

So they'd tried to replace her. Bailey wondered how that had worked. If she remembered them, she might be hurt, but as it was, nothing he'd said yet had triggered even the smallest of memories.

"It turns out I'm a little younger than I thought I was." She made a face. "We guessed I was at least twelve when he left me. Because of the way I was developing."

His gaze flicked to her irritatingly overabundant breasts.

Men always looked. And she never blushed, although—wow—her cheeks definitely felt warm.

"Is Bailey what he called you?" the detective asked.

She shook her head hard. Hard enough her hair clip slipped and she had to reach up to reanchor it. "No. I wouldn't tell anyone my name. Eventually, they gave up and let me pick my own. I went to court to make it legal once I was an adult."

"You know I'm going to want to know that name eventually."

She compressed her mouth.

He took out his phone, his gaze never leaving hers.

SETH SUCCEEDED IN talking her into riding with him to the Lawsons'. She'd wanted to follow him.

Have her car available for a quick getaway, he suspected.

But she reluctantly got into his department issue unmarked car and deposited a sizable handbag at her feet. He started the engine to get the air-conditioning going, reached for the gearshift, then let his hand drop. He sighed and looked at her.

"You know this isn't going to be as simple as meeting and greeting the Lawsons, don't you?"

She eyed him warily. "You mean they're going to want more from me."

"They are, but that isn't what I'm talking about." He hated to even raise this subject, given how obviously close to panic she already was, but felt he had to. "Your reappearance is going to be big news. The biggest. The press will flock to Stimson. You'll be on the cover of *People* magazine. You will give hope to every parent who lost a child who has never been found. It won't be a nine-day wonder, either. They'll keep following up." Seth knew he sounded brutal. "A week from now, a month from now, a year from now, they will want to hear how your family has healed. How you've moved on. They'll dig for all the details. Paparazzi will try to catch you unawares. You will never live an unexamined life again."

As he'd talked, horror had gradually overtaken her face. "Like Elizabeth Smart."

"Yes. You, Bailey Smith, will be famous."

"Oh, God." She was shaking.

Unable to resist, he took one of her fine-boned hands. "Breathe."

"I can't do this."

"I think you've come too far to turn back."

Blue eyes fastened on his with a desperation that wrenched his heart. "If I go now—"

"Do I leave the Lawsons thinking you're probably dead?"

"What if I meet them and we don't tell anyone?" She didn't seem to have noticed they were holding hands. That she was clutching *him*.

"I don't think that would work."

"Why not? You could make it part of the deal. Say I'll talk to them only if they agree to keep it private."

"You have grandparents. Aunts and uncles, cousins. Your parents have friends. Their adopted daughter. I know Karen Lawson. She's incapable of lying to everyone. She won't be able to hide her happiness." He stroked the back of her hand with his thumb. "And then there's your face, Bailey."

The way she stared at him, stricken, told him she understood.

"The stranger that pointed you to the picture. Is this the only person who saw it and noticed the resemblance?"

Her shoulders sagged. "No. A couple of others have said something."

"All it would take is someone getting excited and telling a reporter. Think what a coup it would be. Doing it this way, we have some control over the flow of information. You can give exclusives to reporters who will treat your experience with sensitivity, say 'No comment' to everyone else. We'll hold a press conference, then ask everyone to give you and the Lawsons the privacy you need to come to terms with this new reality."

He'd always thought the idea of drowning in someone's eyes was idiotic. Unable to look away from her, he discovered different.

"But…my life," she whispered.

He had to say this. "Will never be the same."

"Oh, God," she said again. Her struggle to regain her balance was visible. "I should never have told you my name. I could have made one up. Then I could dye my hair. Wear colored contacts. I could still do that," she said on a rising note.

He didn't say anything.

Defeat flattened her expression. It was a long moment before she nodded. She bowed her head and seemed to notice their linked hands for the first time.

He gently disengaged them, however reluctant he was to sever the connection.

"When you called her, why didn't you tell Mrs. Lawson you'd found me?" she asked suddenly. "They probably think you're bringing bad news."

"Me finding your body wouldn't have been bad news." He frowned. "It would have hurt in one way, but been a relief in another. They'd have had closure, at least."

"I can understand that," she conceded.

"The answer to your question is, I don't know." He heard his own uncertainty. "Maybe I just want to see their faces." And it could be that was the answer. He'd worked hard to effect this reunion. Usually his greatest reward was to make an arrest, then see the jury foreman step up and say, "Guilty as charged." He hadn't been able to wall out Karen Lawson's pain as effectively as he usually did. Seeing her joy—he needed that.

"Okay." She sat tensely as he backed out of the slot, then drove across town. The sheriff's department headquarters was on the outskirts of Stimson, the county seat that still had a population of only thirty-five thousand or so. The Lawsons had never moved from the house they'd lived in when their daughter was snatched. He'd read and knew from experience that was usual. People believed they had to be there when their missing family member magically made his or her way home. There was probably a subconscious fear that, if they weren't there, everything as much the same as possible, the lost one wouldn't be able to find them.

He stole glances at Bailey Smith, sitting marble still and almost as pale, staring straight ahead through the windshield. Scared to death and refusing to show it, he diagnosed. She didn't like giving away what she felt.

And him, he kept watching for every tiny give-away. His heart had taken up an unnaturally fast rhythm from the minute she turned around and their eyes met. He'd felt as if he'd taken a blow to the chest. Attraction multiplied times a thousand, an unfamiliar hunger to know everything about her, to soothe her fears and heal her wounds, a breathtaking need to protect her—and pounding at him the whole time was terror that she'd walk away before… What?

I can find out whether she might feel the same. Even close *to the same.*

"Here we are," he said quietly, pulling to a stop in front of a nice two-story white Colonial-style house with dark green shutters. He was willing to bet the Lawsons had never even considered changing so much as the shade of green on the trim when they repainted. Kirk Lawson's pickup was in the driveway. Lawson's Auto Body, it said on the door. So Karen had called him to come home, as Seth had suggested.

Bailey's head had turned and she stared now at the house where she'd grown up. Her breathing had quickened. She might swear she didn't remember the house at all, but he wondered.

Seth turned off the engine but sat there, ready to give her all the time she needed. A minute passed. Two. Mercifully, the front door didn't open and he didn't see anyone at the front window. Probably they hadn't heard the car out in front.

"You okay?" he asked at last.

"I...yes." She drew in a deep breath she probably meant to be steadying. "Yes," she said again, sounding a little more sure.

"Ready?"

Bailey nodded and reached for the door handle.

He met her on the sidewalk and stayed close on the way to the front door. After ringing the bell, he laid a hand on her back. He'd have sworn she leaned into it, just the slightest bit.

After the deep gong, he heard nothing until the door swung open. It was Kirk who looked through the screen door at him before switching his gaze to Bailey. Utter shock transformed his rugged face. "Dear God in heaven," he choked out.

"May we come in?" Seth asked.

He pushed open the screen, his gaze devouring Bailey. "Hope?" Then he gave his head a shake. "Come in. Karen!" he bellowed.

They stepped into the living room. His wife appeared from the direction of the kitchen. She was braced for bad news, Seth saw, in the instant before she set eyes on her daughter, resurrected, and came to a stop.

And yes, everything he'd hoped to see blazed forth on her face, making him realize that most lines on it had been formed by grief.

"Hope?" she said tremulously. She took a few

steps forward then stopped as if disbelieving. Tears brimmed in her eyes and overflowed. "It is you. It is. Oh, Kirk! Hope is home."

Seth laid a seemingly casual hand on Bailey's shoulder. Despite his focus on the two Lawsons, he was attuned to *her*, not them. Aware of her shock as she saw her mother's face, so much like her own. Felt when the waves of emotion hit her, as she absorbed the yearning in these strangers' eyes.

Seth cleared his throat. "I do believe this is Hope. That's why I brought her to meet you. We will need DNA confirmation. You know that."

Predictably, Karen shook her head, not looking away from her daughter. "Of course this is Hope." A smile burst forth despite the tears, and she hurried forward, holding out her hands. "Oh, my dear. Thank God. You don't know what this means to us."

Bailey shrank toward Seth. "I…it's a pleasure to meet you." She turned her head. "Both of you."

Karen stopped short of flinging her arms around the alarmed young woman. "Meet us? You don't remember us?"

"I'm afraid not. I…it's astonishing how much I look like you." She sounded stunned. "I… I've blocked so much out. I suppose I couldn't let myself remember."

"That's why you never came home. Because you didn't know where we were."

Seth squeezed Bailey's shoulder in reassurance. "Why don't we sit down?"

"Yes. Oh, yes!" Karen gestured them toward the sofa. "Oh, my dear. This has to be the best day of my life, except possibly when you were born."

Seth understood the sentiment, but was damn glad Eve wasn't here to hear it expressed.

Bailey cast him a single, desperate glance as they sat, side by side. He smiled at her, hoping to convey without words that she was doing great.

Hoping. He'd never be able to use any variant of that word again without seeing her in his mind's eye.

Karen tore her gaze from Bailey long enough to beam at him. "You brought her home. You accomplished a miracle."

He had. He still felt shell-shocked. He'd found Hope. Or, at least, cast the right lure to draw her home.

Uneasiness stirred, because he knew she didn't think of this house or this town *as* home. He hadn't asked yet where she lived, what her life was like, thinking they had more than enough to deal with. She didn't wear a ring, but that didn't mean she wasn't involved with a man. She could have kids. Who knew?

If she had a guy in her life, where the hell was he? Seth thought savagely. No man who loved her would have let her do this alone.

"Will you…will you tell us about yourself?"

Karen said timidly, seemingly still not realizing her face was wet with tears even as it glowed with joy.

Kirk sat heavily in an armchair. Seth had the impression he hadn't once taken his eyes off Bailey. Both waited expectantly for her answer.

"Well... I live in Southern California. My name..." She floundered at their expressions, but squared her shoulders. "It's Bailey Smith." She hurried on, as if to be sure they didn't have a chance to comment. "I've held all kinds of jobs since I graduated from high school, but I'm currently waitressing because I can do it nights and weekends. I'm about to start my senior year of college. A little late, but I finally got there." Her lips had a wry twist. "Majoring in psychology. I don't know what I want to do with it, but getting a degree feels...important." She lifted her chin a little higher. "I wanted to make something of myself."

"That's wonderful." Karen beamed some more. "What school are you in?"

Seth's hand had been on his thigh, but he moved it to the sofa cushion where his knuckles just touched Bailey's thigh. He waited for her to inch away, but she didn't.

"USC," she said. "Um, the University of Southern California." She smiled weakly. "Go Trojans. Although I'm not really into sports."

"Your father watches football and baseball—"

They all heard the front door open.

"Mom? Dad, why are you home?" Eve entered the living room, worry on her face. "There's a police car here." She stopped dead, her gaze moving from her father to her mother to Seth—and stopping on Bailey. Something dark entered her eyes. "I see." She sounded almost casual. "The *real* daughter returns."

CHAPTER THREE

BAILEY HUGGED HERSELF as Seth drove. "They still
have my bed." Why that blew her away, of all
things, she had no idea, but it did.

She felt his swift glance. "I don't think they
changed a thing in your bedroom."

"The whole room is pink."

"You were only six. Little girls like pink and
purple."

She stole a look at him. "How do you know?
Do you have children?"

Unless it was her imagination, his mouth
curved. Because he liked knowing she was curious about him? "No children. Never been married.
I have two nieces and friends who have kids."

"Oh." She swallowed. "I always pictured this
perfect bedroom." Her voice sounded faraway,
bemused. "It was pink, and I had a canopy bed.
Like a princess."

"You did."

"So... I was actually remembering." She was
stunned to know those dreams had really been
memories. Standing in the door of that bedroom

had left her shaken in a way the faces of her parents hadn't. And how weird was that?

As if he understood, Seth said, "Memories are odd. Unpredictable. A couple of my very earliest memories are of semitraumatic moments, which makes sense. Others are totally random. Why do I remember standing at the foot of a staircase in what my mother tells me was probably my great-grandmother's house, feeling really small? It's just a snapshot, but vivid. Couldn't have been an earth-shattering moment. For you, maybe you really loved having a bed with a canopy."

She gave a funny, broken laugh that didn't sound like her at all. "I did. I mean, I don't know that, but I used to think about what my bedroom would look like if I ever had a home. You know. I'd change the wall color as I got older, but the bed was always there." She sighed. "I hurt their feelings, didn't I?"

"When you wouldn't stay?"

And sleep in that canopy bed, the idea of which had freaked her out. As in, if she'd tried, she just knew she'd have run screaming into the night. More irrationality—it wasn't as if she'd been snatched from her bedroom and therefore had trauma associated with it.

"Or even agree to stay for dinner. And when I didn't fall into their arms."

"Maybe," he said, driving with relaxed competence. "But they're so happy that you're alive, they'll get over it. My impression is they're good people. They probably had fantasies. They'll adjust to the reality, which is that you're essentially strangers. Any sense of family or intimacy will have to be built from the ground up."

Bailey bowed her head and stared at her hands. "I don't know if I want to join the construction crew."

He was quiet for a minute, a small frown furrowing his forehead. But he looked thoughtful, not irritated.

"Why did you come here?" he asked. "What changed your mind?"

Would he understand if she admitted she didn't know? That she'd have sworn her original decision had been final, except that knowing she could find out who she'd been had nibbled at her until she'd finally decided to make this trip?

"Curiosity," she said at last. All she was willing to admit to.

He made a sound in his throat she couldn't interpret.

"You in school right now?" he asked.

She shook her head. "I didn't sign up for summer semester. It gave me a chance to work a lot more hours and save for the tuition. Fall semester starts the last week of August." Which was a month away. She added hastily, "I should get back to my job, though."

"How long did you tell them you'd be gone?"

"I…left it sort of open-ended."

He turned into the parking lot of the sheriff's department. She scanned the lot for her rental car and was reassured to see it.

"Have you found a place to stay yet?" he asked.

God. She almost had to stay for a few days, didn't she? She'd raised expectations, and she didn't want to hurt those people who had looked at her with such hunger and happiness and puzzlement. And then there was the whole press conference thing, which *really* scared her.

Aghast, she suddenly wondered whether Canosa would even want her back. The food and atmosphere were supposed to be the focus, not one of the waitresses. What if people stared? Went there just to see her?

Maybe she could change her appearance. But would brown hair or glasses fool anyone who had once seen a good photo of her? Say, on the cover of *People* magazine?

Her stomach dipped. With an effort, she dragged her attention back to his last question.

"No. I assumed there'd be a hotel in town, or I could drive back to Mount Vernon." It was a county away, but straddled the I-5 freeway, making it busier than off-the-beaten-track Stimson, which wasn't on the way to anything but the Cascade Mountains.

"There's a Quality Inn."

She nodded; she'd seen it as she'd turned into town.

"Also a more rustic place just out of town called the River Inn. And a couple of bed-and-breakfasts."

No B and Bs. She didn't want to have nosy hosts or have to share a breakfast table with other guests. "If they have a vacancy, the Quality Inn will be fine." The more anonymous the room, the better.

"Until the press arrives," Seth said. "Then we'll have to think of something else."

She shuddered.

He gave her a quick look as he finished parking, then gripped her hand again.

"Will you have dinner with me, Bailey?"

"You can't possibly want—" she began in panic.

He interrupted. "I want." There was the smallest of pauses during which she tried to interpret his enigmatic tone. "It'll give us time to talk this out. You can ask some of the questions that must be on your mind. We can plan our strategy."

"You can ask questions," she said with quick hostility.

He did the eyebrow lifting thing really well. "I won't tonight, not if you'd rather I don't. We will need to talk eventually about what you remember about your abductor. I'm a cop, Bailey. If he's still out there grabbing little girls, he needs to be stopped if there's any way in hell I can locate him."

What could she do but nod? She hated the idea *he* might have another little girl right now, who called him Daddy. She had spent most of her life blocking out those images, except they crept into her dreams.

"But this evening—" Seth's voice had softened "—we'll set that aside. I think it would be better for you to talk out what you're feeling than go hide in a hotel room."

"I'm used to being alone." It burst out of her before she could think twice. "I like being alone," she said softly. Not answering to anyone.

He turned off the engine and sat waiting, just as he had in front of the Lawson home. A patient man, he knew when not to push. And that made him a dangerous man, too, she thought, at least to her.

"Fine," she said, disgruntled but grateful all at the same time. She hadn't been ready to stay at the Lawsons' for dinner, but the idea of getting takeout and eating in a hotel room by herself held no appeal, either. At least, Detective Seth Chandler offered distraction.

"Okay," he said, as if the outcome had never been in doubt. "I need to go in and check messages, make a few calls. Why don't you check in at the Quality Inn, and I'll pick you up there?"

"Fine," she muttered again.

He smiled and took out his phone. "Give me your number so I can call when I'm on my way."

She told him. Apparently not trusting her, he touched Send and waited until the phone in her bag rang. Then, satisfied, he put his away. His hand emerged from his pocket with a business card, which he handed her. "My number."

He insisted on walking her to her car. Bailey had no doubt he memorized the license plate number, just in case she ran for it. Then he let her go, but kept watching until she turned onto the main street and she could no longer see him.

At which point she pulled to the curb, put the car into Park and bent forward, resting her forehead against the steering wheel. And then she did her best to breathe as she struggled with the kind of roiling emotions she hadn't let herself feel in something like ten years.

Strangely, it was a picture of the man she'd just left that she fastened on. His physical strength, his relaxed, purely male walk, the big hand he'd touched her with whenever he sensed she needed support.

How did he *know*?

Breathe.

He just did, she admitted. Somehow, those dark

eyes saw deeper than she liked. Except today, she was grateful.

A new swirl of panic joined all her other fears. She couldn't let herself depend on him. She shouldn't have agreed to dinner. When he called, she'd make an excuse.

Bailey moaned, knowing she'd just lied to herself. Yes, she had to be careful where he was concerned, but right now, she needed him. She, who never let herself need anyone, wasn't sure she'd get through these next few days without the man she'd met less than three hours ago.

EVE'S MOTHER—*ADOPTIVE* MOTHER—laid down her fork. "I keep thinking I dreamed it. But Hope really was here, wasn't she?"

This was probably the tenth time she'd said something similar since they sat down for dinner. All she'd done was stir her food around.

Dad laid his big, scarred hand over hers in a gesture more tender than Eve remembered seeing. "She was. We'll see her again in the morning."

Eve didn't have much appetite, either. She'd done a lot of scrambling to make up for opening her big mouth at the sight of her sort-of sister.

"I only meant biological," she had explained.

Apparently that was good enough, because they immediately dropped the subject and went back to exclaiming in shock and awe.

Hope, Hope, Hope.

And I'm being such a bitch, Eve thought miserably. She should be *grateful* to Hope, whose disappearance had given her a chance to have a family. Nobody else had wanted the rail-thin, withdrawn eight-year-old she had been when the Lawsons had taken her in.

She'd always known the truth. They hadn't taken her because they'd fallen in love with her, but rather as penance. They felt guilty because they had failed their perfect daughter. For their own spiritual salvation, they needed to save another child.

Which still didn't mean she hadn't been lucky to be that child.

She remembered her first visit to this house, when Kirk had opened a door partway down the hall and said, "This will be your bedroom."

Now she knew it had been a guest bedroom before she had arrived. Then, given the way she'd lived before she got taken into the foster system, she'd been thrilled because she'd have a queen-size bed all to herself and her own dresser and closet and everything.

Karen had stepped into the room behind Eve and looked around. "We'll paint and decorate once you've decided how you'd like it to look," she said. "What is your favorite color?"

"Pink," she had whispered, and then seen the expression on the face of a woman who was thinking about becoming her mother. "And yellow," she said hurriedly. Yellow, she saw, was safe.

She had lived with them for a week before she worked up the courage to open the door to the other bedroom that nobody went in or out of. *I want* this *bedroom*, she'd thought, indignation swelling in her, but she never said a word, because she knew. It was *her* bedroom. The lost daughter the social worker had told her about. The Lawsons had insisted that of course they would keep Eve even if Hope was restored to them, but then, she wasn't sure she believed that. She'd stared at the pink bedroom with furniture painted white and edged with gilt, and at shelves filled with dolls dressed in beautiful clothes, and most of all at the bed with tall posts and gilt-painted finials and a white lace canopy, and she had envied until she ached.

She had mostly been ashamed of that envy, because the pretty blonde girl in all the pictures was probably dead even though her parents kept her bedroom for her and told everyone that they knew she was alive and would come home someday. But the envy had crept into her heart and stayed no matter what she did to root it out, and today it had made her say, "The *real* daughter returns."

Of course Mom and Dad were ecstatic. They'd been given a miracle. Eve loved them. She had dreamed of seeing them truly happy, and now they were.

Just not because of any accomplishment of hers, any gift she gave them. She'd always believed, in the back of her mind, that she was engaged in a competition. She'd just never let herself see that it was one she *couldn't* win. Her bringing home a gold medal in athletics, being accepted to Harvard Law School or crowned Miss America, none of those achievements would ever have erased the grief that cast its shadow over both of them. Only the return of their precious Hope could do that.

And I am *happy*, Eve told herself. Just…envious, too.

She smiled at her mother. "Hope's coming to breakfast?"

Karen Lawson's face was both softer and younger than Eve had ever seen it. "Yes. But remember she asked us to call her Bailey. Oh!" She hugged herself. "I can't believe it."

Eve offered to come over and make breakfast, but no, Mom wanted to make it with her own hands, because she'd been cheated of the chance of feeding her daughter so many other breakfasts.

"Waffles," she decided. "Or crepes. I have all those lovely raspberries. Oh, my. I should have asked her what she likes." Her expression cleared. "But of course she loved raspberries. Do you remember, Kirk? That time we took her with us to pick berries, and lost sight of her for a minute?" That clouded her face momentarily, but the smile broke through again. "And when we found her she was stuffing herself with berries, and her hands and face were stained with the juice?"

He chuckled. "She tried to claim she hadn't been eating them and was astonished we didn't believe her."

How touching, Eve thought. *My little sister lied. And I am a lousy human being.*

DAMN, SHE WAS BEAUTIFUL. Seth didn't understand this intense reaction to Bailey Smith and wasn't sure he liked it. He didn't want to think it was related to the triumph of finding her. As in, *I'm the creator.*

That was just creepy.

The corner of his mouth twitched. Frankenstein's monster, she wasn't.

He had been tempted to take her home and cook dinner for them, but had had a suspicion she wouldn't like that. Plus, this might be their last chance to go out in public without being noticed.

So he'd taken her to a local diner with high-backed booths and asked for the one in the far corner. Once the waitress led them to it, he didn't give Bailey the choice. Instead, he slid in with his back to the wall facing the room and the door. It would have been his preference anyway, but what he liked tonight was that no one not standing right in front of their table would see her face.

After they ordered, she looked at him with

big, clear eyes that were more gray than blue in this lighting.

"Eve wasn't thrilled by my appearance."

He'd been waiting for this one, and found himself in a spot. He'd silenced a call from Eve on the drive here from the hotel. He'd have to talk to her, if only to tell her he wouldn't be calling again. An uncomfortable conversation he'd been avoiding. The last time they'd had dinner was almost three weeks ago. He'd been taking the coward's way out, hoping she'd clue in to his waning interest.

He'd made no promises and had nothing to feel guilty about, except that it was damn awkward to have these feelings for Eve's sister.

"I noticed that," he admitted. "In a way, I'm not surprised. What did surprise me was that she didn't hide how she felt."

"Her parents were really taken aback."

"I was glad Eve wasn't there when Karen said that about the two best days of her life."

"Because they were both associated with the *real* daughter," Bailey murmured. "The one who doesn't remember them and isn't sure she wants to be bothered to get to know them."

The one, he suspected, who didn't want to admit she hungered for family.

"You knew Eve, too?" she asked.

He hesitated. "She and I dated for a while. I actually became interested in your disappearance after hearing the story from her."

"Really." It was as if he'd confirmed something she had already guessed. "'Dated.' Past tense?"

"Uh… I haven't called her in a few weeks. It was never more than casual."

She scrutinized him for an unnerving moment. "I shouldn't have asked. It's none of my business."

Sure it is. His reaction was immediate and powerful. Seth didn't share it.

"I don't blame her if she resents me," Bailey continued, sounding thoughtful. "When you first mentioned her, I couldn't help thinking, *So they replaced me.* I'd have resented *her,* if I cared. You know."

He knew. She had felt a pang of resentment she refused to acknowledge.

"When Eve first told me the story," he said, "she sounded offhanded about it. 'Here's something out of the ordinary.' I don't think it crossed her mind I'd go anywhere with it, even though she told me because she knew I regularly work cold cases. Once I dug into it…" He hesitated, then shrugged. "She didn't want to talk about it anymore. If I asked a question, she'd claim she didn't know anything. Some bitterness may have been building…" He frowned. "I was going to say because her parents were suddenly obsessed with their loss again, but that isn't really what happened. The truth is, I doubt an hour has passed in the last twenty-three years that Karen and Kirk didn't think about you. They'd quit talking about it, that's all. Until I gave them hope." He grimaced at his choice of words. "Sorry."

"I think I could hate that name." Her voice was sharp. "It's sappy. And, God, so *wrong*, considering what happened. And so wrong for me." She pointed her thumb at herself. "The me I am."

"Who are you, Bailey Smith?" he asked softly.

Her gaze clashed with his. "I'm not a nice person, in case you haven't already figured that out. I don't make close friends. I don't have boyfriends." Her warning was clear. "Don't trust people." Her tone curdled. "I am what *he* made me."

Speaking of bitterness.

"That's not true," he said calmly, reaching for a roll, tearing it open and buttering it.

Her chin jutted. "You don't know."

"You enrolled in college. Did he have a single thing to do with making you the woman who'd do that?"

"My major. There's nothing subtle about that."

"No, I guess there isn't. You're trying to figure yourself out. Maybe him. But he wouldn't have liked you doing either, would he?"

She finally looked away. "No. But my interest is *because* of him." She didn't have to say how much she hated knowing that. "If it never happened, if I'd grown up here as sunny Hope Lawson, who knows? I'd have probably gone off to college at eighteen and majored in literature or biology or dance. But psychology?" She shook her head.

"You're right," he agreed. "You're a more complex person than you would have been. I won't argue with that. Given what happened to you, I think it's remarkable what you've become."

"And what's that?" she asked, the edge present.

"A smart, self-aware, poised woman who may claim she isn't nice, but who was kind today to two people when she didn't have to be."

"Of course I had to be," she grumbled.

He looked past her. "Dinner is coming," he said quietly.

The diner did decent American basics—burgers, steaks, fries, onion rings, roasted chicken. He'd been glad she didn't order one of their salads, which he felt sure came mostly out of a bag. He could be wrong, but he didn't see her as a waitress at Denny's or anyplace like that. With her looks and air of class, she could make a lot bigger bucks at someplace upscale.

Once their meals were in front of them, he asked about her job, thinking it might be a good idea to dial back the tension.

Of course he'd never heard of the restaurant, but it sounded expensive. "Do you get free meals?"

A surprised smile curved her mouth. His heart skipped a couple of beats.

"Of course I do. One per shift. Saves me a lot on the groceries, plus their food is really good. And I love Italian."

"Me, too." He glanced down at his steak.

"Unfortunately, Stimson does not boast a fabulous Italian restaurant."

She chuckled. "Nothing wrong with a hamburger." She took a big bite of hers.

He couldn't remember the last time he'd dined out with a woman who ate with gusto. And red meat and French fries, no less. Apparently she didn't worry too much about her weight. Not that he saw any reason she should.

She got him talking about the town and what it had to offer, seeming intrigued once Seth admitted he hadn't grown up here.

"City life isn't for me. I like to hike and I enjoy white-water rafting. I run to stay in shape and would rather not have to pound the pavement or go to the gym."

"Do you ski?"

"Alpine on occasion—lift tickets aren't cheap. Otherwise Nordic. We don't get a lot of snow at this elevation, but we don't have to drive very far to find it."

She exercised at a gym. "Actually, the university, now. Saves me having to pay a membership. I do the elliptical, treadmill, swim laps. And most semesters I take a phys ed class. I like to try different things. Spring semester, it was African dance. Which turned out to be really good for the thighs," she said ruefully.

He laughed.

Their conversation was starting to feel as if

they were on a date. When she suddenly scowled at him, he wondered if she'd had the same thought and was fighting it.

"What makes you think you know me?" she challenged. "Smart, self-aware, poised. *Kind*?" She said it as if the very idea was ludicrous.

He swirled a fry in ketchup. "You denying any of that?"

"Yes."

"Which part?"

"I'm not kind. I'm…oh, I suppose I'm mostly a decent person. I mean, I don't go out of my way to slap people down. But I don't go out of my way to extend a helping hand, either." She glared as if to say, *How dare you put* that *label on me?*

Seth didn't let himself smile. "We'll see," was all he said.

Her eyes narrowed, but she abruptly shifted gears. "You said my… Karen was a teacher. Elementary or high school or what?"

"Kindergarten."

Looking stricken, she breathed, "Oh."

"You were about to start first grade."

"How…awful."

"That's safe to say."

He stayed quiet, letting her process what he guessed was a real hit: her first true understanding of what losing her had done to them, the couple she didn't want to say were her parents.

"And Eve? Do you know what she does?" She

tilted her head. "Of course you do, since you had a relationship."

"Calling what we had a relationship is a stretch." He tried to sound mild. Easier because he and Eve had never made it to bed. Thank God they hadn't. He'd known she was willing and, at first, he'd fully intended to take her up on it. And why not?

He had a sharp, unsettling realization. *I saw Hope's face, the woman she would be if she had lived to grow up. That's why not. God.* Eve had had good reason to resent his sudden, obsessive interest in the sister who must have haunted that house. Today, he'd had trouble making himself meet her eyes. He hoped she hadn't noticed the way he was looking at Bailey.

He grimaced. *Yeah, what were the odds of that? Of course she'd noticed.*

"What's that face you're making?" Bailey looked wary. "You don't want to tell me what she does for a living. Why?"

"No, I don't mind telling you. I had a passing thought, that's all." An epiphany. "She's a social worker with DSHS. Washington State Department of Social and Health Services. She oversees kids who are dependents of the court."

"Foster children," Bailey said slowly.

"Some of them. Some she supervises in their own homes, making sure the families are showing up for counseling, keeping their kids clean, not abusing them."

She gave a funny laugh. "I suppose she majored in psychology."

"I don't know. She has a master's degree in social work from UW."

"And me, I still have another year just to get my BA."

"Bailey." He waited until she was looking at him. "She's a year younger than you, but she had advantages you didn't. She had parents who put her through college. She didn't have to earn her own way. She had support."

After a moment, she nodded.

"You do have something in common. She lived in foster homes for several years before your parents took her in. All I know is that her mother died, but I don't get the feeling her life was any picnic before that, either."

"So on that watershed day, the seesaw flipped." And she sounded flippant when he knew she felt anything but.

"You know it isn't that simple."

"Kinda seems that way."

"It was three more years before your parents took in Eve."

She scowled. "I wish you'd quit calling them that."

"Your parents? Why? They are."

"Were."

"Ah."

The scowl morphed into a glower. "What's *that* mean?"

He gave into impulse and took her hand again. "It means I get it."

"Does it mean you'll quit calling them that?" She tugged to get her hand free, but half-heartedly.

"I'll try," he said. "No guarantee."

"Great," she muttered.

He smiled, squeezed her hand and let it go. "Hey, you want dessert?"

"Are their pies as good as they look?"

"Why do you think I come here?"

He hadn't seen many of her smiles yet, but he especially liked this one.

"Of course I want dessert." She pushed away her plate, only a few fries uneaten. "I don't suppose you'd like to have breakfast with us tomorrow."

Despite the tone that said, *Of course I'm not serious*, he felt a glow of warmth beneath his breastbone. She might deny it, but she wanted him at her side in the morning.

"I wasn't invited," he pointed out.

"I noticed." She sighed. "And I know I have to do this. It's just…" After a moment she shrugged. "Will you think I'm even more of a coward if I confess I hope your Eve isn't there?"

"Not my Eve," he said curtly, then frowned at his own vehemence. Damn, he *had* to call Eve.

"And no, I don't blame you. I doubt she will be. She'll understand they want time with you. To get to know you, and…" He hesitated.

"Stare at me?"

His mouth quirked. "Probably. I was going to say, to rejoice."

"Fine," she finally said. But then she looked at him, dead serious. "Will you be masterminding the press conference?"

"Yes."

"Can we, um, talk about it?"

"Yeah." He waited until they'd both ordered pie and the waitress was walking away before he took her hand again. "Here's the plan."

She held on tight.

CHAPTER FOUR

"I OWE YOU an apology for yesterday. I mean, for bolting the way I did," Bailey said first thing the next morning, after arriving at the Lawsons' house.

Kirk looked at her kindly. "We understood."

He had a good face, craggy and lined, and his eyes... *I have his eyes*, she thought in shock.

"Of course we did," Karen hastened to add, but less believably. More than Kirk, she made Bailey uneasy. Maybe mother and daughter had been closer than father and daughter. It did make sense. But also, before coming to Washington for this reunion, Bailey had searched online for the original newspaper articles about her disappearance. She knew that she'd been at a swimming lesson at the high school pool, open all summer for community use. That particular day, Karen had decided to run some errands during the time rather than watch. She'd been held up at train tracks while a very long freight train passed, making her a few minutes late. When she arrived at the high school, most of the kids who had taken lessons at the same time were gone with their parents. Others had arrived for the next set of lessons, but nobody had seen Hope. Not struggling with a man, not waiting, not so much as leaving the dressing room although she had apparently changed, because the locker she'd used was empty and her swim bag had disappeared, too. And Karen Lawson had to have struggled for twenty-three years with the knowledge that, if only she'd stayed to watch the lesson, her child wouldn't have been abducted. If only she'd started back to the high school two minutes sooner, she'd have crossed the tracks before the train came by, and would have been there to meet her daughter in the dressing room.

If only.

Bailey hadn't had any reason to feel guilt; she didn't get close enough to people to let them down. But she understood the concept, and *if only* had to be the most damning of phrases.

"Please, come in and sit down," Karen said. "Breakfast is ready."

"Is Eve here this morning?"

"She let me know last night that she couldn't make it," Karen said over her shoulder. "Work, I'm sure."

Relieved though she was, Bailey had to wonder if Eve had really felt welcome. Or did she feel as if she was extraneous to this small nuclear family, now that Hope was home again?

No, they'd probably talked after Bailey fled

yesterday. The Lawsons seemed like nice people. They wouldn't sideline their adopted daughter.

And really, what is it with me? Bailey thought with incredulity. So, okay, she was majoring in psychology. That didn't mean she usually bothered analyzing everyone else's secret motives or wounds.

The dining room was as perfect as the rest of the house. Old-fashioned, as if it hadn't been updated in a while. Say, twenty-three years. But nice, with an antique china hutch, table and chairs, a big tatted doily in the center of the table with a vase of orange, daisylike flowers, and a Persian-looking rug on the hardwood floor.

They sat down to a spread that widened Bailey's eyes. Gorgeous crepes with perfect, red raspberries ready to spoon over them along with luscious Devonshire cream, crisp strips of bacon and a selection of other fruits, all beautifully presented. Karen must have worked for ages.

"Oh, this looks lovely," Bailey made herself say with a smile. The same one she gave diners at Canosa. "As nice as anything I've ever served."

Karen beamed and handed Bailey the crepes. "I remembered how much you loved raspberries."

Did I? Bailey couldn't actually remember the last time she'd eaten one. They were awfully expensive at the grocery store. But she kept the smile pinned in place and said, "I still do."

And then came the questions. Did she remember how much fun they'd had picking raspberries? No. The county fair—she'd always looked forward to it so. She wasn't the slightest bit afraid of heights! Did she remember...? No. She'd begged for horseback riding lessons, and they'd finally found a place to take her that summer. Did she remember...? No.

Bailey's throat grew tight. She smooshed a raspberry with her fork rather than take a bite she wasn't sure she could swallow.

Karen opened her mouth again, and Kirk laid a hand on her arm. Out of the corner of her eye, Bailey saw his slight shake of the head.

"Detective Chandler says you machine-quilt," she said brightly. "I'd love to see what you're working on."

Karen forced a smile. "I'll show you after breakfast. We were lucky to have four bedrooms. Neither of us had any use for a home office, like people all seem to have these days. This way I can close the door on all my mess."

"I don't even have one bedroom," Bailey heard herself saying. "Mine is a studio apartment. Rents are high in LA. I've been tempted to buy a Murphy bed, so I could put it up when I'm entertaining, except—" she was winding down "—well, I don't entertain very often."

"You have a bedroom here."

Her stomach twisted. A bedroom that had been

kept as a shrine for twenty-three years. The idea creeped her out.

"Do you remember anything at all?" Karen begged.

She set down her fork. "The bedroom. I know it's weird, but I remember the bedroom."

The face of this stranger who was her mother lit with happiness. "I'm so glad we didn't change it, then."

"I'm not six anymore," she said, sharper than she'd meant.

The happy expression froze, then slipped away. It was like watching death happen, and Bailey felt like a crummy human being. *See?* she wanted to say to Seth. *I'm* not *kind*.

Smart she'd give him. She'd found her college classes easier than she'd expected. *Poised...* maybe.

"I'm sorry," she said. "I shouldn't have said that. This is..." She moved uncomfortably. "I guess it's harder than I thought it would be."

"No," Karen said with dignity that surprised Bailey for some reason. "I was pushing you. It's difficult to accept that the daughter we missed every day of her life doesn't remember us at all."

"I'm hoping it will come back." *Am I really?* She honestly didn't know. "He didn't want me to remember. So I have this kind of mental block. But...maybe the memories are still there, on the other side of it?"

Some of the happiness bloomed again on Karen's face. The one that looked so much like Bailey's, unsettling her. She'd never had what other people took for granted, the ability to think, *It's Mom's fault I have skin so ridiculously white I burn whenever I step outside*, or, *It's not my fault I can't carry a tune in a bucket, it's Dad's*. Other people could make a face and say, *My family is cursed with freckled redheads*, but her, not a clue who to credit or blame for the thousands of bits and pieces that made her up.

Except for *him*. She'd spent a lot of time wondering about the nature versus nurture thing. How much *was* his fault? Maybe she'd been abused at home, too, which made her easily trained by him. At that point she always felt sick. Had she been dumb enough to let herself be lured by him, or had he taken her forcibly? Why hadn't she run away from him? She still didn't know.

Now, at least she could say, *I have my dad's eyes and Mom's cheekbones. And my mother's smile*. Seeing it made her skin burn and feel too tight.

She could hardly wait to get out of here. But this was why she'd come. To meet these people, to get to know them, open the possibility of some kind of relationship, if they still wanted one when they found out how truly messed up she was. Mostly she didn't mind being alone, but there were times, like the holidays, when she listened to other people complaining about family and buying gifts that probably got returned or tossed in a drawer, and she'd think, *At least you have somewhere to go.* The Neales invited her every year, but they'd had a lot of foster kids since her. Going to their house, she'd have felt like a ghost from Christmases past, chains rattling.

Say something.

"Was I horse crazy?" was what popped out.

It was that easy. A question now and again, and she heard all about her childhood. Listening was surreal. Her life sounded like something out of a storybook, as if nothing had ever gone wrong, nobody had ever argued and Hope had mostly gotten her heart's desires, including a "princess" bed.

No wonder I was in shock, she thought. Maybe... maybe she had quit believing in that perfect childhood. It must have seemed as unreal as Disneyland. A phantasm. Maybe, to survive, she'd *had* to quit believing.

She noticed that Kirk didn't say much. About all he did was murmur agreement when his wife said, Do you remember when...? Those steady blue eyes stayed on Bailey. Seth had told her Kirk was quiet, but she began to suspect he was more sensitive to her mood and discomfort than Karen was.

Finally, he laid his hand over Karen's to prevent another spate of reminiscences. Although she looked startled, she also closed her mouth.

He cleared his throat. "There's so much we don't know, Bailey. Can you tell us what happened?"

As if the air had been sucked out of the room, she suddenly couldn't breathe. It took everything she had not to leap up and say, "I've got to go." But years of therapy paid for by the state of California had brought her to a point where she knew to breathe deeply and clear her mind before she did or said anything. *Be calm. You don't have to do this.*

She shook her head. "I don't like to talk about it."

"Oh, but—"

Once again, Kirk's big hand gently stopped his wife's outburst. Bailey found herself staring at that hand. It filled her vision to the point where she didn't see their faces. Why a hand? That hand? *Don't know.*

"Detective Chandler said you spent years in foster care," he said.

Not the best part of her life, either, but this she could talk about. She wrenched her gaze from Kirk's hand.

"Six years. I didn't know how old I was, so we guessed. I aged out of the foster care system when we thought I was eighteen. As it turns out, I'd have been only seventeen."

Pain showed on a face rough-hewn enough to almost be homely. "Did you have a good home?" he asked.

"I...actually was moved several times." More like seven or eight times, but who was counting? "I was pretty traumatized at first. I hardly spoke at all. He... I was way behind in school." Yep, eleven years old and she had kindergarten under her belt. "Of course they had no idea what was wrong initially. They put me in special ed classes, but I picked things up so fast, I was back in regular classrooms after about a year. I must have already been reading pretty well when—you know."

Tears in her eyes, Karen nodded. "You were reading at a second-grade level after kindergarten."

Bailey nodded. "I kept reading. Books, when I could get my hands on them, or newspapers or just about anything. And I watched TV, so I knew about politics and crime—"

Both flinched.

"Not a clue about multiplication tables," she said lightly. She hadn't had a clue about so many things. "I'd never had a chance to use a computer." She shrugged. "But, like I said, I adapted fast. The first few years were hard, though."

"But...you'd been rescued from so much worse," Karen faltered.

How do you *know?* Bailey thought resentfully, but caught herself. The fact she'd just admitted to receiving no education in those missing years must have given them a hint. Of course *he* hadn't dared put her in school, even aside from the fact that he couldn't produce the identification or records any school district would have demanded. Never mind the fact he kept them on the move. She'd didn't remember ever staying in the same place more than a couple of months.

She tried to think how to explain how fish-out-of-water she'd felt after he left her.

"Any reality gets so it's almost comfortable. The new reality was so extremely different—I didn't fit. I didn't know how to relate to people." Not as if she was an expert at that, even now. "I withdrew, and a lot of foster parents didn't know how to deal with that, even if they were well-meaning." Seeing their faces, she said hastily, "I had some nice ones along the way, though. I lived with the same family my last three years. They're…good people. I've stayed in touch."

"Oh." Karen dabbed at her wet cheeks with her cloth napkin. "I'd love to be able to thank them."

"I…maybe I can introduce you sometime." Weird thought. Weirder was realizing that once the press conference happened, the Neales would read all about her history, just as everyone else she knew would. Maybe she should call them before that happened.

Your life will never be the same. Hearing Seth's voice, she felt panic swell in her, stealing her breath again. Everyone would know. Casual friends, fellow students, employers. Her face would become famous.

It already is.

The Lawsons were both staring at her in alarm, and she wondered what she'd given away.

"Um, have you told anyone else about me?"

"Yes, of course. I called your grandma and grandpa Peters, and your grandma Lawson." Karen looked momentarily sad. "Your grandfather Lawson died two years ago of a stroke. I wish he could have lived to see this day. And, well, I called my sister, and Kirk's brother, and some friends. I'm sure Eve has told people. She was so excited."

Sure she was.

But what boggled Bailey's mind was the number of people *who already knew.*

"You don't think any of them would have called a reporter, do you?" she asked anxiously.

"I can't imagine," Karen exclaimed, looking shocked. "Why would they?"

"Because my reappearance is news? Big news, and they might enjoy the attention?"

"But that's…that's…" She stopped, either unable to describe what that was or because understanding was finally dawning. "You've surely told people, too," she said at last.

Bailey shook her head. "Nobody."

"Not even friends?"

"No. I…wasn't sure I believed it."

"That you're our Hope."

"Yes."

"Do you now?" Kirk asked, eyes keen on her face.

Bailey tried to smile. "It's hard not to. I mean, look at us."

He glanced at Karen's face and back to Bailey. "Nobody could mistake you two for anything but mother and daughter."

"There's the birthmark, too."

He nodded, as if feeling a weight settling onto him. "Your smile. We'll have to show you pictures."

"I'd like that," she lied.

"You think we'll need to have the press conference right away," Karen said suddenly. "I'm sorry. I didn't use my head. I don't believe anybody close to us would go to the press, but everyone I called has probably told everyone *they've* talked to since. I should have kept it quiet until you were ready."

Bailey couldn't help making a face. "Are you ever ready for something like this?"

"No. Oh, my. A press conference. Everyone will be staring at *us*." She sounded appalled. "What should we *wear*?"

Bailey laughed, the familiar, feminine wail providing comic relief. "I have absolutely no idea. I've seen this kind of press conference on TV without ever paying the slightest attention to what people were wearing. I'm not sure anybody cares."

Her mother's back straightened. "*I* care."

"So do I," Bailey admitted, then thought—*wait. Did I just think of her as my* mother?

Yes.

"I suppose we should talk to Seth—I mean, Detective Chandler. He said he'd arrange everything."

"Should we call him?" Karen sounded dithery.

"I agreed to meet him later today," Bailey said. "I'll call you after I do, okay? Um, I should get your phone number."

Adding so many new numbers to her contacts list made this all seem real.

Jarred, she thought, *Another new reality.*

She added the Lawsons' home phone, Kirk's cell phone, and Eve's cell phone.

"She doesn't have a home phone," Karen said, sounding mildly disapproving.

"I don't, either. Most people our age don't."

Her phone rang, startling her. Seth. She answered. "Is something wrong?"

"Not wrong." He hesitated. "I just had an inquiry from a journalist at our local paper asking if there was any truth to the rumor that Hope Lawson had been found alive and well."

Bailey closed her eyes. "We were just talking about that. Karen called everyone in the family as well as some friends. And of course they may have spread the word, too."

"Cat's out of the bag. I think we need to accelerate our timing. I've talked to the sheriff and our PR people. We want to do it this afternoon."

He gave her details. There was apparently a small auditorium of sorts in the new public safety building that held the courthouse as well as the Stimson city police department. The sheriff's department was borrowing it. Someone was already calling news outlets.

"I think we'll have a full house, Bailey."

"Oh, God."

"It might be good if we can get Eve there, too. Otherwise, someone will think to corner her later for a quote. Best to get it over with in one gulp."

She pictured herself slithering down some monster's maw. Lovely thought.

"Um... Karen wants to know what we should wear."

There was a prolonged moment of silence. "Something nice?" He sounded out of his element. "No big prints or gaudy colors. Probably not too dressy."

"No sequins. Check."

"Business casual."

"Gotcha." Sort of. Even as her heart raced, she mentally sorted through the clothes she'd brought with her.

"After you change, I think you're going to want to check out of the Quality Inn. If you feel ready to stay with the Lawsons—"

"No," she said too quickly.

Another silence. "All right." He said it so gently. "We'll talk about it when I see you. Lunch?"

She glanced guiltily at her plate. She really hadn't done justice to this breakfast, and Karen must have worked so hard on it.

Pathetic though it was, she'd have begged if she'd had to. She swallowed. "Yes, please."

"I'll get takeout. We can park somewhere."

"That…sounds good." Her gaze slid sideways again to the amount of food left on her plate. Maybe by then she'd have conquered this roiling in her belly and be hungry.

Letting him go, she then had to detail the plans to the Lawsons, watching Karen's eyes widen again.

"Eve? Oh, my."

"I hope this isn't a problem for her, given her job. She'll suffer from some reflected notoriety."

"Oh, my."

Which pretty well said it all.

SETH STEPPED BACK into the small staging room where all four Lawsons huddled like a herd of deer unsure which way to leap. Kirk looked his usual stoic self, if uncomfortable in a white shirt and tie, Karen excited and terrified all at once, Bailey resigned and Eve… He couldn't quite tell.

He'd call her tonight. Or even take her aside after the circus was over, if he had a chance.

"We're set up," he told them. "There are a lot

of cameras out there. Ignore them. Look people in the eyes when you talk. Along with reporters, we have some curiosity seekers." His mouth quirked. "I saw the Stimson police chief himself standing at the back."

Over lunch, eaten at a relatively deserted riverside park, Bailey had finally thought to ask why a detective with the county sheriff's department was investigating, given that the Lawsons lived in Stimson. The high school, she'd learned, was outside city limits. Since that's where the crime had occurred, the original and any continuing investigation had been the responsibility of the sheriff's department.

The sheriff himself had shaken all their hands and been briefed to do the initial talking. Usually detectives stayed in the background, but under the circumstances he'd warned Seth to expect to have to answer questions.

"All right," he said quietly. "Let's do this."

He ushered them all onto the stage. Flashes momentarily blinded him. He blinked as they continued. The forest of big-ass cameras was intimidating as hell. He'd ended up by design with a hand on Bailey's back. He felt her stiffen, but a sidelong glance reassured him that she and Eve looked remarkably poised. The parents...well, everyone would expect out-of-control emotions.

An experienced, folksy speaker, Sheriff Jaccard had his audience bespelled from the moment he began.

"Twenty-three years ago, a little girl who'd been born and grown up in Stimson vanished into thin air. The community was shaken when news of the abduction spread. Even then, we had our share of crime, but having a child snatched by a stranger under the noses of a whole lot of other parents scared the daylights out of everyone. How was it that not a soul, adult or child, had seen anything at all? This department's best efforts never produced a fruitful lead. The FBI had no more success. Six-year-old Hope Lawson was gone, for all intents and purposes, from the face of the earth. Her parents were left to grieve and yet cling to their belief that she would someday come home. The rest of us…well, we came to assume she was dead." He swept the audience with a gaze that commanded attention. "We were wrong."

Exclamations and shouted questions filled the auditorium.

When they died down briefly, he raised his voice. "We'll take questions eventually, but first let me finish. Hope Lawson is with us today because of Detective Seth Chandler, who has a special interest in pursuing cold cases. He moved to Stimson only three years ago and had never heard of Hope until someone mentioned her disappearance to him. He's had some success in tracing missing people, in part because law enforcement agencies are getting a lot better at communicating with each other. But Hope didn't appear in any of those databases, either. He took the extra step of having an artist create an age-progressed picture." The sheriff used his laptop, open on the podium, to project a picture on the white screen behind him. He turned to look at it, as everyone in the audience did the same. "This is that picture."

The flashes dazzled Seth's eyes again. Photographers, crouching, got as close to the stage as they could, probably trying to get Bailey and the picture in the same frame.

The sheriff explained how Seth had created interest in the case and how the picture had spread across social media sites until someone had said to a young woman, "Your picture is online." He smiled and stepped aside, motioning Bailey to join him. "Meet Hope Lawson."

Again questions flew before she could open her mouth. Again he waited for quiet and said, "She's prepared a statement."

Poised had been a good word to use for her, Seth thought. Given her background, it was hard to understand where she'd come by so much strength and confidence. Confidence that hid a whole lot of damage and a mess of insecurities, he suspected, but the beautiful woman who gazed calmly at the roomful of people and cameras had one fine facade.

"I do not remember the abduction itself," she

began. "I spent the next five years with a man I do remember. I presume he was the one to take me, although he might have acquired me from someone else. Eventually, he abandoned me in a motel room in Bakersfield, California." Head high, she looked around. "By then, I no longer remembered my name or family. He had taught me to call him Daddy. Authorities were unable to locate him, but assumed he was my father. I was placed in the foster care system, where I was fortunate enough to have some fine people to help me heal." She talked about graduating from high school and working a variety of jobs before deciding to get a college degree. "A part of me was afraid to walk into the sheriff's department and say, 'I think I'm Hope Lawson.' I wasn't at all sure I really was, and also…acknowledging it forces me to face a great deal from my past. I know you have questions, and I will answer some, but not all. I ask you to respect my right to privacy."

The questions flew. She did answer some. Seth answered others. Yes, he told them, Bailey had that day submitted a sample for a DNA test, but along with the obvious family resemblance and Bailey's memory of her background, a birthmark had solidified their certainty that she was Hope. Karen did most of the talking for the Lawsons, but Eve told everyone there how thrilled she was to have Hope home.

"After I came to live with the Lawsons, I felt

incredibly lucky. But I was always conscious of a hole in our family. Hope was missing. Somewhere, I had a sister out there. Now—" she aimed a shy but warm smile at Hope "—she's home."

Truth, Seth thought, *but not all of it.*

Tears ran down Karen's face. Kirk swiped some from his own cheeks. Cameras caught it all.

At last the sheriff stepped up to the podium again and made a plea for everyone to respect the Lawsons' need for privacy and space to move ahead with their lives. Trying for unobtrusive, Seth opened the door at the back of the stage and signaled for the family to fade back.

The moment he'd closed the door, Karen burst into sobs. Looking helpless, Kirk put his arms around her. Eve hovered close, murmuring comforting words, while Bailey stood apart looking helpless and awkward.

"I'm so happy!" Karen wailed, and Seth sort of understood. Twenty-three years' worth of agony, despair, guilt and hope—yeah, *hope*—had all been released today to fly free.

Whether she liked it or not, Bailey Smith now had a family, with all the complications that entailed.

CHAPTER FIVE

"MOM TOLD ME you need a place to stay," Eve said in a low voice her parents wouldn't hear. "That Seth insists you move out of the hotel."

They had been ushered into a conference room in the public safety building to wait for the tumult to die down so they could all slip away.

"He thinks some members of the press might be staying there," Bailey agreed. "That they're all going to try to get me by myself. I packed and checked out earlier."

"You can stay with me if you want." Eve sounded offhanded, even abrupt. "I don't have a spare bedroom, but I do have a pullout couch."

Bailey tilted her head, assessing the sincerity of this woman whom she'd barely met. Eve was trying to hide it, but, if Bailey read her right, she fairly bristled with dislike and resentment. It seemed ludicrous they had to pretend to have a sisterly relationship.

Was there any chance she actually did want them to get better acquainted? But all Bailey had to do was meet that expressionless gaze to know the answer. No. Her parents had thought it would be wonderful if Bailey stayed with her. She'd just about had to make the offer. But she wanted Bailey in her apartment about as much as Bailey wanted to be there.

Of course, there was the little problem of where she *would* go. One of those freeway exit hotels back in Mount Vernon, she thought, even as she studied Eve.

Her adopted sister was beautiful. Bailey knew when she was outshone. The other thing that stood out was how very different they looked, making her wonder if the Lawsons had asked for a foster daughter who bore no resemblance to their lost child. Had that occurred to Eve? Something else that might sting.

Masses of dark, curly hair fell to the middle of Eve's back and framed a delicate, heart-shaped face. She had huge, brown eyes accentuated by long, dark lashes. *She* didn't have to plaster on mascara to make her eyelashes visible, or use a pencil to color in pale eyebrows. Her complexion was dark enough to suggest she might be half Latina or Italian or—who knew?—Philippine or Arabic. Arabian nights, was what Bailey had thought, seeing her. Eve's looks were somehow exotic, although she didn't have the lush body that would make her a fortune at belly dancing. She was slimmer than Eve, almost slight, and small-breasted.

"Thank you for offering," she said pleasantly, "but I already have something arranged."

Eve's nostrils flared. "I suppose Seth has taken care of you."

Bailey refused to give anything away. "He's been thoughtful."

"Oh, he can be that." Her lip curled the tiniest amount. "Until he's not." Eve turned her back, excluding Bailey. "Mom, Dad, if we go out the side door we ought to be able to make our getaway."

Karen gazed beseechingly at Bailey. "Oh, but… Hope."

"She has someplace else to stay." Eve didn't so much as glance over her shoulder.

Bailey took a deep breath, centered herself and smiled at Karen. *My mother.* "Could we have lunch tomorrow?"

"Oh!" Her cheeks pink, she turned her head as if it was a given she'd consult her husband. "Kirk, can you make it?"

He patted her back. "I think Bailey was inviting just you. It might be easier for her to get to know us one-on-one."

"You don't mind?"

He shook his head. "Of course I don't. Bailey and I, well, we'll have a chance."

For some reason, the idea of spending time with him caused jolts of anxiety. Not fear—she didn't think she'd ever been afraid of him, but…there was something.

Karen smiled. "Then I would love to have lunch with you, Hope."

"I'll call you in the morning, if that's all right," Bailey suggested.

"Perfect."

Eve gave one narrow-eyed look over her shoulder, then escorted her parents out of the room. Bailey heard the deep grit of Seth's voice speaking to them. From where she was standing, she couldn't hear every word, but she made out enough to gather he was trying to separate Eve from her parents and failing because they were oblivious. The voices all faded as he apparently walked them out.

She sank into a chair at the long table, wishing she could take off, too. If she knew where to go—

Hostility masking all-too-familiar panic had her stiffening. Who said she had to consult him? She didn't need Seth Chandler. Yes, he had been nice, but she knew damn well how he saw her. His ticket to fame and advancement. He'd be damn near as famous as she would be. The dedicated, caring detective who worked tirelessly to bring Hope Lawson home despite the heavy weight of his caseload. She could just hear it, said solemnly by a newscaster introducing the story.

Her suitcase was in the trunk of her rental. If she was lucky, she could dodge him and just go. To a hotel that wasn't in Stimson. Maybe even one all the way south of Seattle by SeaTac. She could fly out in the morning. Call and apologize to Karen. Promise to stay in touch.

She jumped up from the chair, snatched up her bag and made for the door.

A couple of heads turned when she appeared in the hall, but she saw only one person. Seth, striding toward her, lines creasing his forehead. Frustration? Irritation? She couldn't tell. But his expression changed when his gaze locked on her like a heat-seeking missile.

Her knees inexplicably wobbled. She squared her shoulders and raised her chin. "Detective."

"Where do you think you're going?" he demanded.

"Leaving?"

He gripped her arm. "I thought this would be a good time for us to talk."

Her heart contracted. "Talk?"

"I want to put that son of a bitch behind bars where he can never touch a little girl again," he said with controlled ferocity. "Never so much as set eyes on one."

Without volition, she retreated a step. "I...didn't realize you intended to do that so soon." She was infuriated by the die-away tone. Gothic heroine, ready to swoon. Unfortunately, she felt close.

His hand on her arm tightened. "Are you all right, Bailey?"

"No." She tried to keep backing away. "This has been a really hard day. I don't... I can't..."

"Will it be any easier tomorrow?"

This gentler tone weakened her. *Damn him*, she

thought furiously. It was as if he knew exactly what buttons to push.

"I don't know, but forgive me if I'm not eager to dredge up the nightmare I've spent a whole lot of years doing my damnedest to suppress."

"You want to let him get away with what he did to you?" His stare was hard now, all cop. Tactic number two: lay some guilt on her.

Trembling, she said, "What I *want* is to erase him from my memory."

"What if he's stalking a little girl right now?"

"Oh, that's low," she whispered.

He closed his eyes briefly. "It was. I'm sorry, Bailey. Being pushy… I guess it gets to be a habit."

Still trembling in his grasp, she looked up at the strong-boned face that, despite everything, reassured her. And then she was the one to close her eyes in shame. "It was also true."

"What? That I'm pushy?"

"That *he* could have his eye on another little girl now. Only…mightn't he be too old?"

"Depends on how old he is."

"Oh." Her shoulders sagged. "You win. Let's get this over with."

He looked disturbed. "I win? Bailey, this isn't about me putting something over on you."

"I didn't mean it that way."

He grunted, accepting what she'd said but not necessarily buying into it. Still, he steered her into the same room, his hand warm on her back.

She was becoming accustomed to the feel of that hand, solid, comforting and… Realizing what she felt was a shimmer of excitement, she put on the brakes. Whoa. Not going there.

Seth closed the door behind them, waiting until she'd pulled out a chair before sitting down directly across the table from her. His gaze on her face, he pulled a pen and small spiral notebook from a pocket. He'd come prepared.

"Start anywhere you want," he said in a tone obviously meant to calm her. Animal control officer coaxing a terrified, possibly vicious dog. "Or, if you prefer, I'll ask questions."

"No." She turned her gaze away to the bland, textured wall usual for these kind of rooms. She didn't look forward to seeing pity and disgust in those eyes. "His name—" Oh, God, this was hard to say. She forced the rest out, her voice rusty "—was Les Hamby. At least, that's what he called himself then."

Describing the monster who haunted her dreams was worse than speaking his name aloud. The more mundane she made him sound, the more pitiable she felt. If he wasn't huge and snarling… what was her excuse for not escaping?

"You think five foot eight or nine," Seth said, making notes. "Skinny."

"Wiry," she said, still not meeting his eyes. "He was strong, or at least, he seemed so to me."

"Will you sit down with an artist to try to come up with a drawing?"

See his face again? A scream bounced around in her head, so piercing it was hard to believe Seth didn't hear it. But, "Yes," she murmured.

"His hair wasn't graying," Seth said thoughtfully.

"No."

"Picture him, Bailey. You're an adult now. Can you estimate his age?"

Beneath the table, her hands fisted, her fingernails biting into her palms. "I...don't know. When I see him, I'm a child. He wasn't graying, or..." God, was she rocking? *Yes*. "Thirties, maybe. I suppose he could have been younger. Late twenties. Old enough to not look like a college student."

"Not forties."

"No." Surprised at her certainty, she sucked in a breath, then repeated, "No."

"Did he use the same name the whole time you were with him?"

"Yes. I thought—" There was the naive child again.

"You thought?"

She jerked one shoulder. "That was his real name."

"Did you ever see his ID?"

"No." Her pulse picked up. "He'd have killed me if he saw me looking in his wallet."

"But you know he *had* ID."

"Yes. I mean, he had to show something when he rented rooms. And…one time he was pulled over. A taillight was out. Nothing happened, so he must have had a driver's license and registration and maybe even an insurance card."

Seth contemplated her. "Do you remember when and where that happened?"

Breathe.

"It was…" *Close your eyes. Think.* "California. Maybe. I don't remember where. It was a sheriff's deputy. Not a state patrol officer. We were in really dry country, like desert. So it might have been Nevada. We were there for a while."

"And how old were you?"

"I don't know." The first birthday party she remembered was in her second foster home. "By that time, I'd forgotten where I came from."

She felt herself rocking again and hoped the movement was slight enough he wouldn't notice. After her daddy had pulled to the side of the road, he'd twisted her arm like a pretzel. It hurt for so long, she guessed he had broken or at least cracked it. "Call me Daddy," he'd hissed, while they waited for the policeman to walk forward. "Look happy. Do you hear me?"

She blocked that part of the memory. "I might have been eight or nine?"

"Good." His voice was deep, but also capable of sounding so patient and even tender. *Just another weapon in his arsenal*, she thought, arming herself with cynicism. "Let's talk about where you lived."

She'd forgotten so much. Tried so hard to forget. But some towns stuck in her memory anyway. They'd wandered the west—Idaho, Nevada, Oregon, California. "I don't think we ever went to Utah, but maybe Arizona? I'm not sure." She told him the kinds of places they'd stayed. A few flashing motel signs had stuck with her.

"No big cities," he said thoughtfully.

Bailey shook her head. "Not really little towns, either, or at least not for more than a night. Big enough that nobody noticed us, and economically depressed. Or maybe that was only the parts of town I saw. He'd get work sometimes and leave me locked in the room while he was gone."

Seth didn't say, *Why the hell didn't you take off? Ask for help?* Maybe he knew. *This* was why she had never told anyone the whole story. Because they wouldn't understand.

Or maybe they would, which might be worse. Her own self-loathing was sufficient, thank you very much.

Of course Seth wanted to know what kind of work *he* had done. She tried never to think of *him* by his name and certainly not as Daddy.

"Handyman. He had tools in the trunk. But he was a mechanic, too. Sometimes he got a job working on cars. I don't know what else."

"Did he have friends? Did you ever meet other people who seemed to know him?"

She shook her head emphatically at that. "He never brought anybody to our room. He did go out to bars. He got drunk, but not falling down." She had to close her eyes to say this. "Mean. He especially liked to hurt me when he was drunk."

Seth made a pained sound that had her looking at him, really looking, for the first time since she'd started telling him about those terrible years.

"Goddamn," he whispered. "I would do anything to go back and keep him from ever laying a hand on you."

"Why? You didn't know me. You still don't really."

"I know you well enough to want to protect you." He lifted a hand that shook to his face, rubbed his jaw, then pinched the bridge of his nose. "Remind me to show you the pictures I have of you."

"Pictures? I've seen the ones that were online. I mean, the school picture."

"Your mother—Karen—has been bringing me a snapshot a week," he said with a grimace. "Baby pictures. Toddler pictures. You laughing, staring solemnly at the camera, playing, reading. It was torture."

"You could have told her to stop."

"No. It was her way of keeping me invested." He gusted out a sigh. "A very effective way. Your smile haunted me. Your eyes." He stopped. "You were such a happy child, Bailey. Your smile was like…turning on a light in a dark room." He frowned. "You still have a beautiful smile. I just have this feeling it's not lit from within like it was then. It's only on the outside. I'd like to see you smile again as if you mean it," he finished roughly.

She stared at him, unable to figure out why he sounded as if he cared so much. It didn't make any sense. Sexual come-ons, those she got. But this…this was unfamiliar. It made a lump rise in her throat.

Fighting perplexing emotions she didn't understand, she lifted her chin. "Are we done?"

"No." And he kept asking questions. She'd said she watched TV. Maybe she remembered channels, local ads, specific news stories that would pinpoint where she and Mr. Hamby had been at specific times. To her astonishment, she had some answers. Stupid commercial jingles catchy enough she could still hum them.

"There was a murder," she said slowly, this memory rising from deep within. "The body was found in a room in the motel where we were staying. He had parked out back. He always did if he could. He grabbed me and we walked toward the diner like we were going to eat, then got in the car and left before the police could start knocking on doors. I remember the flashing lights and people gathering to stare. We had to leave some of our stuff behind."

Seth leaned forward. "What about the name of the motel? Or the town?"

"Walla Walla," she said without hesitation, surprising herself. "I thought the name was so funny. Mostly everyone I heard there spoke Spanish, so I guess there were a lot of migrant workers. But the man who was murdered didn't have a Hispanic name. It was a funny name, too. Peter… Penny something." The name hovered at the edge of her consciousness. The idea of a person *dead*, killed right there a few rooms away from them, had loomed large in her limited world. "Baker. Pennybaker. I don't know how it would be spelled."

"You have an extraordinary memory." Seth sounded admiring, unless he was putting her on.

"I didn't know I remembered any of this."

"Have you really succeeded in putting any of this away? Or does it come out in nightmares?"

She flinched, not sure she liked the compassion in his eyes any more than she would the pity she was sure he also felt. And disdain—Seth had to feel that, too, because she could have asked for help instead of enduring until *he* cast her off and she had no option. And even then, when the police might have been able to catch and arrest him, she hadn't told them enough about him.

How many other girls had he abducted since? Used sexually? Discarded, too…or had he started killing them at some point when he was done with them? There had been a few times she had thought he was going to kill her.

I have to live with knowing I could have stopped him, she thought bleakly. *Please, God, don't let there have been any others.*

But she knew. Of course there had been.

Reacting to the last thing Seth had asked, she tried to blank her expression. "You know my nightmares. Can we be done?"

"Yes, Bailey." He closed the notebook. "You've given me enough to work on for now." Before she could move, he held up a hand. "One more thing. The FBI will be getting involved now."

She stared. "Why?"

"Because child abduction is one of their specialties, and because Hamby took you across state lines. This is standard procedure. An agent will be coming over from Seattle to interview you."

"But I can go now?" When he nodded, she pushed back the chair, grabbed her bag and jumped to her feet.

He rose to his more slowly, his gaze never leaving her. "You have someplace in mind?"

She thought wistfully of that airport hotel, of being home by lunchtime tomorrow, but knew she couldn't do it, not when her departure would hurt the Lawsons so much. Anyway, she was realist enough to know it wouldn't be home as she'd known it, not if her face had appeared on national news. Which it would by tomorrow.

Your life will never be the same. She couldn't say she hadn't been warned.

"I thought a hotel in Mount Vernon."

"That would be better than here," he said, "but I have another suggestion. The parents of one of our deputies offered to let you use their summer cabin right on the river. They aren't here right now and he gave me the key."

"They…aren't afraid I'll steal or something?"

"I don't think there's much to steal. I get the feeling it's pretty stripped down. Private, though."

Private was good.

"I'll need groceries."

"Let me take you out there, and you can make a list. I'll shop for you. You don't want to show your face in the grocery store right now."

"I was going to take Karen out for lunch tomorrow."

"That's fine, if you don't mind everyone staring, cameras shoved in front of you, microphones under your nose. Hell, everyone else in the restaurant will be using their phones to get pictures they can upload to Facebook or YouTube."

Anxiety prickled her skin. "You're telling me I have to hide out."

"For now."

"Oh, God." She crossed her arms, squeezing hard.

"Hey." He circled the table, laid a hand on her shoulder and kneaded. "Interest will die down. People may keep noticing you, but you'll quit being news just because you're out in public. I promise."

Will die down—was that nicely vague, or what? *When* would her notoriety wane? Next week? Three months from now? A year?

She should never have come. If she'd gone on with her life...

Yes, but three people had said, "Wow, you look like that picture." Once classes started, more would have. Sooner or later, someone would have taken *her* picture and posted it online with a caption, *I found her!* Or called a reporter.

And it was too late now. Second thoughts were useless.

She practiced her deep breathing again, then nodded, hitching the strap of her bag over her shoulder. "Okay. Shall I follow you?"

"Yep. Let's do it."

Suddenly this completely boring conference room felt like the safest place in the world. Ready to flee not so long ago, Bailey was now reluctant to emerge. But if life had taught her anything, it was to forge on.

"Sure," she said, as if she wasn't cringing inside at the idea of people staring.

THE CABIN WAS even more rustic than Theo Leighton had implied. Seth had stepped inside first, but Bailey was right behind him. He couldn't imagine what she thought.

Moss had been growing over the cedar shingled roof, and the whole structure was set on concrete blocks, more of which made up the steps to the minuscule porch. The interior was dim, given that the three windows were small, their frames warped, the panes dirty. A single bulb came on overhead when he flipped the switch, which helped some but not much.

The plank floor was rough enough to give her slivers if she was foolish enough to walk barefoot. The refrigerator had been replaced in the past fifteen years, but the gas stove looked ancient. The bed was really a bunk built against the wall with unfinished lumber. The only room walled off was a bathroom. Seth was afraid to see what it looked like.

"Ah…maybe we should rethink this," he said.

Her glance held surprise. "You said rustic— that's what it is. At least the electricity is on. I might have balked if it wasn't. Basic is fine."

Oh, damn, he thought; to her this was *fine* because she'd lived in a whole lot worse. He tried not to envision those roach-infested rooms with stained mattresses.

"It's clean enough," she commented, "except for the dust." She swiped some off the table. "The owners must not have come at all this summer."

"No, Theo's dad had cancer. They live in Olympia. He's been having chemo and staying close to home."

"Well." Bailey visibly squared her shoulders. "Let me see if there are any cleaning supplies."

One of the cupboards held some spray bottles, and she found dishes, silverware and old but usable pans. When he tore a page from his spiral notebook, she sat down to make a grocery list.

Watching her, he tried to picture delivering her groceries, saying, "Sorry there's no TV," and leaving her while he went home to his big-screen, his primo speakers, nice kitchen, air conditioner in his bedroom window, big bed.

"Sheets," he said. "I'll bring something from home."

"Or a sleeping bag, if you have one."

"I do." Yeah, that was a good idea. The mattress here had a venerable history. He'd rather she be tucked in his sleeping bag. "All right," he said finally. "I'll be back in a couple hours."

"Thank you."

He didn't think she'd like knowing how very vulnerable she appeared at this moment, sitting with her back straight and her hands clasped on her lap like a good little girl. He wondered unhappily whether him leaving her in this crap place had thrown her back to all the hundreds—no, thousands—of times *Daddy* had left her by herself in places a whole lot worse.

But Seth left anyway, because what else could he do?

At Safeway, he was stopped several times by people asking about Hope Lawson. He nodded, smiled, said, "I wanted to think we'd get this lucky, but I'm not sure I believed it myself." Two cars followed him after he left the grocery store parking lot. He considered shaking them, but finally decided it would be better if it appeared he was innocently heading home with the groceries he'd stocked up on for himself. He didn't like leading reporters to his house, but that seemed the lesser of two evils.

He drove into his garage and hit the remote to close the door behind him. Finding a spare mattress pad, the sleeping bag, a pillow and a few more comforts of home didn't take very long, but he ended up lingering until he didn't see the cars parked down the block anymore.

He called to order a pizza and picked it up on his way back out to the Leightons' cabin, keeping an eye on his rearview mirror for pursuers. No other vehicle was in sight on the river road when he turned into the narrow, rutted driveway that led between a thick stand of firs and cedars.

Whippets of vine maple and blackberry scratched at the finish on his SUV. Except for the presence of Bailey's rental car out in front, the cabin looked as abandoned as it had when he led her here. With days so long at this time of year, the sun was high still, so there wasn't even a comforting glow of light from the windows. As he parked and carried the first load toward the decrepit porch, he looked toward the river, running low, barely strands of shimmering silver between boulders.

Her face brightening at the sight of him, Bailey let him in immediately and insisted on going out for the second load. "Pizza!" she exclaimed. "What a nice thought. Can you stay?"

"If you don't mind me inviting myself."

She cast him an oddly wry look. "You went to a great deal of effort to invite *me* in the first place."

Invite her…? Oh. As in, spreading her picture all over the internet.

He grimaced. "I did, didn't I? Are you sorry you accepted?"

"Did I have any choice?"

No. Not really. Not given how distinctive her face was.

"I'd say I'm sorry," he said, "except that knowing you survived means so much to the Lawsons."

After a moment she dipped her head in acknowledgment. She busied herself putting away groceries in cupboards and the refrigerator, which he realized she had managed to scrub clean while he was gone. While she was doing that, he hoisted the mattress off the bunk to be sure no spiders lurked in dark cracks, then put the mattress pad on before thumping it back in place and spreading the sleeping bag.

"Thank you," Bailey said behind him. "That looks comfy. Even a pillow." This smile was the warmest he'd seen, and made his rib cage feel as if it had contracted.

They each had a beer as they ate pizza, Seth careful to steer the conversation into casual pathways. News that didn't involve her, the rare movie he'd seen recently. He didn't tell her he intended to call Eve as soon as he got home. Bailey cooperated by sharing a few funny stories about incidents at the restaurant where she waited tables. He asked about her last foster parents, the ones who'd kept her until she "aged out"—he hated that term—and she said they were in their early seventies now and still almost always had two to three foster children.

"The Neales have a son, but their daughter died when she was nine. Riding her bike, she was clipped by a car and hit her head on the curb." Bailey was silent for a moment. "I don't know if they were filling an empty place, like the Lawsons did when they took in Eve, or if they blamed themselves and we foster kids were a penance." She shrugged as if it didn't matter, although of course it did. "They were good to me."

Seth ached to touch her but didn't. God, what was it about her? He had to be careful. Odds were, she'd stay a few more days, a week, then go back to LA. He'd swear she felt something for him, too, but it seemed to scare her more than please her. Anyway, what was he going to do, quit his job and follow her?

Say good-night, he told himself. *Now. Before you step in it any deeper than you already have.*

But, damn, he did hate leaving her in this isolated cabin even if she repeated twice more, sturdily, "It's fine. Private. That's good."

She'd gone back inside and shut the door before he so much as had the key in the ignition. No lingering in the open door to watch a visitor depart, not for Bailey.

She might feel safest alone, it occurred to him. He swore aloud, his mood dark as he drove home.

CHAPTER SIX

WHEN EVE'S PHONE RANG a little after eight and she saw Seth's number, she almost didn't answer. If she didn't talk to him, he couldn't kindly, honorably tell her that their brief relationship was over. Plus, this was Friday night, and she would have liked leaving him to assume she was in such demand she'd gone out with some other guy.

But really, why put off the inevitable? Suddenly more angry than hurt, she snatched up the phone. "Seth."

"Hey," he said. "I tried to catch you today, but your parents were clinging to you."

Were they? From her perspective, it had been more a matter of *her* pretending they needed her, when she wasn't sure they'd so much as noticed she was there.

He waited for a response, and when he didn't get one, he said, "Eve, sometimes it's easiest just not to call again, but I've always thought that's a lousy thing for a guy to do."

She closed her eyes. Said nothing.

"You're a lovely woman. I like you, and I enjoyed the time we spent together." His explanation came across as rehearsed, which it probably had been. "There just was never enough of a spark to make me think the thing between us would go anywhere. I hope you felt the same and I'm not hurting your feelings."

"Somehow this isn't a surprise, given that you haven't called in a while," she said tartly. Oh, God—did she sound bitter? *Yes*. She closed her eyes. "But thank you for not leaving me wondering what was wrong."

"I'm sorry." For the first time he sounded awkward. "The timing is bad, with us likely to keep running into each other because of Bailey. Ah, Hope."

"Well, it's not likely she'll stay around, is it?" she said maliciously, then was ashamed of herself. She'd seen the way he looked at Hope.

The pause was shorter than she'd expected. "No," he said, and shifted gears. "You did a great job in front of the cameras today, Eve."

No mention of how she did when *not* in front of the cameras, of course. Perhaps because she hadn't done very well, at all.

"Thank you," she said, with more composure than she felt. "It must have been really difficult for her."

"Considering her history, she has amazing strength." The warmth in his voice, missing until now, made her fingers tighten on the phone. "Even so, she can use your support, Eve."

Wow. Was he blind, deaf and dumb? Her lips curled. No, he was just being a typical man. Contempt joined her anger and hurt.

"Is that's all you called for?" she asked.

"Uh...yeah."

"Then goodbye." She ended the call before he could tangle himself up in adding details about why their *thing* wasn't going anywhere.

Very carefully, she set down the phone. She was still paying for the latest model. She'd added insurance, so maybe she could get away with some creative explanation of why it was smashed rather than saying, *I threw it*, but why take the chance?

She was a little shocked to realize her vision had blurred. Oh, God, she was crying. Swiping furiously at the tears with the back of her hand, she admitted the truth.

No, Seth, I didn't feel the same. And, yes, you did hurt my feelings.

And, no, it wasn't fair, but Eve thought she could easily hate Hope, blonde, beautiful and *amazingly strong*.

LUNCH, OF NECESSITY, had to be at the Lawson home again. Eve had offered to bring takeout or groceries to cook, but Karen, of course, had declared that she'd love to make lunch.

Once she arrived, Bailey insisted on helping, though, and the two women worked together more harmoniously than she might have expected. She reminded herself that Karen was used to sharing her kitchen with another woman—her adopted daughter. And Bailey had done the dance often enough in her last foster home and then in restaurant kitchens.

At her suggestion, they sat down to eat in the kitchen, at a table set in front of windows looking out at the backyard. Conversation was easier today. Karen chatted about her quilting and asked questions about Bailey's classes, job and friends.

But all good things must end. Bailey's quesadilla was only half-eaten when Karen set down her fork. "I can't get over this." She gestured helplessly. "Sitting here with you, talking. I feel like I should pinch myself. I swore I'd know if you were dead, but…when the years pass…"

Seeing this woman's pain hit Bailey hard. There'd been a time she'd wanted quite desperately to know what her mother looked like. One of her fantasies involved a mother who was out there somewhere, searching frantically for her. When she'd quit dreaming altogether, she didn't know. To find that her fantasy was reality, that she had loving parents who had never stopped looking for her, made her feel a whole lot she hardly understood. A fairy godmother somewhere had waved her magic wand, and the sparkles had floated down to touch her, Bailey Smith. But it couldn't be real. She wanted to believe it had something to do with her, but just couldn't.

Only…if she had started to walk past Karen Lawson at the mall one day, she would have stopped dead and stared. She'd have known: *This is my mother.* The resemblance was that uncanny.

"I'm sorry." Her voice sounded weird, not her own. She was actually choked up. "So sorry I never tried to find out who I was."

"Can you tell me why you didn't?" Karen asked, sounding timid.

Not Karen—my mother. Mom? Bailey couldn't imagine ever calling Karen that.

"I don't exactly know," she admitted. "*He* didn't want me to remember. I guess… I gave up. Maybe to survive I *had* to block any belief that I'd ever had better or deserved better."

Seeing the tears in Karen's eyes, she regretted saying as much as she had, but how could they avoid it forever?

"He…wasn't kind to you at all?"

To save this woman more pain, Bailey was willing to soften jagged edges of her life, but not when it came to *him*. He was evil. She could only shake her head. "Abandoning me was the best thing he did for me."

Karen wiped her eyes, nodded and looked at Bailey steadily. "What were you like then? When you realized he was gone?"

"Terrified," Bailey admitted. "First that he'd come back, then that he wouldn't." Ashamed as always to admit that, she launched into automatic justification that was also truth. "I…knew nothing but life with him. I didn't talk much for a long time. With him, I was supposed to answer when he asked me something, but otherwise keep my mouth shut. I learned—" No, she didn't have to say this: that she'd learned not to scream when he hit her or did *that*, no matter how much it hurt. Not to cry until she was alone. Eventually, not to cry at all. Sharing that much would only hurt this woman, who loved Hope, if not Bailey.

"You learned?"

She scrambled for something else to say. "I tried to drink up as much knowledge as I could without him noticing. A lot of the time, he didn't pay much attention to me. I could pick up old newspapers, or magazines that had been left in the lobby of the motels or diners or wherever, and watch TV when he wasn't there. I listened to conversations whenever I could. Despite everything, I was curious."

"You were a very bright little girl. You'd taught yourself to read before you started kindergarten. It was a shock when you started reading road signs to me." Despite tears in her eyes, Karen smiled. "And the speedometer. One day, you said, 'Mommy, that sign says thirty-five, but there it says forty.' You pointed at the speedometer and looked so disapproving."

On a tiny flare of shock, Bailey remembered silently noticing the speedometer when *he* was going too fast, too, although he didn't very often. Of course he'd been afraid of being pulled over. She would never have said anything to him anyway.

She had educated herself. When she was first put into school—into special ed—she'd felt so stupid. But one day a teacher's aide working with her had smiled when Bailey finished reading a passage aloud, and she'd gushed, "I can't believe how fast you've advanced. You should be proud of yourself. You must be a very smart girl, Bailey."

That was the first time she remembered anyone ever telling her she was smart. Or maybe they had and she just didn't believe it. But that day she felt a glow, and she did believe. After high school, she let herself forget for a few years, but the time had come when she'd taken a hard look at her life and thought, *I can do more than this.*

She had the sudden wish she'd told the aide how much those words had meant to her. Maybe hugged her. She knew she hadn't. She'd still been very withdrawn.

Now she felt her lips curving. "To this day, I never exceed the speed limit. Friends have teased me about driving like a little old lady."

Karen chuckled, then teared up again. "Oh, my," she murmured, dabbing at her eyes again.

"Will you tell me more about us as a family, before I disappeared?" Bailey asked impulsively.

"If I liked pink so much, I must have been into girlie things."

That had the other woman smiling again. "Yes, you loved dressing up, and insisted on being a princess for Halloween. You took dance lessons, but you played soccer, too. Considering your age, you were a fearsome goalie!" The smile became sad. Bailey could tell that for this moment, Karen Lawson saw the past more clearly than the present. "You were a daddy's girl. You'd run to meet him when he came in the door after a day's work. He'd have grease embedded in his hands, and you didn't care! When you were little, you wanted *up*. Kirk would swing you into the air, and you'd chortle and he'd laugh." Grief moved through her eyes. "I haven't heard him laugh like that since." So softly, Bailey barely heard her, she added, "Or at all."

For an instant, Bailey heard that laugh, deep and happy, as if a ghost hovered in the room with them. *My imagination*, she told herself sharply. Words came from her against her will. "He... doesn't look like a man who often laughs."

"He's never been much of a talker. It took him longer than it should have to ask me to marry him, because he was convinced he wasn't good enough for me, a teacher with a college degree. I didn't know what was holding him back. I thought he couldn't figure out how to put it in words. I was about to propose to *him* when he finally said, 'I'll understand if you say no, but…'"

The rising amusement surprised Bailey. "Doom and gloom, huh?"

"He did the voice of Eeyore in Winnie the Pooh really well."

They both giggled.

Bailey had a panicked thought. *How do I know what she's talking about?* At twelve years old—as it turned out, really eleven—she'd been way too old to be read Winnie the Pooh stories. She knew vaguely about Pooh Bear and his honey and all that, but not because she'd ever read the books or seen a video. But Eeyore's deep, slow, hopeless voice was there, embedded in her memory.

The suffocating feeling came from nowhere. "I…remember," she whispered.

"What?" Her mother stared at her.

"I think… I must remember." She pressed a hand to her chest. *Breathe.*

"Oh, sweetheart."

"No. Maybe I saw a video somewhere. One of the younger kids in a foster home was watching it." She talked faster and faster. "That makes sense." Relief freed her chest from that crushing grip. "I can't possibly remember—"

"You can." Her mother touched her hand, tentative but gentle. "You will, when you're ready."

Deep inside was a cry: *No, no, I can't.*

Long habit made her deft at changing the subject, but even so she saw that Karen—*Mom*—knew what she was doing and why but chose to let it go.

HAVING DECIDED TO go into work today, Saturday or not, Seth was on a call when Bailey's number came up. "I'll get back to you," he said hastily, and transferred to the incoming call. "Bailey?"

He heard her voice, muffled. "Please allow me to shop in peace."

He surged to his feet, understanding immediately what was happening. "Where are you?"

"Walgreens. If you're busy… I shouldn't have called." Just like that, she was gone.

He bounded down the stairs and ran across the parking lot to his vehicle, ignoring stares. Fortunately, the drugstore was on his side of town, a distance he covered in about three minutes. Barely suppressing his rage, he pushed his way through the glass doors. A clerk to his left was gaping at the small crowd blocking the end of an aisle.

"Where is your manager?" Seth snapped. "Get him. *Now.*"

She was fumbling with her phone when he passed.

He found what he expected—Bailey trapped midaisle, bodies blocking her way from all directions, microphones thrust at her.

"Police in Bakersfield say you didn't remember

the name of your abductor. Will you comment, Ms. Lawson?"

"Were you sexually molested?"

Seth's voice boomed above them as he pushed his way through. "That's enough. If you're not here to shop, you're trespassing. Back off," he snarled at a cameraman who tried to block him.

Bailey was utterly expressionless, so pale she looked like a marble statue. Only her eyes teemed with distress.

"She has no comment," he declared, looking from one avid face to another. "Under these circumstances, she will accept no questions. Do you hear me?"

"Detective, has she given you any more information than she did Bakersfield police?"

"I cannot comment about an ongoing investigation. Now please excuse us."

He gripped her arm and moved forward. They had broken through the crowd when he spotted the manager hurrying from the back of the store. Seth knew Troy Gaskins, who had always seemed like a good guy. He looked almost as mad as Seth felt.

"All of you!" he snapped. "Out of here. I will not allow a customer to be treated this way. Detective Chandler, if they don't depart now, I'm going to request you start making arrests."

Protesting, they shuffled out. Camera flashes went off. Bailey stood rigid beside him, gripping the handles of a shopping basket that held several items. Her white-knuckled hands held on as if they were all that kept her from plunging into an abyss. She said nothing until the last reporter had gone outside. Then she said, "I need to pay for these things." Her voice was almost steady.

"No need," the manager said. "Sonia, please bag Ms. Lawson's items for her." When she tried to argue, he shook his head. "I regret that an incident like this occurred in my store. It's the least I can do."

"I don't mind—"

"Please," he said simply.

She bit her lip, then nodded and set the basket on the counter. "Thank you."

Still gaping, the clerk moved the few items into a plastic bag and handed it over. "Have a nice day," she said, then flushed at the inappropriateness.

Bailey managed a weak smile for her. "Thank you."

Seth steered her toward the doors. She balked when he put out a hand to open one.

"They're still out there."

"They know better than to get in our way," he said grimly.

"But…they'll follow me."

"Come to the station. You can hang out for a while, until they give up."

Her laugh broke. "Hang out at the police station."

Goddamn it. He'd found Hope Lawson, achieved a miracle. And this was the result.

He unclenched his jaw. "Do you have a better idea?"

"No. No, I suppose I don't." She peeked at him, almost shyly. Color tinged formerly colorless cheeks. "I'm sorry. This is my fault. I didn't think. I needed—"

He'd seen what she needed, and, yes, she'd had to shop unless she were to ask him to pick up something so personal to any woman.

"It's not your fault," he said roughly. "This was an obscenity. I half expected it, but I deluded myself the press would behave with some decency. I was wrong."

"You warned me."

"They must have seen why you were here."

Her blush deepened. "Yes." Suddenly a smile curved her mouth. "At least they didn't ask whether I'm secretly pregnant. You know, with a monstrous eighteen-year-old fetus."

Startled into a bark of laughter, Seth said, "God. I can see it on the cover of a tabloid."

"Complete with picture of the newborn, already needing to shave," she agreed, still smiling.

"You're a gutsy woman, Bailey Smith." Damn, he wanted to kiss her. "So, what do you say? I know the safest hangout in town."

The humor sparkling in her eyes and lingering on her lips, she shrugged the straps of her handbag over her shoulder. "How can I say no to an offer like that?"

He wanted to kiss her as he'd never wanted anything in his life.

"Let's move fast," he said brusquely, ignoring her startled look as he pushed open the door.

BAILEY FELT LIKE a kid stuck waiting in a doctor's or attorney's office while the adults held conversations that passed right over her head. It was ridiculous—she had a book, she could have played a game on her phone, but instead she sat in an oversize, not very comfortable chair and felt petulant. Did her lower lip stick out? At least she hadn't yet whined, *I'm bored.*

Part of the trouble was that all she wanted to do was watch Seth Chandler, and she'd been doing her best not to let herself. This...fascination wasn't normal for her. She couldn't afford to feel like this for a man. Couldn't trust the feelings *or* him, even if he had been nothing but kind to her so far and had rushed to her rescue like some kind of superhero leaping into the air, cape flying behind him.

Okay, exaggeration. But still.

She had entertained herself watching the other detectives come and go, eavesdropping shamelessly on their phone conversations, which unfortunately lacked drama. She heard a lot of things like, "Yes, I can wait." Or, "Uh-huh."

"Please repeat that," was another frequent flyer.

This being Saturday, she was surprised to see so many detectives working. There were empty desks, but some of their owners might be working, too, just out at crime scenes or doing interviews or whatever else detectives did. Out of the seven she saw, only one was female. Another young woman, Bailey pegged as a clerk. The woman detective was middle-aged, with enough crow's feet beside her eyes, Bailey felt sure the lack of gray in her hair was thanks to her hairdresser. She looked and sounded maternal, which Bailey could see really working with some witnesses or suspects.

Most of the men were middle-aged and older, too. A number sported potbellies and had to hoist their pants when they rose from behind their desks to pour another cup of coffee. The two youngest were Seth and the guy who sat behind him, who somebody had called Kemper. Kemper had a face almost attractive enough to qualify him as a model. Every angle and plane was sharply, beautifully cut. Blond hair was still considerably darker than Bailey's and cut short, emphasizing the pure lines of his face. Occasionally she felt his scrutiny but refused to turn and look at him. Once their eyes met, his brows rose slightly and he nodded, his mouth quirking with what she thought was amusement. His eyes were blue, also like hers, but darker, shadowed somehow. Objectively, he was really much better looking than Seth, she decided, but her body didn't soften for him the way it did for Seth's rough-cast face and stockier, stronger body.

She spent an embarrassing amount of time eyeing Seth sidelong, taking care that he didn't catch her ogling him. And really, that's not what she was doing. She was more…assessing him. Trying to figure out why just looking at him made her feel so much that was unfamiliar.

Small, wiry men repelled her, no surprise there. Even during her high school years and early twenties, when she believed her ability to attract guys was all she had going for her, she wouldn't have touched someone who looked like *him* with a ten-foot pole. Otherwise, she hadn't been discriminating enough to be able to say what attracted her or what didn't. The guy had never been the point. Whether she especially liked him or not wasn't the point. Her needing some kind of validation—*that* was the point. She didn't know any other way to be noticed, wanted. Something. Going cold turkey had been something she had to do for herself. It took her a while to realize what a relief it had been not to do or say anything because of what a guy would think, to dress to please herself and no one else, to refuse to let her body feel anything sexual, which—face it—had ugly connotations for her.

So she couldn't understand this. It was circumstances, she tried to convince herself. He'd cared enough to search for her, and now had become her anchor in a world turned on end. And, yes, he had a great body, muscular but not in a hulking way. If he lifted weights at all, he probably had a bench set up in a spare bedroom or his garage, and she seriously doubted he studied himself in a mirror anytime he wasn't shaving. His dark hair was shaggier than Detective Kemper's, and in midafternoon like this, his jaw was dark with the beginning of stubble. Which, God help her, was sexy on him. Maybe sexier, because she knew it wasn't a conscious look for him, like it was for so many guys where she came from. Hollywood had made stubble *the* look. She wondered what Seth would say if she told him he was trendy right now.

She made herself pretend she was engrossed in checking messages on her phone. There were none, thank God; apparently no member of the press or paparazzi had coaxed anyone to give out her number yet.

That sent a wave of disbelief crashing over her. Paparazzi and Bailey Smith in the same sentence. Impossible. And terrifying, if she let herself think about it, because she couldn't go back to the life she'd had and had no idea what the alternative was. The future had just become a giant whiteboard, clean and pristine, without even a trace of writing on it to guide her.

The panic filled her until she shot to her feet. When Seth lifted his head in surprise, she said, "It's been ages. I think I can go now."

The lines in his face deepened. "I wouldn't bet on that."

"Will you look?"

"All right." Gaze never leaving hers, he pushed his chair back and stood. Only when he reached the window did he look away from her. After a moment, he said, "I don't see anyone. Doesn't mean they aren't watching your car."

"What difference will another hour make?" She needed to get out of here *now*. The cabin sounded like heaven right now. She could sit on a rock and watch the water flow by, breathe in the stillness and scent of evergreens.

He sighed. "Maybe none. All right. I'll walk you down."

She was ahead of him going down the stairs. Partway, he said heavily, "I'm sorry, Bailey."

Stopping, she gripped the handrail and turned. "For what?"

"My crusade has made your life hellish. It's not something I foresaw."

She believed in his regret, but remembered what he'd said the other time they'd talked about this: that, even knowing what would come of it he'd do the same again, because finding her had meant so much to the Lawsons. He'd known them longer; it made sense that they ranked higher in his list of priorities than she did. So why was he the only person here in Stimson who actually saw her, Bailey, not Hope all grown-up?

She shook off the perplexing thought. "You didn't foresee what's happening because you didn't think you'd find me alive."

He winced. "Something like that."

"We can't go back," she said briskly, and started down the stairs again. The question inevitably rose in her mind: Would she go back if she could?

Not answering that.

She considered herself a fatalist. So much in her life had been out of her control. Everything, when she was with *him*. Her only privacy was inside her head. He couldn't tell her what to *think*. So that's where she'd retreated.

The foster care system had much the same impact. She had no say over where she lived, what the house rules were, even what was for dinner or who she shared a bedroom with. Only in the past few years had she finally taken control, understood that she could shape her own life.

Wow, and see how that's turned out, she thought. She ought to hate Detective Seth Chandler for what he'd done to her.

Brooding over that, she crossed the lobby and almost pushed open the glass door before he stopped her.

"Let me go first, Bailey."

Goose bumps prickled her skin. God. What if she'd carelessly stepped out only to be mobbed again? She blinked a couple of times, fast, as if flashbulbs were exploding in front of her.

"All right," he said. "Let's go."

They made it without incident to her car. She slung her bag in and got behind the wheel, Seth standing in the open door. "Watch out that you're not being followed," he instructed her. "If you think you are, take a few turns to see if the vehicle behind stays with you. If you can't shake someone, come back here or call me. Don't drive to the cabin. Okay?"

She gripped the wheel to hide the fact that her hands were shaking. "Got it."

"What if I bring dinner out there tonight?"

The depth of her longing rattled her as much as the idea of pursuers. It made her shake her head hard. "You've done a lot, Seth. You don't have to feel responsible for me 24/7. It's Saturday night. You must have a life."

The silence had her finally turning her head to look at him. The muscles in his jaw were bunched, and he stared at her. Then whatever it was she was seeing on his face disappeared.

"Not as much as you'd think," he said, tone unrevealing. "Enjoy an evening on your own, Bailey." He nodded, stepped back and closed the door.

She found herself looking at his back as he strode across the parking lot. She was aware, however, that he didn't go in until she'd turned onto the street so that he lost sight of her anyway.

CHAPTER SEVEN

SETH POPPED THE top of a can of beer the minute he walked in his door at almost six. He was hungry and should have stopped to get something on the way home. He sure wasn't in the mood to cook.

You must have a life.

He scowled. Of course he did. He was perfectly happy with his life, and don't let anyone try to say differently. Kemper, for example; he was good at mocking. It had taken Seth a while to figure out that it was a form of self-defense for Ben: hold up a mirror so whoever was getting too close had to look at himself instead. Seth didn't usually let it bother him, but right now...

Right now, what? he asked himself, and didn't have a ready answer. All he knew was that Bailey had knocked him off balance today, with her "Thank you for helping, but I don't need you anymore" dismissal.

He turned on the Mariners game, but was too restless to sit and watch. He finished the beer and went to the kitchen for another, not caring when a burst of excitement from his television suggested some pivotal action.

Maybe he needed to take a couple of days and head into the back country, remind himself why he'd sought a job in this rural county backed by the Cascade Mountains instead of with a more respected urban police force. Rivers were too low for rafting, and he didn't feel ambitious enough to aim for a climb, but backpacking…that sounded good.

Except it didn't. It sounded lonely.

He wondered whether Bailey had ever done anything like that. Stupid damn thing to wonder. Of course she hadn't. When would she have? Unless she'd had a boyfriend along the way who'd taken her up into the Sierra Nevadas. He had no idea what her life had been like since she "aged out" of her foster home. It hadn't included college, obviously, until she'd made the decision to go back when she was— He had to think. She was twenty-nine now, and said she would be a senior this year, so she'd started as a freshman when she was twenty-six. Assuming she'd gone full-time, of course, which he didn't know for a fact.

In the act of opening a second beer, he went still. He wanted to know everything about her, which wasn't a good sign.

Truth was, he told himself, he *didn't* know her. He'd been fascinated by her ever since he'd set eyes on the age-progressed drawing. He'd go so far as to say it had haunted him. But what did that have to do with Bailey in the flesh? Not much. No more than did the photos Karen had pressed on him of Hope as a baby, a toddler, a kindergartner. That child had been innocent, hopeful, secure. Bailey wasn't any of those things. Never would be.

Except secure. The time could come when she'd feel safe, at least. Physically and emotionally both. A good start would be accepting the parents who had never stopped loving her, held on to faith that someday they would find her. She was resisting believing that, he knew, and yet a seed of longing must be inside her or she wouldn't have made the trip up here to find out about her past.

Seth wondered what kind of relationships she'd had with men. Maybe she didn't want anything to do with them, given what she'd experienced. That would make sense. Except he didn't believe it. She felt the same spark he did. He'd caught her a few times looking at him with a kind of hunger he understood. As if she was fascinated, too. Unwillingly, maybe, but he could work with what was there.

Sure, to accomplish what?

He dropped into his recliner, tipped his head back and groaned. Bailey didn't need a hot fling with the cop she depended on to guide her through the troubles she faced. She needed something he didn't see how he could give her. Their lives were too far apart.

So get it out of your head, he ordered himself, but knew it wasn't going to be that easy.

His phone rang and he felt an unfamiliar burst of hope. There was his favorite word these days. But the caller was his mother, not Bailey. Having always felt her sadness, he'd never been a rebellious kid. As long as he could remember, his goal had been to protect her from more hurt. An impulse to dodge her call wasn't usual for him.

Ignoring it, he answered. "Hey, Mom."

IF SHE WENT to town tomorrow, it could be a repeat of today, Bailey thought, but she couldn't hide out here forever. The view from the cabin porch was pretty, and she'd relaxed for the first time in days this afternoon when she picked her way among the rocks to a place where the river ran deep enough she could dangle her legs in and feel the tug of the current—until her feet went numb, that was.

The day's heat lingered in the cabin, making the air stuffy. Since she hadn't seen a mosquito yet, she opened the door wide and also wrenched open a couple of windows in hopes of creating some airflow, then took her salad outside. She sat on the porch with her feet on the first step. From here, as she ate she could see the river and the dark, forested bulk of the ridge beyond. One strip looked as if the trees had been clear-cut, which made sense, given that logging was still a big industry in northwestern Washington, except she couldn't imagine how anyone had done it on such a steep hillside.

Bailey pondered that for a few minutes before reverting to the decisions she had to make.

Logically, what she ought to do was go stay with Karen and Kirk. She could get to know her parents. She could make them happy.

She could not see Seth Chandler, which would mean she didn't have to deal with her worrisome feelings about him. Or, if he came by at all, she'd be insulated from him, in a way, there in the bosom of her family.

A shudder rolled through her as if the ground was moving. She looked down to see that goose bumps stood out on her bare arms. It was that pink bedroom she saw in her mind's eye. Going back to being the little girl who had loved it…no. She couldn't do it. Couldn't.

If they'd let her sleep in Eve's room… But what excuse could she give? Wouldn't that seem weird?

It was weird. Not even for herself could she put into words why she felt such horror at the idea of so much as setting foot into her childhood bedroom. Nothing bad had happened there. It didn't make sense!

I'm not her. I can't be her.

Not her first freak-out of the day. There'd been that moment when she'd thought she remembered her father's laugh. His voice lending appropriate gloom to Eeyore, too. Of course, neither was really a memory. She knew that.

Having finished her salad, she set the bowl

aside. The sound of an approaching car made her stiffen momentarily, until it passed without ever slowing at the head of the driveway.

So. She needed a plan. She couldn't hang around here forever. She hadn't intended to stay more than a few days. Thank goodness she wasn't having to spend money on a hotel, given that she *was* still paying the rent on her apartment. Tuition for fall semester would be due soon. As usual, that would wipe her out. What she should be doing right now was working and adding to her stash.

Waitress jobs weren't hard to get, but she sort of suspected the manager of the Denny's here in town wouldn't be thrilled when the press descended on the restaurant to follow the new waitress around while shouting questions like, *Did he sexually molest you?*

Chilled, she wrapped her arms around herself. It took her a minute to push her demons back down where they belonged and slam the lid on them.

Plan. Number one: let an FBI agent interview her. Another new life experience. Number two: spend some time with Kirk.

For whatever reason, that made knots form in her stomach. It was as if…she didn't know. He didn't *scare* her, she knew that. It was more as if she'd clung to the memory of him longer. Had she believed with all her heart that her daddy would rescue her? When he didn't, the disillusionment would have been severe.

You were a daddy's girl.

And yet, something in her shied from the idea of spending time with him alone. What she would do was call Karen and invite herself to dinner tomorrow night. She could even suggest they ask if Eve could be there, too. Like her or not, she was part of the family.

Unsettling thought. *My family.*

Number three: tomorrow she'd drive to Mount Vernon or Burlington—she'd seen an ad for an outlet mall there—and do some shopping. How hard could it be to disguise herself enough that she wasn't immediately recognizable? Makeup, maybe a baseball cap, dark glasses. That would be a start.

IT WASN'T AS if he didn't have other investigations, but Seth justified beginning the hunt for Bailey's abductor immediately by telling himself he should take advantage of her presence in Stimson. Asking follow-up questions would be considerably easier.

A sergeant in Walla Walla was glad to look up information on the murder Bailey remembered, but the police report contained no mention of anyone registered at the motel who'd done a bunk. In fact, investigators probably hadn't done more than talk to people in the rooms to each side. Turned out, there'd been no mystery about who the killer was; a drunken fight had escalated, and the guy had been arrested on the spot. Unfortunately, the motel had been condemned twelve years before and demolished shortly thereafter. The very co-operative sergeant, who had seen the press conference about Hope Lawson being brought home, promised to try to find out if the former owner of the motel was still around and had kept records, but was frank that chances were slim to none.

What would confirmation that Hamby had checked in under that name tell him, anyway? That had been a lot of years ago.

He'd fought the desire to call Bailey all day, only the memory of how firmly she'd sent him on his way stopping him. But, damn it—he wanted to know what she was doing. Who she was doing it with. He hated the idea she might be stuck alone at the cabin, afraid now to venture out.

He was frowning at his computer when the answer to one of his queries popped up and adrenaline had Seth sitting up straight. Les Hamby had been ticketed once in the state of Oregon for driving with an expired license—and he'd been arrested once for trespassing in an elementary school in La Grande. He'd paid the fine for the ticket, and the arrest never came to trial. But that arrest had happened thirteen years ago—ten years and two months after he'd ditched Hope Lawson because her body was developing into a woman's.

The math was simple and had Seth swearing aloud. Hamby had kept Hope for five years. If that was usual for him, he could have had two other little girls in those intervening years. And, although he'd failed to grab his target the day he intruded on school grounds, he'd sure as hell found another girl not long thereafter. Odds were he'd cut his losses and left La Grande—the arrest would have been a red cape waved in front of a bull if a child who attended that school had been abducted shortly thereafter. But Seth would check, anyway. Unfortunately, police incompetence wasn't unknown.

It took him the rest of the day to determine that no girl had been abducted in La Grande in that window of time, but a five-year-old female child had vanished from her bed in the middle of the night in Nampa, Idaho. Easy drive from La Grande, but different state, investigators unaware of the near miss in another town just over the border. Hell, they might have dismissed it if they had heard about it—Seth could just imagine Hamby claiming he'd sneaked in to use the john, didn't mean to scare anyone, and cops shaking their heads and telling him to get out of town.

The five-year-old girl's name was Gail Engstrom—and it so happened she was an exceptionally pretty blue-eyed blonde. Staring at her picture, Seth felt sick.

He put in a call to the Nampa PD and ended up

talking to a detective who remembered the case well. He'd been a patrol officer then, and that kind of crime wasn't common in their town.

"The detective who investigated her disappearance is near retirement now. He's stayed in touch with them, talks about 'em sometimes. The Engstroms ended up divorced. He sold the car dealership he owned and moved away. Mrs. Engstrom is still here, in the same house."

"Waiting," Seth said.

There was a little silence. Then, "Not hard to understand. I have a girl in kindergarten this year." He cleared his throat. "You want to tell me why you're asking?"

Seth did. While they were talking, the guy evidently looked online for Hope Lawson and found not only the news story but also one of Seth's postings that had resulted in her return.

"Damn," he breathed. "She looks one hell of a lot like Gail."

"I don't think there's any doubt the same guy snatched both."

"I always figured Gail was dead."

Seth hesitated, but decided he had to say this. "She might be. He took a hell of a risk, leaving Hope alive. What if she'd talked right away? He wasn't sophisticated enough to constantly change identities—maybe couldn't afford to buy forged ID or to pay for a new driver's license, buy a different car, get insurance again. Hope says he was pulled over once and everything was in order. He may have quit bothering with insurance and whatnot later, though. He was picked up for an expired license in Oregon." Seth gave the particulars. "He'd succeeded in terrorizing Hope into forgetting her real name, but what if he let a kid go who remembered?"

"Yeah. Shit. Although Gail was a year younger when he grabbed her. Might have been even easier to wipe her mind clean." Energized, the guy committed himself to doing his damnedest to trace Hamby's every move in Idaho. They agreed to stay in touch.

Seth set down his phone and stretched. Looking around, he realized most people had closed up shop for the day. No wonder he was hungry.

He could call Bailey, see what she was doing for dinner.

You must have a life.

He grunted unhappily and shut down his computer.

EVE KICKED OFF her shoes and curled her feet under her, pretending a nonchalance she didn't feel in the presence of the real daughter.

Mom had clearly been pleased with herself when she insisted she didn't need any help with dinner. "No, no," she'd said, beaming. "My two girls need time to get to know each other."

Apparently she didn't have a clue.

Eve could tell Hope wasn't any more enthusiastic; she'd looked as if she wanted to grab Mom to keep her from heading for the kitchen. And Dad—well, who knew where he was? Mom had probably given him his orders.

Hope sat gingerly on Mom's favorite chair, a glider, and gave a tentative push to start it moving. She studied Eve. "So."

"So."

"Karen says you're a social worker. That you deal with foster kids."

"I do. Go with what you know, I always say."

Hope's blue eyes, so like Dad's, narrowed. "How long did you live in foster care?"

"Four years."

"What happened to you? Um, if you don't mind telling me."

Eve shrugged. "My mother was into crack. She died. Or that's what they tell me, anyway."

"You don't remember her?"

"Not very well." And what memories she had, she wasn't sharing with Hope.

Who nodded meaninglessly and looked away. Silence stretched to the snapping point, although it might feel that way only to Eve, who had hostility all but choking her.

"Why won't you stay here at the house?" she asked.

Hope looked at her again. "It's too soon. It would feel like staying with strangers."

"You don't believe they're your parents?"

Her forehead crinkled. "No, I do. I mean, it's sort of hard to deny, isn't it?" She waved a hand at herself.

Eve didn't understand herself why the fact that the sainted daughter looked *exactly* like Mom enraged her so. No, that was a lie; of course she knew. It was because she'd longed so desperately to belong. And she would, she'd convinced herself, if only *she* was pretty and blonde instead of so dark and exotic enough people always looked surprised when she checked "Caucasian" on a survey. Of course, eventually she'd figured out the Lawsons never would have wanted her if she'd looked too much like their lost daughter.

The real daughter.

"It is," she agreed, simmering. "So why do you act like you don't really want them to be your parents?"

Her sort-of sister—now, *there* was a joke—went absolutely still. "It all seems unreal to me."

"You're hurting their feelings, you know."

She almost hid her flinch. "I know."

"Do you know how hard it is to watch this? Them so hopeful—" her laugh grated "—you shutting them down."

"I'm not."

"You are."

"You're jealous," Hope said after a minute, as if she'd had a sudden revelation. "You wish I'd never been found. You must have hated it when Seth decided to launch a new search for me."

Seth. Not Detective Chandler. Of course.

"I did." She leaned forward, her body wound tight. "And do you know why? Because I thought all he was doing was getting their hopes up. Especially Mom's. She went to see him at least once a week. Did you know that? She took him pictures." She spat that out. "I'd find her going through albums, looking for the one that would captivate him. She'd make *me* look at them all again to help her. She baked him cookies. She cried. How could he quit, then? It was such a stupid thing for him to do. What did he think—it was going to make them *happy* to move your dead body from one grave to another and put your name on a headstone?" Oh, God, she was dripping vitriol and couldn't seem to help herself. "Or to have it go on and on and on, endlessly, painfully, like it did after you disappeared?"

"Knowing what happened would have given them resolution." Her eyebrows arched. "But that isn't what happened, is it? Instead, I walked in the door. And guess what? *You* were here."

Eve wouldn't have thought it was possible to stiffen further, but she did. "What's that supposed to mean?"

"You kind of stepped into my shoes and stole the life that was supposed to be mine, didn't you?"

Eve's laugh corroded her lungs and throat. "Oh,

like that was possible. You're right—I tried desperately to fill this giant hole in their lives and their hearts, but I always knew I was failing. Hard to miss, when practically every room in this house has a shrine to *you*."

Too late, she heard a gasp. A few feet into the living room, Mom stood staring at her in shock and desolation. She'd pressed her fingers to her mouth after the one sound.

"Mom." Eve started to rise. Anguish replaced the anger.

"You thought we didn't love you?" her mother whispered.

"I didn't say that!" She wasn't sure her legs would hold her if she did try to stand.

"Oh, dear God. I'm the one who failed." She turned a tearful gaze from Eve to Hope and back again. "Both of you," she cried, and fled the room.

Eve sat frozen. When she looked, she saw that Hope wasn't so much as breathing, either. "Why didn't I keep my big mouth shut?"

"I think... I goaded you."

Surprised, Eve focused on Hope, who had a hand pressed to her stomach as if she was about to be sick.

"You're right," she said. "I shouldn't have come, should I? They want me to be Hope, and I can't be. All I'm doing is making us all miserable." She scrambled to her feet. "Tell them—"

"You can't just *leave*," Eve cried. "How do you think that would make them feel?"

They stared at each other. After a moment, Hope sank back onto the chair, which seemed to startle her by rocking. She grabbed for the padded arms.

"Maybe I should go talk to her," Eve said after a minute.

"I don't know. I don't know her."

Eve absorbed what Hope had said a minute ago. About *not* being Hope.

"Would you rather I call you Bailey?" she asked tentatively.

"Please." Hope—Bailey—swallowed. "Kirk does, but Karen won't."

Words pushed themselves out. "I shouldn't have said all that."

"I shouldn't have said what I did, either. I think—" Bailey's gaze shied from Eve's.

"You think?"

"That it's natural for us to both be jealous. Even though…" She stopped again, made a face. "Nobody has ever been jealous of my life before."

"A lot of kids who were never adopted would be jealous of mine." Knowing that was true made Eve feel even smaller than she already had. "I was the lucky one."

Bailey looked right into her eyes and said the unexpected. "Except there was that other bedroom."

Eve grimaced. "I wanted that bedroom so bad. Except I didn't, too."

"But it was always there, no matter what."

She shrugged.

Hope looked down at her hands. "You want to know something? I can't make myself so much as take a step into that bedroom, and I don't even know why."

Eve gaped at her. "You don't think something bad happened to you there?"

Bailey shook her head. "It's like they expect me to *be* that little girl. I guess it's symbolic." Then she said something else, in a voice so low Eve barely heard it. "I'm afraid I'll remember."

"I used to sneak in there sometimes," Eve heard herself confessing. "They never said I couldn't, but somehow I knew it was…sacred. You know."

Bailey nodded.

"I'd open drawers and look at your clothes and touch your dolls, and I imagined I was you. How thrilled they'd be. How happy."

Bailey's eyes closed again. "And here I am, not making them happy at all."

Thinking of her as Bailey instead of Hope was easier than Eve would have thought. She found herself seeing her through different eyes, too.

Managing a sort of smile, she said, "Yeah, you are. Why else am I being such a bitch?"

This new sister answered with a smile as wry. "Because it comes naturally?"

Eve laughed. "Maybe." Now she was able to stand up. "So, what do you say we go find out what the damage was?"

"Only if I can bring up the rear."

"Coward."

The truce was probably temporary, Eve thought as they both stood. Maybe they'd cleared the air a little, but the mutual resentment was still there. And then there was the fact that Seth quit seeing her once he got Bailey on his mind. And, no, that wasn't exactly Bailey's fault, but… *Who says I have to be fair?* Eve asked herself, and answered, *Don't have to be.*

But hurting Mom the way she just had—that was totally on her. Deep inside burrowed a painful knowledge: words once said couldn't be unsaid, and forgiven wasn't the same as forgotten.

BAILEY DROVE HOME in a daze. She didn't know how it was possible, but each meeting with the Lawsons felt more stressful than the last.

When she and Eve had tracked Karen down to her bedroom, she insisted she understood they'd said things they didn't mean and told them not to worry about it. "Of course emotions are high," she said softly.

She even let them help her finish getting dinner on the table, but was subdued enough during the meal that Kirk noticed, his worried gaze resting on her often.

Bailey's only consolation was that she could tell Eve felt as guilty as she did.

At this point, her feelings for Eve were more than a little mixed. The hostility, she got. It probably wasn't anybody's fault, but they'd been set up from the beginning to resent each other.

It was almost funny, when she thought about it. Sibling rivalry, to the nth degree. And between two women who had never even met a week ago. In fact, Bailey hadn't so much as suspected Eve's existence.

Of course, she hadn't believed in her parents' existence, either.

Brooding as she drove, Bailey decided maybe she and Eve had cleared the air a little. The sting she felt because Eve had taken her place was so recent, getting past it wasn't a big deal for her, but Eve had had twenty years to learn to hate Bailey. No, Hope. The real daughter.

Could they be friends? Her mind boggled. Polite? Probably. They'd done pretty well at dinner and after. Bailey thought she might have liked Eve, if they'd met under other circumstances. Even aside from Kirk and Karen, they had something in common: painful childhoods and years in foster care.

Dusk had arrived without her noticing. She had to watch carefully for the driveway, not that different from a dozen others along this narrow country road. With the thick undergrowth pressing close and dark evergreen trees rearing above, it felt like full night. She was relieved to emerge into the clearing around the cabin. Home, sweet home, of sorts.

She'd stayed later at the Lawsons' than she'd meant. It was sort of hard, she'd found, to make excuses for a getaway when the people you were making them to knew perfectly well you had nowhere else to be. As a result, she'd felt compelled to agree that she'd love to look at photo albums. *Love* did not accurately describe her confusion of emotions that swung between deep reluctance and shy curiosity. While Eve and Bailey cleared the table, Karen bustled off to get the albums, after which they all resumed their seats, Karen having moved her chair to sit right next to Bailey.

Naturally, she'd already seen her kindergarten school picture, but this— There was a much younger Karen, who looked frighteningly like Bailey did now, in the hospital holding a newborn. Bailey's gaze switched to the next photo and the next as her mind grappled with the idea that this was *her*. The vague gaze of that baby, who was almost bald with only a little colorless fuzz. That baby grinning toothlessly, a pink bow somehow stuck to her head. Crawling. Pulling herself up to stand. Walking. Running. Laughing. *Me.*

There were two fat photo albums, only a couple of pages left empty at the end of the second one. When Karen turned the last page, where one of

Hope in her swimsuit grinning was the last, and they all saw the blank, facing page, there'd been a long silence. Even Eve, who'd endured the reminiscences, had looked pained.

Bailey asked to see pictures of Eve growing up. Eve had shot her a quick, unreadable look but said nothing. Delighted, Karen went off to fetch a heaping pile that almost made Bailey groan. Thank God they hadn't had Eve from the time she was a baby. That would have taken until midnight.

She'd found herself unwillingly interested, however, once she saw the first photo taken when a social worker brought Eve with her single suitcase to stay.

"She was eight, then," Karen murmured. "Nine when we adopted her."

At eight, Eve had been scrawny, all eyes and dark, tangled hair. Still petite now, then she'd looked like a wild child, raised in the woods by wolves. Bailey had no trouble at all interpreting the wary stare or the body language, her arms pressed tight to her sides. *That's probably what I looked like, too*, she thought with an uncomfortable cramp beneath her breastbone.

Seeing the change from that suspicious, neglected-looking child to a pretty preteen, who became beautiful by her prom picture, was illuminating. *It wouldn't have happened if the Lawsons* hadn't *loved that child*, Bailey thought, and hoped Eve saw the same thing she did.

Bailey shook off the thoughts of the evening as she pulled to a stop in what had become her spot in front of the cabin. Locking from habit, she hurried up the steps to let herself in. She wished she'd thought to leave on a light. Not that it was completely dark, but still.

She had the door open when she was surprised to hear a car engine that sounded like it was coming down the driveway. Turning, she saw headlights spear the night and glint off her car. Could it be Seth? But he'd have called, not arrived unexpectedly this late, wouldn't he?

And then she realized a second vehicle was behind the first.

Understanding came in time for her to leap inside, slam the door and lock it. She'd been stupid, so wrapped up in everything she'd learned tonight, she hadn't paid attention to whether she was being followed.

She pressed her back against the door and stayed completely still, a small creature desperate to avoid a predator's notice. A moment later, someone hammered on the door.

"Ms. Lawson? I'd like to talk to you."

Light glinted off to one side. She turned her head and was almost blinded by the flashlight beam shining in one of the small windows. A voice called excitedly, "I see her! She's in there."

Her teeth chattered, and she fumbled for her phone.

CHAPTER EIGHT

SETH TOOK THAT damn driveway so fast, his head whacked against the roof of his SUV when he hit a rut wrong. He'd made the drive with lights flashing and siren screaming. He was ready to kill someone, to hell with the consequences.

His headlights swept over three separate vehicles besides Bailey's in the small clearing and a bunch of people who all swung his way. Son of a bitch, wasn't there a grain of conscience among them?

Slamming to a stop, he turned off the siren but left on the flashing light to make a point. He climbed out and stalked toward the porch, his hand resting on the hilt of his weapon. To make *another* point.

"Anyone still on this property thirty seconds from now will be under arrest," he said loudly.

The two people on the porch began to protest.

"There's no law says we can't knock on someone's door," one of them argued.

He began to count. "One thousand one, one thousand two, one thousand three."

The yellow beams of flashlights pierced the

near-complete darkness as shapes behind them materialized from the darkness to each side of the cabin. Christ. They'd been looking in the windows? Imagining Bailey's fear made him pause in his counting.

"Ten-thirty at night, this is an isolated home, and you're shining flashlights in the windows in hopes of terrifying a lone woman into coming out?" His voice was harsh. "By God, I *want* to arrest every last one of you."

"We're going, we're going," one of them said as she scuttled by him.

A woman. He wondered how *she* would have felt, huddled by herself in that cabin.

He took up his count to allow for the time since he'd left off. "One thousand and twenty. One thousand and twenty-one. One thousand and twenty-two."

One set of headlights came on, then another. Car doors slammed. Vehicles backed up, maneuvered around each other and his SUV, and he saw red taillights.

He turned then. "Bailey? You okay?"

After a moment, the door opened a crack. He saw only darkness inside. "Are they gone?" Her voice shook.

Son of a bitch. "Yeah. Can I come in?"

"Yes. Okay." The door swung wider. She must have reached for the light switch, because that bare overhead bulb came on.

The rage in him swelled when he saw her face, pale and pinched, and her body held tight as if to make herself small. He took one step inside and gathered her into his arms.

For an instant, she stayed stiff, so tense it was like gathering in a bundle of high-tension wires. Then she made a muffled sound, threw her arms around him and sagged against him.

He pressed his cheek to her head. "I can't believe they did that," he growled.

"It was my fault."

"What?"

"I forgot to watch for someone following me," she said miserably. "It was…kind of a full evening, and I got careless."

"There's no excuse for that bunch of weasels. They were trying to scare you out."

"You warned me," she mumbled into his chest.

"I didn't expect anything like this." His hands moved up and down her back. "I doubt any of this bunch were working for the *Seattle Times* or any reputable national magazines. They don't operate this way."

Bailey pulled back a little, crying, "Then who *were* they?"

One hand now wrapped her nape. He squeezed gently. "At a guess, freelancers. People who don't get a paycheck unless they produce a story. Apparently, any way they can."

Her breath came out in a gust, as if she'd taken

a blow, and she let herself lean against him again. A couple of minutes passed. He didn't say anything, just gave her time to gather strength. Unfortunately, he became increasingly aware of her breasts pressing against his chest, the silky texture of her hair beneath his cheek and mouth, a scent that was indefinably her, and the delicate lines of her back, shoulders and neck. He tried to hold her so she wouldn't notice he was becoming aroused, but, damn, he didn't want to push her away, either.

When finally she sighed and straightened, it took him a beat too long to let her go.

If she noticed, she didn't comment. "Will they come back once they see you leave?" she asked.

He frowned. "I doubt it, but we're not taking the chance. You can't stay here anymore, Bailey. It's time for Plan B." Or were they on C?

"Which is?" Her tartness sounded more like the gutsy woman he was getting to know, the one who hated needing to be rescued. "One of those freeway motels?"

He shook his head. "You'd be lucky to make it through the night before the vultures descended again. They'll be watching for you. Desk clerks at that kind of place can be bribed."

Her expression became mulish. "Then what?"

"You do have a bedroom waiting for you at the Lawsons, you know."

She closed her eyes. "I can't."

Seth didn't say anything, but he wrapped his hands around her upper arms and felt her shiver.

"I know it's dumb. I mean, they're nice people." She fell silent for a minute. "Maybe...maybe they'd let me sleep on the sofa. Or...or in Eve's room."

He couldn't pretend to understand what was bothering her—he wasn't even sure *she* knew—but her horror seemed genuine.

She drew a shuddering breath and met his eyes. "I don't have a lot of choice, do I? Um...give me a few minutes to get my stuff. And I shouldn't leave the food to rot, should I?"

"I'll pack the food while you gather your things." When she started toward the bathroom, he said, "Bailey."

Her teeth had closed on her lower lip when she turned.

"I'm going to take you home with me tonight." Oh, man. Was he nuts? "It's late to knock on the Lawsons' door no matter what. I have a spare bedroom," he finished gruffly. "Nobody will bother you at my place."

She searched his face with those desperate eyes. "I've sort of cornered you, haven't I? I didn't mean to."

Seth shook his head. "My house is the most secure place for you right now."

"Won't you get in trouble? I mean, since I'm part of, well, an investigation?"

He had no idea what his lieutenant would have to say about it, never mind the sheriff himself, enough of a politician to make Seth queasy on occasion. He discovered, however, that he didn't give a damn what anyone else thought. "It's not like you're a suspect, Bailey."

"No, but—"

"We can talk in the morning about alternatives," he said quietly.

Instinct told him she'd hate knowing how much vulnerability she was betraying at that moment, as she hesitated. But finally she nodded.

More relieved than he'd have admitted, he found where she'd stashed the plastic grocery bags and began repacking what he'd bought for her... not today, yesterday. By the time he was done, she was ready, the handle of her rolling suitcase clutched in one hand, the sleeping bag efficiently rolled.

"You okay to drive?" he asked.

"Of course I am."

Her indignation made him smile. "Okay, just follow me, then."

She turned out the light, locked up and handed him the key. As they made their careful way in the dark to their respective vehicles, her voice came to him. "I kind of liked it here." She sounded wistful.

"Didn't turn out to be as peaceful as I'd hoped."

"No." She hopped in her car and the slam of the door brought an end to the conversation.

There wasn't much traffic at this time of night, which made it easy to watch for anyone following them. Apparently he'd scared that last bunch enough; none of them had hung around hoping for another shot at her. Bailey stuck so close behind him during the drive he could have ticketed her for tailgating. He understood, though; whether she was happy about it or not, he was her rock right now. The Lawsons would be there for her, too—she had to know that—but she must feel a lot of confusion about them right now. He was neutral.

Yeah, he thought, unless she blamed him for the nightmare her life had turned into since she walked into the sheriff's department that first day. Man, he hoped she didn't hate him. But he kind of thought she wouldn't have leaned against him so trustingly if she did.

His house was nothing special—an older rambler with the typical two-car garage that really only had room for one car along with the workbench, tools, lawn mower and sports equipment. He used the remote to open the garage door, but parked as close to one side of the driveway as he could get and jumped out to wave her in. She gestured for confirmation; he nodded, and she finally, tentatively, edged inside the garage.

He grabbed the bags of groceries, locked his SUV and walked into the garage, where she was getting her suitcase out of her trunk.

"You're trying to hide me," she said.

Seth raised his eyebrows. "Wouldn't you rather have your car out of sight?"

She made a face at him. "You know I would. I feel bad you couldn't park in your own garage, though."

He smiled. "If it was pouring or snowing, I might mind."

He ushered her inside, closing the garage behind them, and set the bags down on the kitchen counter. "Spare room is over here," he said casually, and led the way. The house was your basic three bedrooms, two bathrooms boxy. He had a guest room set up only because his mother or sister and her family visited. A double bed and simple dresser were the sole furnishings. A cot kept in the closet could be unfolded for one of the kids.

"The bathroom across the hall is all yours," he told her. "If you want to go straight to bed, that's fine. If not, why don't you come along to the kitchen. I have coffee, tea, cocoa."

She nodded, not moving, and he left. Not anywhere close to ready to go to bed himself, he'd be disappointed if she didn't want to talk. Listening to the silence, he started putting away her groceries. He was wadding the plastic bags up again when she appeared, expression tentative. Normally a graceful woman, right now the way she held herself was awkward, shoulders rounded and arms as far from relaxed as they could be, betraying how uncertain of herself she felt. She had brushed her hair, pulling it into some kind of bundle at the back of her head, only wisps of bangs softening her face. Whatever makeup she'd started the day with was mostly gone, though, leaving dark smudges under her eyes.

"Don't you need to get to bed?" she asked.

"I'm not on the clock. I work long hours. If I show up a little later tomorrow, no one will complain."

"Oh." Keeping a wary eye on him, she climbed onto one of the stools pulled up to the breakfast bar that formed the end of the countertop. "You really have cocoa?"

Seth smiled, careful to appear relaxed. "Coffee would keep me awake. Anyway, I have a sweet tooth. Want some?"

"Please."

The teakettle whistled. He silenced it long enough to dump mix into a couple of mugs, and then poured. He handed her one mug and a spoon and kept the second, leaning back against the counter edge. He liked to think he was a smart man, which meant keeping his distance.

"I miscalculated what was going to happen after the press conference," he said. "My fault."

Her forehead crinkled. "What do you mean?"

"We didn't give enough detail."

She absorbed that. "You mean, whether he sexually molested me."

"That's the biggie," he agreed. "They want the

whole story. What your life was like with him. How you could have forgotten your own name. Some of the stuff you've told me."

Her chin came up. Her eyes were dark and turbulent. "And if I don't tell them what they want to know?"

"They're going to keep after you. At least for a while."

Bailey ducked her head and sipped cocoa. Finally, she asked, "What do you think I should do?"

He sighed. "I don't know. Probably I should have said something tonight. Told them I've asked you not to say any more since this is an ongoing investigation."

"Would they respect that?"

He shook his head and repeated, "I don't know. The scene tonight was out of my experience."

"If I tell them...it would be like stripping naked so they could critique my body. Them all circling me, poking at me, prying open my mouth to look at my teeth, telling me to spread my legs." She shuddered. "You know?"

The picture she painted was a vivid one. And, God help him, he wished she'd strip naked for him. But he also understood what she was telling him. Much of the composure that seemed innate to her wasn't. It was more like armor she donned to face the world. Stripped of that, she would be naked in a sense, exposed for everyone to see.

"We can hold out. Most of them will give up

eventually. Alternatively, we can choose one journalist and you can give an exclusive. That might work best. Think about it."

She nodded.

He hesitated. "There's something else I need to tell you."

She went still and her eyes widened. He almost didn't go on. He hadn't even asked why she'd described her evening as "full." Was that a euphemism for shitty?

But she was waiting, and he doubted she'd let him put her off.

"Today, I started tracing Les Hamby's footsteps. The murder you told me about didn't get me anywhere, but I found a couple of more recent citations in Oregon." He told her about them.

"He was going to snatch a girl from that school." Her voice vibrated with outrage and something like fear.

"That's my take," he agreed. "As it was, a parent spotted him loitering between the girls' bathroom and an exit door and confronted him. A teacher called an administrator, who called the police. He was arrested but never brought to trial. He didn't dare grab a girl in La Grande after that." Here came the part he was telling Bailey only because he thought she deserved to know the truth. "A five-year-old girl was abducted less than two weeks later from her home in Nampa, Idaho, not very far away. Bailey…" He hesitated. "She looked a lot like you at that age."

"Oh, God." Obviously stricken, she set down the mug. "So…so it wasn't just me. He didn't stop."

"No."

And then her stare became fierce. "When was that?"

He told her, and saw her making the same calculations he had. "Oh, God," she whispered again. "How many lives has he ruined?"

Her self-assessment gave him an uncomfortable jolt. "You're triumphing over what he did to you," he argued.

"Am I?" Her laugh broke. "I can't make myself take a step inside my childhood bedroom. My head believes the Lawsons are my parents, but my heart—" she tapped her chest "—doesn't. I don't make close friends, I don't have boyfriends. I'm getting a degree in psychology, but what am I going to do with it? Become a therapist, telling other people how to run their lives when I'm so obviously dysfunctional?"

Seth scowled at her. "Bailey, in my eyes you've made something remarkable of yourself, considering the terrified, damaged child you were when he left you. From the sound of it, you've done it all on your own. What I'm seeing is a woman who may be new to the idea of family, but has the compassion to be kind even when she's feeling lost herself. That's a woman who'd be one hell of a fine therapist for kids dealing with traumatic events and shattered families."

She blinked a couple of times. "You're mad."

"Hell, yes, I'm mad." Belatedly, he realized he'd flattened his hands on the countertop so he could lean in on her. He probably looked as combative as he felt. Damn, he hoped he wasn't scaring her.

"Thank you," she said, utterly confounding him. "What you said, that's nice. Um… I suppose I do put myself down more than I should. Sometimes I'm proud of myself, but…"

When she hesitated, he finished. "But not as often as you should be."

She tried to smile. "I guess."

"What kind of grades are you getting?"

"Really good." This smile was wider and remarkably sweet, not like the one she used as a form of self-defense, but it died too soon. "That doesn't negate my point. I don't know how to be… oh, a daughter, a sister, really even a friend."

She didn't bother listing *girlfriend*, he noticed. Or *lover*. A lurch in his chest reminded him she had good reason not to want a lover.

Blocking it out, he said, "I've set up an appointment for you with Special Agent Andrew Stuart of the FBI. Tomorrow afternoon at two-thirty."

"Oh, joy," she mumbled.

He cast his mind back. "What happened tonight? You sounded shaken."

She cocked her head. "You mean, before people started peering in my window, spotlighting me with their flashlights?"

"Yeah." He permitted himself a small grin. "Before that."

Bailey made a face, then took a swallow of her cocoa. "Eve and I, well, sort of went at it."

He raised his eyebrows.

"You don't need to hear about that. I mean, considering."

"Considering?" His temper rose to a simmer again. Presumably she was talking about his non-existent relationship with Eve.

"You know what I mean. The thing is, Karen heard some stuff we said, and that upset *her*." Emotions crossed Bailey's face too quickly to all be identified. "We apologized—she insisted she understood, but of course I felt guilty, so after dinner instead of leaving while it was still light, I agreed to sit down and look at photo albums."

"Ah."

She traced the rim of her mug, her head bent. "It was…so bizarre." Her voice was very soft. If he'd stood much farther away, he wouldn't have been able to hear her. "Seeing myself. Pretty, and happy. Chubby cheeked." Her shoulders hunched. "Karen was so delighted, and I kept thinking, that *looks* like me but how can it be when I don't remember?" She looked up, so much hurt and perplexity in her eyes, Seth felt it like a blow.

He was a cop; he dealt every day with people who had just been injured or victimized, who were enraged, scared, sobbing, and he didn't let himself feel what they felt. He couldn't afford to. But he couldn't seem to shut out this woman's emotions. Although his chest felt bruised, he was shaken by the realization that he didn't *want* to shut her out. For her, he'd bear almost anything.

Partly because much of what she felt was on him. Instead of appearing on scene after the fact, as was usual, *he* was the one who'd torn open the life she'd created, exposed her to the public eye, brought her home to face a forgotten past.

But that wasn't the only reason why, and he knew it.

"Despite the grief she's lived with, Karen is an optimist." He managed to sound calmer than he felt. "She can't let herself believe that you might never remember anything."

Bailey nodded. "It would be like losing me all over again. I'm not sure knowing I'm alive is enough for her. You know? She needs me to be Hope."

He wouldn't have been able to keep his hands off her if not for the width of the counter separating them. Lucky thing. She'd accepted his comfort earlier, but he had a feeling that didn't come naturally. No wonder.

"Maybe you're both expecting too much, too soon," he said gently.

"She is. Me…" Her mouth twisted. "I don't have any expectations. When I came—" She shrugged. "I think I'd have been relieved if you'd said, sorry, you do look like Hope Lawson, but you can't possibly be her."

Watching her closely, he suggested, "And disappointed, too."

One shoulder jerked. "Maybe."

She wanted to be tough enough to shake off anything life threw at her, he diagnosed, but this homecoming had battered her defenses.

Before he could say anything, she continued. "Then we looked at Eve's photo albums." She raised her gaze to his. "The early pictures? I identified with them more than I did the ones of me. I *knew* that girl."

"Damn, Bailey."

"But then… I could see what their care did for her. She became beautiful and confident, because she felt loved. It was like—" She stopped, obviously unwilling to finish.

"She took up where that little girl Hope left off."

"Yes," she whispered. "It was like…a seesaw. I said that before, didn't I? But it's true. When I was up, she was down. I went down, she soared."

"Except I heard Eve. She called you the *real* daughter."

Creases formed on Bailey's smooth forehead. "Yes. She said…more than that this evening. You know. When we, um…"

"Went at it."

"Right."

Seth frowned. "Bailey, what you saw in the photo album—in both photo albums—was partly truth, partly facade. The pictures of you don't tell the whole story of your life before you were abducted. They represent the high points. I'm pretty sure you threw temper tantrums, were sometimes mad at your mommy or daddy, might have been a spoiled brat on occasion."

She watched him, unblinking.

"And Eve. You're right. The Lawsons helped her become a beautiful woman who is confident on the outside. But inside, you'd find the scared girl who didn't think anybody would ever want her."

"You're right." Her grimace turned into rolled eyes. "Just don't make me say that too often."

Protecting herself again. But he let her get away with it. He just smiled. "I'm frequently right, you know. I'd go so far as to say—"

Her eyes narrowed. "Don't you dare."

"Hey, when it's the truth…" He spread his hands.

She laughed and shook her head, then gazed into her mug as if reading tea leaves at the bottom. When she looked up, the vulnerability that got to him was very apparent. "Here you came to my rescue again, and what do I do but dump on you. Speaking of therapists."

"Bailey." His voice came out rough. Whatever his face showed had her eyes widening. "I prodded you into talking. I want to hear anything you have to say. I deal with a lot of people on the job. I don't bring them home to stay with me."

Whoa, he thought. Maybe that was more than he should have said. She looked stunned. Possibly alarmed.

"That's…nice of you to say." She sounded cautious. "But I think I've unloaded enough for one night. You don't mind if I go to bed?"

"You don't need permission." He made an effort to keep it light. Too little, too late, he feared. "If you get up before me in the morning, help yourself to any food you find."

"Okay." She smiled tentatively. "Good night, Seth."

He lifted his mug to her and stayed right where he was. "Sleep tight."

Her mouth was curving as she turned away, making his heart feel light in his chest.

Left alone, he didn't move for a long time.

HAVING BREAKFAST WITH a man was beyond weird. Bailey guessed there must have been times in foster homes when it was just her and the foster dad eating at the same time. She didn't remember. Otherwise—she hadn't so much as had a female roommate in aeons. When she went out on her own, she'd had to share a place, like it or not.

Minimum wage didn't go very far. Her first apartment, there'd been three of them crammed into a one-bedroom. She'd hated it. She'd had years of sharing bedrooms in foster homes. She'd have given anything for her very own room. As soon as she could manage, she lived alone. Which usually meant crummy neighborhoods and microsize studio apartments, but having her own space was really important to her.

Sharing the newspaper with Seth, him grunting his thanks when she handed him a bagel that had just popped up in the toaster, her murmuring her thanks when he poured her a second cup of coffee, felt both surreal and oddly comfortable. It helped that he apparently wasn't a morning person any more than she was. He looked heavy-eyed and didn't seem interested in talking. Or encouraging *her* to talk.

Maybe he'd had his fill last night.

But Bailey knew better.

I want to hear anything you have to say.

She would swear he'd meant it. She didn't understand why, but believed unwillingly in his sincerity. Probably he thought of her as part of his job, which she was, in a way.

Not "in a way"—who was she kidding? He'd been all cop when he arrived tonight, not to mention when he came to her rescue at the pharmacy. Once he'd delivered her to the Lawsons and presented her to the world, she should have quit being his job, but, oh, oops, turned out she still needed help and he felt obligated. And then there was his hunt for her abductor.

Telling herself she was satisfied and even relieved by the explanation, she finished the front section and folded it neatly. Looking up, she found him watching her with those intense dark eyes.

"Do you have plans today?" he asked.

"I saw an ad for a discount mall in Skagit County. It's not that far, right?"

Lines gathered on his forehead. "Right."

Seeing that he was about to ask why the hell she needed to go shopping right now, she told him.

"I could use some different things to wear. I didn't pack for a long stay."

He jerked his head toward the door leading into the garage. "I have a washer and dryer. Feel free."

"Thanks. But I think I could disguise myself a little. Not be so obvious," she explained, and he nodded.

"They'll be watching for your car, but just covering your hair would make you a little less conspicuous."

She didn't take offense. Her white-blond hair didn't occur naturally very often. In kids, sure, but then it darkened. Hers never had.

"All right." He sounded grudging.

"Ooh. I have permission."

The slant of one eyebrow suggested he was not

amused. "Just so you make it to the police station by two-thirty."

She rolled her eyes. "If the shopping doesn't take very long, I thought I'd stop by Kirk's shop and see if we could have lunch. With Karen around, he doesn't say much. And maybe he won't be enthusiastic, but…" She let herself trail off, not quite wanting to admit how curious she was about him. *You were a daddy's girl.* Sometimes, looking at him, she felt movement deep inside, just a shiver, as if something well below the surface stirred the water.

Focusing again on Seth's craggy face, she had the uncomfortable feeling he'd seen more than she meant to give away. And not for the first time. Resentment mixed with unease. She was *good* at hiding. What was it with him, anyway?

"We haven't talked about where you're going to stay."

Bailey tensed. "I can call Karen. I'm sure they'd be okay—"

But he was shaking his head. "I'd rather you stay here."

"Because?"

"Lot of pressure on you when you're with them."

Yes! She could spend an hour or two at a time with them, then wanted to get away so desperately, she understood why animals chewed a leg off to escape the steel jaws of a trap.

He frowned again. "Once the vultures know you're there, you might find yourself stuck."

"They can follow me here."

"Not if you're careful. Even if they do, they'd have to deal with me. They wouldn't like that."

"It's not fair to you."

"Bailey." His voice had dropped an octave. He kept watching her in that unnerving way. Apparently two cups of coffee had really woken him up. "I mean what I say. I want to provide a refuge for you. I want to hear about your day. How you feel about what's happening. I know—" he hesitated slightly "—trust isn't easy for you. I'm asking for yours anyway."

Her throat closed up and for a minute she couldn't have spoken even if she knew what to say. But at last she said gruffly, "You're right. I mean, it's not. But I do. Mostly. It's not like you haven't earned it. So… I'm trying."

He surprised her by laughing. "You should have stopped while you were ahead. Another ten seconds, you'll be admitting you don't trust me at all."

"No, that's not true—"

Still smiling, he said, "I think it is, but that's okay. We'll get there, Bailey. Now I need to be off. Do what you have to today, but if you're cornered, you have no comment. You take out your phone and say, 'If you don't back off, I'm calling 911.' They don't, you call me. Okay?"

She nodded, that lump clogging her throat again.

"Oh." He went around to the kitchen side of the breakfast bar, opened a drawer and took out a key and a flat black *something* she realized after a puzzled moment was the remote for the garage. "You keep parking inside. And do *not* open the door to anyone. Got that?"

All she could do was nod.

He came back around the breakfast bar and bent to kiss her cheek. "See you this afternoon."

And then he was gone, leaving her not understanding at all why that casual kiss had sent shock waves through her, and why the idea of having the key to his house—living here—didn't make her want to bolt.

CHAPTER NINE

WHEN SHE WALKED into Lawson's Auto Body & Towing, Kirk stood behind the cash register, smiling as he listened to whatever the man on this side of the counter was saying. A customer, presumably. Kirk tore something from a printer, folded it neatly, put it in an envelope and handed it over. As she approached, she heard him say, "Now, you let me know if you have any problem, Jim."

His smile slid from his face when he saw her. The beefy, middle-aged man departing looked at her with curiosity and a kind of *knowing* in his eyes she was growing to hate before he nodded, said, "Ms. Lawson," and left.

Her momentary fear that her father was dismayed to see her vanished when she saw his eyes crinkling with a smile far warmer than the one that had just left his face. "Bailey."

"Hi," she said, feeling shy for no good reason. "I wondered if I could take you to lunch."

"I'd like that," he said, "but I've had reporters coming by all morning asking questions. Unless you hanker for something fancy—"

She shook her head.

"Then what say we sneak down the alley, grab something from the taco truck on the next block and just sit out back to eat?"

"That sounds perfect. I was cornered yesterday at Walgreens and again—" She wasn't so sure she wanted to tell him where she was staying now. "Well, it wasn't fun."

He frowned. "Hope the manager sent them on their way."

"Yes, with help from Seth. I shouldn't have called him, but I did on impulse. I was—" Scared. *Daddy*, she wanted to say, *I was scared.*

He heard what she didn't say. "I'm here, too, honey."

Bailey was momentarily unable to speak. Seth wasn't the only one who made her feel like she had a gumball stuck in her throat. She could only nod.

Appearing satisfied, her father went off to tell his employees he'd be out and to wash his hands.

When he returned, her gaze dropped to those big hands, scarred and nicked—he wore a bandage on one finger—and she saw that, yes, grease was embedded in his skin. Her heartbeat sped up. A memory teased, but to her relief didn't quite take shape.

He nodded toward the back. "Like I said, I recommend the scenic route."

She made a face, hiding her underlying turmoil. "That sounds like a good idea."

He didn't say anything as they walked, but the silence didn't feel uncomfortable. It...eased something in her.

They had to emerge into a parking lot where the truck was set up, but they were early enough no one else was waiting. They ordered a bunch of tacos and carried them in a couple of greasy sacks back to the cinder block rear of his business, where some molded plastic lawn chairs served the function of employee break room. A pile of more loose cinder blocks made a table of sorts, and Kirk quickly carried an overfull ashtray away, although the smell lingered.

He went in and returned with cold cans of soda from a machine, shaking his head at the idea of two of the young guys who worked for him being smokers. "Fools," he muttered.

She smiled and enthusiastically started in on a taco.

"Wouldn't want your mother to know how often I eat there," he said after a minute. "I'm supposed to be watching my cholesterol."

New disquiet struck at the idea of losing this kind man before she even got to know him. "Have you had heart trouble?"

"Just family history." He pondered that for a minute. "Guess we need to let you know that kind of thing."

"I'm a little young to worry about my cholesterol."

"I had a sister who died young with breast cancer."

Well, okay. That could be familial.

Such an astonishing concept.

"Karen—Mom," she corrected herself, "said I was a daddy's girl when I was little."

As seemed to be his way, he gave that some thought. "I guess you were." He was quiet for a minute, not eating. "Losing you…" He shook his head. "I didn't think we'd survive that."

By an instinct she didn't know she had, Bailey covered his hand with hers. "I'm sorry."

The lines on his face seemed to have been carved by grief, but in his eyes—the same shade of blue as hers—she saw astonishment and happiness that squeezed her heart.

"Mom said she felt as if she should pinch herself." *Mom. There. I've said it twice.* Her voice was husky. "That she was having trouble believing."

"When you're right here, I believe it's you." His Adam's apple bobbed. "Last night, lying in bed, I kept wondering if any of this had happened."

With some difficulty, she smiled. "Even Detective Chandler feels that way. His goal was to make it possible for you to bury me. He looked like he'd seen a ghost when he set eyes on me."

Her father gave a rough chuckle. "I guess that's it. Takes some getting used to."

"You...you don't have any doubt I'm really Hope, do you?"

His smile was gentle, filling her with warmth that penetrated deep. "No, Bailey. I know my own little girl when I see her."

Suddenly, tears burned in her eyes and overflowed. "I think," she whispered, "I think I remember you. I didn't have any idea I did."

He took the taco from her hand and set it down, then wrapped an arm around her and offered her a paper napkin with his free hand. Bailey let herself lean against him and absorb his scent into her pores.

WITH HER PERMISSION, Seth chose to sit in when the FBI agent interviewed Bailey. He told himself he wanted to hear anything new she came up with. Different questions produced different answers. Mostly, he felt protective. He hadn't forgotten how reluctant she'd been to talk about those years, how wrenching it had been to relive her worst nightmare. If this got too intrusive, too hard for her, Seth intended to stop it.

Special Agent Andrew Stuart—he told them both to call him Drew—turned out to be a decent guy, at least to all appearances. He was maybe forty, lean and dark-haired, gray appearing at his temples. He told Seth and Bailey both that he worked on the Child Abduction Rapid Deployment team the FBI mobilized when a child was

missing or abducted. It was clear he'd heard stories like hers before. Yeah, she had to tell him
all the same things she'd already told Seth and a
few more besides, but to Stuart's credit, he made
it as easy as possible. He skimmed over the sala-
cious or brutal details, focusing on usable information. He intended to contact any agencies in
Bakersfield that would have been part of the response when Bailey had been abandoned there. He
wanted to see the police reports, results of a physical exam, X-rays if there were any. She dredged
up a good idea of the car make Hamby had then
driven, names of a few more towns she was able
to recall from their travels. Stuart wanted to know
if Hamby had a regular route—did he revisit the
same places? Maybe knew people who saved up
jobs for him as a handyman, for example.

Bailey kept shaking her head. She didn't know,
but also didn't think so. If her recollections were
right, Hamby had wandered but deliberately chosen *not* to return to the same towns, the same
seedy motels.

"He didn't want anyone to get too curious about
his 'daughter,'" Agent Stuart murmured.

"And he wouldn't have dared go back to the
same places later, if he had a different 'daughter,'" Seth growled.

Bailey stayed remarkably composed, although
her very stillness gave away her tension. Seth was
proud of her. At the end, she even summoned a

reasonably convincing smile for the agent, thanking him for any efforts he could make toward finding Les Hamby.

Seth walked her out to her car to make sure no vultures loitered in wait for her, then returned to talk to Stuart, mostly to make sure the guy planned to stay in touch and actually share anything he learned. He swore he would, and Seth did the same. They scrutinized each other as they shook hands. Seth felt cautiously optimistic that he wouldn't be stonewalled.

He didn't get one hell of a lot else accomplished in what remained of the afternoon. When he walked in his front door at five forty-five, the house was eerily quiet. He called hello, got no answer. There was no reason for apprehension—what, paparrazzi had kidnapped Bailey and were torturing the answers out of her? But tension crackled through him anyway. He checked the garage first. The sight of her car right where it should be didn't bring relief. If it was here—where in hell was *she*?

Moving quietly, listening for the slightest noise, he rapped on the guest room door, and then opened it without waiting for a response. The room was dim, but he made out a lump in the bed. Relief at last, powerful and knee-weakening.

Bailey rolled over and peered at him. "Seth?" she said, sounding groggy.

"Hey, sorry to wake you up," he said. "I'm putting dinner on. It'll take maybe an hour."

"I should have…"

"I had something planned."

He backed out before the temptation to go sit on the edge of the bed and smooth her hair out of her face could grow.

As he whipped up a curry sauce for the chicken he'd defrosted, he heard the shower start up. That gave him a nice visual—water shimmering as it sluiced over her generous breasts, long slim torso, womanly hips. All that skin, as white as if she'd never lain out in the sun in a bikini. The small, dark heart nature had tattooed on her hip. And, damn, he bet the triangle of hair at the juncture of her thighs was as pale as the hair on her head.

The oven dinged to let him know it had preheated. He drained broccoli and put it with the chicken in a casserole dish, then poured the sauce over it. He was just closing the oven when he heard a soft sound behind him. Lucky she'd taken that extra five minutes to appear. Otherwise he wouldn't have been able to turn around without embarrassing himself and scaring her off.

For some reason, she looked shy. Barefoot, all she'd put on was a knit peach-colored dress that clung to her body and bared her shoulders and collarbone. He couldn't even see a panty line. God. Was there any chance—?

"I really should have made dinner," she said. "I will tomorrow if I'm still here."

"Okay." He opened the refrigerator to give him something to do. "Want something to drink? I have bottled water, soda, beer. No wine, I'm afraid."

"Too sissy for a big tough cop?" she teased.

Smiling, he said, "Something like that."

"Um…just a water. I don't really like beer."

"I can pick up a bottle of wine tomorrow if you'd like."

She shook her head. "I actually don't drink much. *He* did, you know." The darkness was in her voice, as it was every time she said *he* with that mixed horror and hate. "And then I had a foster father who was a closet drunk, too."

Seth felt bad that he'd made her think of Hamby, but recognized there wasn't much he could do about it. Conversations with Bailey were bound to be a minefield. So much shit had happened to her, they'd only skated over the surface so far.

So he only nodded. "I rarely have more than one beer. I've scraped too many victims of drunk drivers off the road, dealt with too many belligerent drunks."

He handed her the water and popped open the one beer he did allow himself. Then he studied her. "New dress?"

She glanced down at herself, and he couldn't help noticing the way her toes curled, as if she'd suddenly become self-conscious. She had narrow feet, a hint of gold revealing the white lines from flip-flops. "Yes. Not exactly a disguise, is it?"

"No." He had to clear his throat. "No, it doesn't hide a lot."

Cheeks pink, she said, "I thought it would be cool."

Oh, yeah. Easy to whip off over her head, too, he couldn't help thinking. No buttons, zipper, tight sleeves. Underclothes?

"I did buy a couple of hats," she said defensively. "One big straw one—" she waved to suggest a broad brim "—and a baseball cap that says Seahawks instead of Mariners." She frowned. "Why is that?"

"People around here got pretty excited when the Seahawks won the Super Bowl. First preseason game is anytime. And yes, baseball season is still going, but the Mariners are in the basement, so the level of excitement isn't there."

"Oh. Um… Is there anything I can do?"

He tensed, thinking of a lot of things she could do, but shook his head. "This is an all-in-one dinner. Curry chicken with broccoli. I'll stick some biscuits in the oven as soon as the chicken comes out."

Her face brightened. "The kind from a tube?"

She was excited? "Yeah."

"Can I open them? I love that pop."

Laughing, he shook his head. "Knock yourself

out." He got out the cookie sheet and the tube, then watched as she rapped it against the sharp counter edge and smiled when it popped open.

"The small pleasures of life," he observed.

She chuckled as she arranged biscuits on the cookie sheet. "I never make these because, gee, there's only me. But Mrs. Neale did."

A good memory. He was glad to have stumbled on one.

"Nice lady?"

"Yes. Kind of grandmotherly. Mr. Neale still worked. He said he'd be bored if he quit. But she was always home. It was..." Tiny lines formed on her forehead as she sought words to express a concept that, if life was fair, would be everyday to her. *Homey* was the word she settled on. "I mean, coming home from school, and she'd have cookies and milk for us even though a couple of us were teenagers." She laughed. "Didn't mean we refused homemade cookies."

"Who does? My mother bakes when she visits. It takes me back."

"Just your mom? Is your dad dead?"

"Yeah." He hesitated, not sure he wanted to open this can of worms. "Probably."

The compassion in her eyes weakened him. "Did he just...leave you?"

"Not like you mean. He was a marine. I don't remember him at all. He was a lot younger than

I am when he died or disappeared, depending on who you believe."

"I don't understand."

"He was deployed to Lebanon in the early 1980s. It was after the Israeli invasion. I guess it was a mess. There was a multinational force there trying to restore order. The part you might have read about is that a truck bomb blew up the marine headquarters. Killed 241 of them."

She listened, her expression troubled. "But he wasn't one of those?"

"See, that's where it gets hazy. There was some suggestion he was missing up to a couple of days before that. His body was never identified. Mom thinks the military was being evasive when she asked questions. Basically, he was just gone. She held out hope for a long time that he was being held captive, that there might be a ransom request, he might escape..." He shrugged. "Something."

"They wouldn't have just left him there if anyone really thought he was alive, would they?"

"I doubt it. Like I said, he probably died when that bomb went off. Or, conceivably, was already dead. Mom and he were really in love, I think. Having there be any doubt really ate at her. She blew up at any suggestion he disappeared on purpose."

Bailey scrutinized him with those crystal clear eyes. He had trouble not squirming.

"So that's why," she said finally.

"Why what?" Seth asked, although he knew.

"You work on cold cases. Because you know what it's like to have to live with doubt."

"I imagine it is," he conceded, "although it's not a conscious objective like, 'I'm going to bring Hope home because I can't bring my father home.'"

"No?"

"No," he said firmly, but didn't expect her to believe it. He wasn't sure he believed himself.

With a small nod, she let him off the hook. "Dinner smells really good."

"Did you get lunch?" He hadn't let himself ask in the brief moments they had alone that afternoon.

Her face clouded. "Yes, but I didn't eat very much."

Did that mean her time with Kirk hadn't gone very well?

The timer went off, and Bailey hopped down to set the table while he took out the casserole dish and put the biscuits into the oven. This was the first time they'd eaten in the dining room, which, like the rest of his house, was pretty minimally furnished. Table and four chairs. He didn't entertain on any kind of scale. The dining room, accessed by open doorways from the kitchen on one side and the living room on the other, wasn't huge, but it looked kind of empty without at least a china cabinet. Not as if he owned any china. His mother dreamed of him choosing a bride, who naturally would register for a china pattern and probably silverware and all that other stuff he still couldn't imagine using. He knew it wasn't the lack of china that bothered his mom; it was that she didn't like to think of him living alone.

Of course, *she* lived alone, with him and his sister long since moved out. His mother hadn't dated when he was a kid, and as far as he knew she hadn't since, either, even though she was a pretty woman who was still only—he had to stop and think—fifty-seven. Could she even see his father's face anymore without looking at a picture? Seth couldn't imagine. But the subject was one she shut down anytime he tried to raise it. "I'm happy," she insisted, but Seth had always known she wasn't. He didn't pursue cold cases because of his father's disappearance/death; he pursued them because of the sadness he caught on his mother's face in unguarded moments.

He waited until the biscuits came out of the oven and he and Bailey sat down to eat before he said, "Are you going to tell me about your day?"

Now she wouldn't meet his eyes. "It was okay."

When she concentrated on buttering a biscuit as if that was the most important thing in the world, he raised his eyebrows. "If you don't want to tell me, just say so."

Bailey lifted her head, her cheeks flushing. "I'm sorry."

"No. I mean it. You really don't have to tell me anything. All I was saying is if you want to talk about it, I'm listening."

She set down the butter knife, picked up her fork and poked at the chicken. "It was... I don't know how I feel about it," she said in a sudden burst. "Okay?"

"Okay," he said mildly. "Me, I arrested an eighteen-year-old punk for knifing the guy his ex-girlfriend had taken up with. So far the new boyfriend hasn't died, but he's in critical condition. Seventeen, supposed to be a senior in high school this year. The girl, too. Previous boyfriend, who graduated in June, doesn't seem to quite get that this was a little more than macho posturing. If he'd still been seventeen, and if the guy he stabbed doesn't die, it might not have been the end of the world. As it is..." Seth shrugged.

"And the girl?"

"She's hysterical. The ex-boyfriend has apparently been making threats. Ugly stuff on his Facebook page. He's texted her some ominous stuff. Of course, neither she nor any of the friends and acquaintances who looked at his Facebook page thought to tell any adults." He shook his head. "There's no getting through to kids. We talk at the middle school and the high school regularly—"

"You, too?"

"Not anymore, but I used to." He gave a ghost

of a smile. "The idea is to send in the really young officers. That way the kids can identify."

Bailey made a face. "I remember being the age when there's this great divide. I think I would have told if I knew of a girl being raped or something like that."

He nodded, not letting her see how that made him feel.

"Otherwise…who knows? Plus, kids are always so melodramatic. Don't you remember? Dark poetry. The world is ending. It's hard to pick out when one of them is actually going to act on it."

"I do know that." Seth stared down at his food, suddenly feeling a lot more tired than he should. Old, too.

Bailey tentatively touched his hand. He couldn't move for a moment. *She* was reaching out to *him*.

He turned his hand over and gripped her much smaller one, feeling the delicacy of her bones. "Thank you," he said hoarsely.

"Your day was a lot worse than my day. You should have said that in the first place," she scolded. "I can't believe I prattled on about *shopping*."

He smiled at the way she said it, as if the fact that she'd hit the discount mall that morning made her an incredibly shallow human being. "Buying a disguise was important."

"Yes, but—" she wrinkled her nose at him "—I bought this dress, too, and some shoes, and I don't even know *why*, considering my tuition bill will be waiting when I get home and I'm not even working."

"Has it occurred to you the Lawsons will want to help with tuition?"

Bailey's eyes widened and she didn't move for a long moment. "No!" she exclaimed. "Do you think that's why I'm here?" She tugged her hand free. "So I can soak them?"

Seth laughed, releasing her hand against his inclination. "No, Bailey, I can honestly say that never crossed my mind. If you were a gold digger, you'd be playing this a lot differently than you are."

She scowled at him. "What's *that* mean?"

"You'd have fallen into their arms. Moved right into that pink bedroom. Cooed over photo albums."

"I did that," she mumbled. "I told you."

"Cooed?"

She grimaced. "I made noises. I couldn't sit there in dead silence."

His smile grew. "I can just see you."

Her eyes narrowed. "You're laughing at me."

"Maybe. Just a little."

She heaved a sigh. "I didn't actually see Karen today."

"But you did have lunch with Kirk."

She nodded.

Seth continued eating, letting the silence extend. He hadn't intended using an interrogation technique, but... If it worked, it worked.

"I remembered, okay?" she burst out. "That freaks me out." And, yes, her eyes were dark with panic.

"Remembered what?" he asked.

"Him. Dad. I did from the first time I saw him. His smile, but mostly his hands. Isn't that weird? I almost wondered—" She broke off.

"Whether there was a bad reason," he said slowly.

Her face went through some contortions. "I guess. But I didn't really think so. It was more like... I wasn't afraid of him... I was afraid to remember."

"Because you were conditioned not to."

"Yes." She looked so unhappy, he suddenly couldn't stand it.

That son of a bitch.

But he also knew he'd scare Bailey all over again if he suggested she come sit on his lap and let him hold her. So he settled for saying, "I'm sorry, honey. Pushing past a block like that isn't going to be easy."

"No." She looked skittish, and he thought, *Shit, an endearment? What are you* thinking? Dumb question. He knew.

Trying to sound matter-of-fact, he asked, "Did you tell Kirk you remembered him?"

Bailey nodded. "I sort of cried on him. It's embarrassing."

"No, it's healthy. It's normal."

She looked at him as if he was speaking Greek.

"Eat," he said, nodding at her plate.

After a moment she picked up her fork.

"Any more plans?" he asked.

"I'm having a girls-only lunch tomorrow. Karen and Eve. At the Lawsons', unfortunately. Reality is, neither of us wants to get emotional where a cell phone camera might capture it. Or, God, a forest of news cameras."

"Makes sense." He frowned. "Anybody still following you?"

"I think so, but I've gotten really good at racing through a yellow traffic light, or making enough quick turns I lose anyone behind me."

He made some grumbling sounds. After a discernible pause, she asked a few questions about the town and the area, which he answered. Maybe she was curious, maybe it was filler.

"Where did you grow up?" she asked finally.

"Vancouver. Washington state, not Canada. Mom works in Portland."

She kept sneaking looks at him. "Did you go to college?"

"Yes, WSU. Washington State University in Pullman. Top-notch program in criminology."

"So you always knew what you wanted to do."

He took a minute to answer that. "I wanted to

get a degree first, but I thought about joining the Marines. Then I saw what my mother was trying to hide when I talked about it, and I realized I couldn't do that to her. I wouldn't have been making her proud because I was walking in my father's footsteps. I was scaring the shit out of her."

"For the armed forces, this hasn't exactly been a peaceful couple of decades, either."

"No, I'd have been in a lot of action." He shrugged. "I don't have any regrets. I was probably like any boy, trying to convince myself I could be a real man."

Bailey smiled at him. "No, you were being romantic."

"Romantic?" he echoed, with mock loathing.

A teasing grin lit her face, although what she said was spot-on. "Wanting to make your dad proud. Vindicate him."

He let himself smile, if wryly. "Yeah, probably. A young male's form of romanticism, anyway."

Bailey's smile faded. "Is your mom okay with what you do?"

He couldn't be sure, but he thought so. "She was happier when I left Spokane PD and took the job here. She thought rural county, no crime. I haven't disillusioned her on that. She liked it when I was promoted to detective, which tends to be less dangerous." His mouth curved. "Despite the way we're *romanticized* on TV and in movies."

"I think—" suddenly she was entirely serious

"—you ought to be. What you did...looking for me, I mean, that was pretty amazing."

He shifted, uncomfortable with such direct praise. "But not exactly heroic."

"I suspect Karen and Kirk would argue with that."

He suspected they would, too, but that hadn't been what he meant. He was rarely in physical danger anymore. But he also guessed Bailey knew exactly what he was saying and still wanted to make her point. So he dipped his head in some kind of acknowledgment and had the appalled realization that his face felt warm. Good God, was he *blushing*?

Bailey had bent her head and didn't see, to his relief. She pushed her food around her plate some more.

"You're not eating much." He dished himself up a second helping.

"Oh! And it's so good, too." She immediately took a bite.

Seth hoped she wasn't cramming unwanted food in just to please him. But she continued until her plate was clean, as if she'd just needed a jump start.

"I'd suggest we go do something, if you weren't, uh..."

"Notorious?" she supplied with a sigh. "And what do you mean by 'something'?"

"There's a local bar that has pretty decent

bands. We could dance." Or maybe that wasn't such a good idea, given that he'd taken Eve to that same bar on one of their dates.

Bailey's eyes sparkled. "Really? You like to dance?"

"I like to shuffle around and cop a feel."

Man, she looked good when she laughed.

"We could put some music on here and dance."

Hell. That's all it took for his blood to rush south. He retained enough of something like common sense, though, to motivate him to say, "That might be dangerous."

"Dangerous?" Her surprise morphed by degrees into comprehension. He must be giving away too much. "Because..." She put the brakes on.

Because we'd be alone. Because it would be all too easy to dance her down the hall to his bedroom.

"You're a beautiful woman, Bailey. You must know that."

She shook her head, then nodded, then shook it again. "I try to look good, but not—" she bit her lip "—for guys."

"You don't like men."

"It's not that." She folded her napkin, then folded it again, concentrating on her task as if she was creating a bird that would have the ability to fly away. "I mean, I'm not a lesbian, if that's what you're thinking. I just..." She lifted those big blue eyes to him. "Sex seems..."

"Dirty." His jaw tightened.

She shrugged, looking almost brazen. As if she didn't want to admit to any weakness. "I guess so. Do you blame me?"

Seth frowned. "Have you had counseling?"

"Years' worth of it," she said flippantly. "Courtesy of the state of California."

"Did it help?"

He could see that she wanted to keep being flip, but gave up. "Sure. You wouldn't ask if you'd ever met my twelve—I mean, eleven-year-old self. But sex, that's complicated."

"You must have tried it later."

"Of course I did. Lots of it."

Not what he wanted to hear, and something told him it was going to get worse.

"Until I was ashamed of myself." Her eyes were more navy than slate blue. "I didn't even like it. Big surprise there, huh? But it was the only way I knew to get attention, okay? Only, one day I thought, why is it important to see myself through a man's eyes?" The hint of darkness when she said "man" was much like her tone when she mentioned Hamby. "It wasn't like I was actually impressing those guys anyway. I'm sure they all thought I was a slut. I was a slut," she said more quietly, but then her chin came up defiantly. "So I quit. I'm trying to be worth something in *my* eyes, not in anybody else's."

"Well, you've impressed the hell out of me," he

said. "And, Bailey, you were never a slut. That's a shitty word to apply to yourself. You knew only one way to ever have any control. Isn't that right?"

She stared at him. "How do you know?" she whispered.

"It's logical. And I get the feeling you're big on staying in control."

"And you aren't?" she shot back.

"Yeah, I probably am. My mother loved me, but I always knew I didn't have what it took to make up for what she'd lost. To make her really happy." *Jesus*, he thought. *I'm laying myself bare here. For her.* "So you're right. I don't like feeling helpless." Now he was the one to shrug, as if his skin wasn't crawling at the admissions he'd just made. At his shocked realization that Bailey, too, made him feel helpless because he wanted to make everything better for her and knew he couldn't. "Cops tend to be control freaks no matter what. We kind of have to be."

She stared for long enough, he couldn't take it anymore. He shoved back his chair and stood, grabbing his dirty dishes. "There's ice cream if you want dessert. Let me get the dishwasher loaded."

"I can do that—"

"Tomorrow night." If he could survive another evening with her. Or even this one. "I brought stuff home to work on reports. I'd better get on with it."

"Oh. Okay." She followed him to the kitchen carrying her own dishes, then went back for the serving dishes when he yanked open the dishwasher.

He rinsed and loaded from habit, his awareness of her like the brush of fingers down his spine. He was done too soon. Closing the dishwasher, he turned to see her standing on the other side of the kitchen. In the dress that molded itself to every ripe, tempting swell of female flesh. But then his gaze rose to her face, and the shyness on it made him feel like a creep, lusting after a woman who'd just told him she hated sex and didn't want anything to do with men.

"Thank you," she said softly, utterly confounding him. "For everything you said."

"Everything?" he echoed hoarsely.

"Understanding why I did what I did. Saying I impressed you. Admitting—" she lifted one slender shoulder in a way that went with her now-rueful expression "—that you're not always as confident as you look. That's really nice."

"You don't believe me?"

"I do." Her smile held all the complexities that made up this woman. "That's why it means so much. Well...that's all I wanted to say. Except I'll get out of your way so you can work. I think I'll watch TV, if you don't mind."

"I don't mind."

"Okay." She backed through the doorway.

He let her go, even though he wanted to say, *What about that dance?*

No. Hell. What he wanted to know was whether she thought she could ever make love instead of having sex, and enjoy it. With him.

The man who'd royally screwed up her life, whatever she was saying now.

Yeah, fat chance.

He retreated to his bedroom, where he was pretty damn sure he wouldn't be able to concentrate on the report he could have put off until tomorrow.

CHAPTER TEN

MAYBE THE NAP was to blame—she didn't take those very often. All Bailey knew was that she couldn't sleep. Instead, she lay in bed, staring at her door, which she'd carefully positioned about three inches ajar. She'd done the same with the bathroom door. The light she'd left on in there served as a night-light, something she'd needed ever since *him*. She'd been relieved when she heard Seth's footsteps come down the hall a while ago and he hadn't turned off the light.

It wasn't so much that she feared the dark or what might come out of it. She thought it had more to do with the run-down motels where they'd stayed. There was never real darkness, or silence, for that matter. City lights, headlights, the neon light of the motel sign, sometimes flickering, all seeped through bent blinds. They were always in the kind of neighborhood where there'd be traffic most of the night as well as sirens now and again. Low-voiced conversations took place just outside, and fights penetrated thin walls. Sex, too—the squeak of the bed frame or noise it made hammering against the wall, the slap of flesh, the cries from the women and the guttural sound men made. She always thought the men must be hurting the women, because he hurt her, every time. But she had learned to be completely silent, so nobody would hear her through those walls.

To this day, she couldn't sleep without some light. In her apartment, she had a night-light plugged into a wall socket, even though in LA there was always some light sneaking through the blinds, too. The never-ending sounds of traffic were familiar, too.

Here, it was so quiet she'd find herself straining her ears to hear *something*. She couldn't believe the whole town shut down, but it must, or at least mostly. There were no taverns in Seth's residential neighborhood. She'd seen that most businesses in town closed at five-thirty, and even restaurants by ten except on Friday and Saturday nights when they stayed open until a crazy, late eleven o'clock. Stimson was Mayberry, and she should have grown up here.

The thought was as surreal as practically everything else that had happened since she first set eyes on her own face online.

In her heart, she knew that having taken a nap wasn't all that kept her awake. Her current state had more to do with the fact that she couldn't stop thinking about that conversation with Seth.

She could not *believe* she'd said all that. Not

since that last counselor, a woman, of course, who'd helped her work some stuff out, had she so much as talked about her slutty—okay, sexually active—days. And that was a *long* time ago. She'd been barely twenty when she decided to call a halt to the need to use her body to garner attention. Or, a creepier way to look at it, to replicate the years when that was her only worth.

The stunning part was that Seth had understood immediately what it took her a long time to grasp. And he hadn't looked repulsed by her past, either, unless he'd just hidden that. Although, now that she thought about it, he had been awfully anxious to get rid of her. So maybe…

But she couldn't quite believe that, which was part of what had her vibrating with tension instead of relaxing into sleep. He'd paused outside her bedroom door on the way to his, long enough she'd gone rigid in bed, waiting, waiting. Until finally his footsteps continued and she heard his bedroom door open and close.

Why *wasn't* he disgusted? She'd seen rage flicker on his face when she first started telling him, but then it cleared. And she would swear that was heat in his eyes as he watched her fumble through her thanks and beat an awkward retreat from the kitchen. As if he wanted her but was holding back.

Well, duh. Because she'd told him she didn't

do guys. Because she'd said she hadn't enjoyed sex even when she'd had it frequently. Because she was part of his investigation, because he felt responsible for her, because he was afraid she'd latch on to him emotionally and he didn't want *that* much responsibility. She could take her pick.

He was being smart, and she didn't know why she was even thinking about this. If nothing else, she'd be heading back to California soon.

But she kept thinking about him anyway. His strong, athletic body and his incredible gentleness with her. Big hands, thick wrists, broad, muscular shoulders and deep, intense eyes. All of which, for reasons she didn't understand at all, warmed her inside until she had a melting sensation that was entirely new. She kept picturing the sex act and visualizing him being the one who touched her, kissed her, penetrated her, and she ached so much she had to squeeze her thighs together to try to contain it.

She'd written off the idea of ever feeling any of that. What if she actually could enjoy being with a man? The idea was unexpectedly seductive.

Of course—what if he was the *only* man she could ever enjoy being with?

One step forward, two back. Because she couldn't imagine he'd want her long-term even if, well, *she* wanted anything like that.

She moaned and rolled over, presenting her back to the door, but she couldn't stand it for long and flipped back over so she could at least see the faint light out of the corner of her eye.

Then she made herself think about Kirk again and how she'd felt when he said, "I know my own little girl when I see her." But *that* made her melt in an entirely different way that left her feeling equally vulnerable, so she thought about Karen instead, and Eve, who wanted to hate her. And how much fun they were going to have, sharing another meal.

But, please, no more photo albums.

Her eyes popped open. Was that a phone ringing? She was sure about it when she heard a muffled voice. A couple of minutes passed before Seth's bedroom door opened. Once again, he paused in front of hers.

"Bailey? Sorry if I'm waking you."

"You're not."

"I have to go in. Don't know when I'll be home."

"Someone was killed?"

Momentary silence. "Yeah. This is what I do."

"I know." She cleared her throat. "Be careful."

"Gunman is long gone. Don't answer the door." He didn't wait for an answer, only walked away. The soft sound of the front door opening and closing was followed by his SUV backing out a minute later.

More of that unsettling silence. Apparently in Mayberry, police officers didn't use their sirens on the way to murder scenes.

"WHAT'S WITH YOU TODAY?" Ben asked, scowling. "As if I can't guess."

Seth had been leaning way back in his chair, his feet propped on a corner of Kemper's desk. Now he lurched upright, planting his feet on the floor, his eyes narrowing. "What's that supposed to mean?"

"C'mon, have you been able to concentrate on anything but Hope Lawson from the minute you set eyes on her? Or, shit, from the minute you started hunting for her?"

"Don't tell me I'm not doing my job," Seth snapped.

Kemper leaned forward aggressively. "Yeah, gazing off into space while I'm trying to *talk* to you."

They had a glaring match. Seth broke it off by swearing and scrubbing a hand over his face.

"I'm tired. That's all." And he was. Fatigue pulled at him in a way it wouldn't have a few years ago even after a missed night's sleep. He was too young to be feeling old. He wasn't about to admit to how inadequate the previous night's sleep had been, too, because that would feed right back into Ben's accusation. Yes, he hadn't slept because he'd been rescuing Bailey again. Because he'd tucked her into bed across the hall from *his* bed. Because he hadn't been able to turn off his awareness of how close she was, how little she was likely wearing. He wanted her with an unfamiliar fierceness.

The other detective grunted. "Yeah. Sorry. Nicole called."

Nicole being his ex, which made his grumpiness understandable. Seth dragged his mind from Bailey to his partner.

"This is supposed to be my weekend to have Rachel," Ben grumbled, "and wouldn't you know, Nicole had her scheduled in a bunch of things she couldn't possibly miss. She's five years old. How important can some other kid's birthday party possibly be?"

Dredging up memories of some of his kid sister's temper tantrums, he said, "Ah... I guess it depends on whether it's a best friend or just some other kid in her day care."

"Crap, I don't know. I could have taken her to the damn party." Ben brooded for a minute. "It was at a roller-skating rink. Can five-year-olds stand up on roller skates?"

"Taking a wild guess... I'd say no. Or only if all parents are on deck to hold them up."

"That's my take, too."

"Have you ever roller-skated?"

Ben looked at him as if he was crazy. "How hard can it be?"

Seth shrugged. "Just asking."

"I skateboarded. I snowboard."

"Okay."

"Nicole insisted I wouldn't have a clue what to buy as a present for the birthday girl. And I'd make all the mothers there uncomfortable. Would I be willing to go unarmed? she asked snidely."

"If you were carrying, that might scare some of the moms."

He gave a short, incredulous laugh. "Who goes armed to take their kid to a birthday party?"

Some guys Seth knew probably would. "Maybe she didn't like the idea of all those young mothers flirting with you."

The fleeting expression on Ben's face made Seth wish he hadn't said that. It looked like hope. Seth didn't know a lot about their breakup, but got the impression it had been her decision, not Ben's. What if he still thought—? Nah. They'd been divorced for, what, a year now? What he mostly bitched about was not seeing his kid often enough, which Seth understood.

"Maybe you need to get tough," he suggested. "Don't you have a court-ordered parenting plan? If she's in violation…"

"And wouldn't that piss her off and make her want to be cooperative."

True—but the alternative wasn't looking so good, either. Not Seth's business. He shrugged and let it go. "What deep thoughts were you trying to convey that I wasn't hearing?"

There was a pause as Ben switched gears. "Did

you catch the hesitation from his partner when we asked how solid the marriage was?"

Seth's attention sharpened. Geoffrey Stephen Moore, attorney-at-law, had evidently been gunned down when he opened the front door after the doorbell rang at almost ten o'clock at night. Wife was in the family room at the back of the house. They were looking into the possibility of a pissed-off client or ex-client, but had to seriously consider his nearest and dearest, too. And, while his wife was distraught, some of her hysteria had a staged look, feeding Seth's inclination always to put the wife or girlfriend—or husband/boyfriend, depending on who the victim was—in the number one suspect slot until evidence indicated otherwise.

In this case, they were leaning toward believing she couldn't have killed her husband herself—she'd been on the phone with another woman who said she heard a muffled sound that must have been the gunshot just moments before Heather Moore cried, "What was that? Geoff?" Then, a minute later, she screamed, "Oh, my God. Oh, my God." She had no gunpowder residue on her hands, and no handgun was registered to either of the Moores.

"I did notice," he agreed. "I'm thinking ole Geoff was cheating on her."

"Which opens all kinds of possibilities." Ben was the one to rock back in his chair now. "Office should be long since open unless they closed down for the day."

"The partner said something about motions," Seth said. "I'm thinking no. If anything, he has to be having nightmares about how much slack he's going to have to take up."

Ben rose to his feet. "I looked the firm up. They have a junior attorney and a summer intern as well as a paralegal and two clerks. We can lean on 'em all."

"Works for me." Seth was energized enough to make it to his feet, too. "Now that she's past the first shock, I say we go back to talk to the wife again, too. She must have said 'What if I'd been alone and *I* was the one to answer the door?' three times. Was she often alone at ten in the evening on a weeknight? If so, where did she think he was the evenings he was out?"

Ben glanced at his watch. "I vote we start at the office. The wife is going to be more of a challenge. You can bet her mother and sister are still in pit-bull mode."

Far as Seth could see, the mother had egged her daughter on to bouts of sobbing rather than making any effort to comfort her, which he'd also wondered a little about. Maybe she was whispering, "Make it look good. Really let loose, honey."

Seth waited while Ben detoured into the john before the two men walked out. Good timing—

they'd catch Geoff Moore's coworkers just before they broke for lunch.

He wondered if Bailey had made it to the Lawsons' yet and, if so, how it was going. Eve's hostility surprised him. He'd feared he might be part of Eve's problem with her newfound sister, except she'd have no way of knowing how damnably attracted he was to Bailey, or that Bailey was now staying with him.

An uncomfortable thought stirred. Eve wouldn't know unless Bailey had told her. And why wouldn't she?

BAILEY DIDN'T OFTEN covet anything, but every once in a while she was hit by a bolt out of the blue. Unable to stop herself, she reached out to stroke the quilt Karen had just flung open across the bed for her to admire. Even the texture wasn't what she'd expected; the only quilts she'd touched before were the cheap kind, imported from China, with great big stitches. This was intricate, with tiny stitches, forming ripples that occasionally spun into spirals, which made her think of whirlpools amidst the watery blues and greens of the fabric.

"This is stunning." She looked at Karen. "Do you at least take pictures before you give them back?"

Karen laughed. "I do. I have whole albums full of pictures." The humor in her eyes told Bailey she'd guessed at her painful reluctance the other night when presented with those albums. "As it happens, though, I made this quilt from scratch. When I have time, I design and piece my own as well as machine-quilt them. I enter some in shows—it's good advertising for my business— and I sell most of them in local stores. This one..." She smiled. "Actually, I think it's yours."

"What? Mine?" Bailey took a step back. "You can't just give me something like this." She sounded as freaked as she felt, but Karen only tilted her head to one side and considered her.

"Of course I can. I've already made one for Eve. For hers I used gypsy colors—reds and purples, vivid motion like women dancing with skirts swirling. You need something different." She hesitated. "Maybe I'm wrong and these aren't your colors..."

"They are," Bailey said in a choked voice, her gaze drawn back to a quilt that wasn't made up of the standard, symmetrical blocks but rather of pieces that curved and flowed into each other. "This makes me think of a pool in a Japanese garden."

"Serenity." She nodded. "It's yours." She began to fold it with brisk, practiced movements. "I don't know what size your bed is."

"Twin, actually."

"Oh." She stopped. "Oh, dear. This one is queen-size. It would be fine on a double bed, but— Maybe I should make you one instead."

Seized by alarm, Bailey said, "No. Please. I'll buy a new bed. I love this quilt."

"Oh, good." Karen had a quiet glow as she gently stuffed the quilt into a zippered bag. "There. This will protect it. Although I should probably ship it to you, shouldn't I?"

"I can carry it on my flight." She didn't want to let it out of her sight. "No one's ever given me anything like this. I don't know what to say." And, to her chagrin, she was close to tears.

Karen straightened and gave her a gentle hug that was so quick, she didn't have time to pull back or return it. Bailey was aware of a faint, lingering scent that might be lavender.

Sounding matter-of-fact, Karen said, "Shall we go have dessert? Eve is probably feeling abandoned."

"I...yes. Of course." Eve had shrugged and declined to join the tour of her mother's studio, which she'd have seen a million times. She'd probably sat on the floor playing with her dolls while her mother worked. She had made a teasing reference to mom wanting to show off her new quilting machine.

Bailey had expected a sewing machine, and been fascinated by something more like a quilting frame that had to be ten feet long, with a high-tech machine poised over it that could be maneuvered with ergonomic handles. Karen had even given her a brief demonstration on the quilt currently stretched on the frame. She said the pattern was called Bear's Paw, which Bailey could see.

Returning to the dining room, Bailey clutched her quilt as if it was a baby. Eve glanced up from her phone, her gaze going to the bundle in Bailey's arms.

"Your first heirloom." Her tone was kind instead of sardonic, to Bailey's surprise.

"It's so beautiful. Not anything like I pictured when I heard the word *quilt*."

"No, Mom's an artist." Eve laid her phone on the table. "Pie, anyone?"

"Oh, I can dish it up," Karen fussed.

"Don't be silly, Mom." Eve rose to her feet and gave her a passing hug. To her, it was so natural. "You did the cooking, for heaven's sake."

"The coffee should be ready—"

It was. Bailey poured and carried cups to the table while Eve sliced a key lime pie that looked way better than it should considering how much lunch Bailey had eaten.

She'd barely picked up her fork when Karen said, "You haven't had any more trouble with reporters, have you?" She knew about the incident at Walgreens. "I'm glad you're not still at the Quality Inn. I'm sure anyone could find you there. But, goodness, that cabin sounds so primitive."

Bailey hesitated. This was supposed to be her

family. They wouldn't tell anyone where she was actually staying, would they?

"Unfortunately, they tracked me down to the cabin, too. It was kind of scary. I mean, it was late at night and they were shining flashlights in the windows." She shuddered. "Seth—Detective Chandler—thinks these were freelancers because they were so ruthless. You know, no story, no payday."

Eve arched her eyebrows. "I suppose he came and scared them away for you."

Bailey met her eyes. "Yes, actually he did."

"So now what?" Eve asked, her voice holding just enough of an edge to have Karen looking surprised before she transferred her gaze to Bailey.

"You do know we'd love to have you here, don't you?"

Bailey forced a smile, aware Eve was watching. "I assumed. I just…don't feel ready. I'm used to having my own space."

Wow, how could she tell them that she was staying at Seth's house? Something like panic bubbled in her chest. She *shouldn't* stay with him. She could just imagine what people would think. Starting with Eve.

"We understand, of course," Karen assured her. "It's such a miracle having you here, I can hardly take my eyes off you, and that must make you uncomfortable. I'm afraid I can't help it. It's going to take time."

"I feel…really shaken up," Bailey confessed. In lieu of that other confession: *I am sleeping across the hall from Seth Chandler, the police detective who found me.* The one who'd dated Eve until…when? Maybe a question she should have asked.

"Of course you do." Karen patted her arm. "I pray you can accept that we love you and that we *are* your family."

"I do believe you are." Somehow she managed another smile, even as she battled the claustrophobic need to make hasty excuses and leave.

Eve's stare remained cool and direct. "So, where *are* you staying?"

Being caught out in a lie would be worse than telling the truth. "For the moment, at Seth's." She made it utterly casual. "He has a guest room. He thinks he knows of someone else who is away and might let me use their place, though." That was what *might* happen, she told herself, and therefore not exactly a lie.

Eve pushed back from the table and carried her plate with half-finished pie into the kitchen.

Seemingly not noticing, Karen looked at Bailey with distress. "Oh, but when you have family—" She made a moue. "No, I won't say any more, I promise."

Eve reappeared. As she picked up her phone, Bailey said hastily, "I won't be able to stay in town

JANICE KAY JOHNSON 221

much longer anyway. I don't want to lose my job, and I'll need to get ready to start classes."

Ignoring her, Eve announced, "I need to be off."

Karen blinked at her. "Oh, but…"

"Thanks for lunch, Mom." She breezed out, leaving silence in her wake.

"I didn't realize she had to be back so early," Karen said.

That would be because she didn't, but Karen must be wearing blindfolds these days. Bailey felt a cramp of empathy. Once again, she was struck by the realization that she understood Eve a whole lot better than she did Karen or Kirk—or even Seth. *Seesaw*, she reminded herself. Right now, Eve probably felt as if she'd slammed down hard enough to bruise her tailbone. And her, she felt light-headed and queasy from the height.

Never happy, she mocked herself.

Since she had no place she needed to be and she could make one other person happy, she asked to see the quilt photos.

Karen lit up. After she'd hustled away to fetch the albums, Bailey picked up her gift from where she'd carefully set it by her feet and unzipped just far enough to let her see a few inches of the tight stitches spiraling inward over a finger of sea-green batik fabric. Her chest felt tight, and she hurriedly zipped it up again before Karen could come back and see her sneaking a peek. Even though *that* would have made her happy, too.

SETH DIDN'T LET himself in the house until almost seven. The first thing that hit him was a great smell that made his stomach rumble. Oh, damn—she'd promised to make dinner, hadn't she? And he'd been a no-show.

This was a big reason even his slightly more serious relationships never took off.

"Hey." Bailey appeared from the kitchen, wearing jeans that showed an amazing length of leg despite the really sacky Seahawks sweatshirt that disguised her breasts and hips and fell to midthigh. *Mine*, he realized.

She glanced down at herself. "I hope you don't mind. I was cold."

Seth shook his head. "Of course not."

"When I left, it was hot there and hot here. I didn't expect the temperature to plummet."

"That's the great Northwest for you." After a roasting hot couple of weeks, the sky had clouded over and even showed signs of threatening rain. Happened quick in these parts. "I should have called. It smells like you made dinner. I'm sorry."

"No, that's okay. I didn't know when you'd get home, so I made pizzas. I already ate. I loaded them both with veggies, but if you want me to take some off…"

"Whatever I smell will be perfect."

"You haven't eaten?"

His stomach grumbled again. "Fast food for lunch. An aeon ago."

Bailey smiled. "I'll go put it in the oven."

"That'll give me time to take a quick shower."

He hadn't last night, intending his usual morning shower. Now he felt foul, more in a figurative sense than literal. Unpleasant people rubbed off on you.

The hot water felt great. He didn't stay under it as long as he would have if he'd been alone in the house, though. The anticipation he'd felt since the minute he decided to head home was new.

Bailey was perched on one of the bar stools with that morning's newspaper open in front of her when he returned to the kitchen. She looked up. "Can I get you a beer?"

"No, I'd take two swallows and topple over." Unless the buzz he felt because she was here kept him awake. He passed her and reached up into a cupboard for a glass. She watched as he poured himself milk.

"Milk and pizza." She laughed. "Not your usual combo."

Seth tipped the glass back and guzzled before replying. "I've had so much coffee the last twenty-four hours, I think it burned a layer off my stomach lining. I'm trying to restore it."

Her smile faded. "Was it awful?"

"Awful?" The murder. "I've seen worse. It was unusual for this town, though. We mostly have bar fights that get out of hand, domestics." He shrugged. "This one is a genuine mystery."

"Really?" She looked fascinated, those big blue eyes fastened on him.

He told her a little. Some would be in the morning paper for anyone to read. Some was still speculative. Apparently Geoff Moore had trouble keeping his pants zipped. His wife and he had fought about it often, but so far the benefits of being married to a successful attorney had outweighed her hurt and fury. His latest affair had been more serious, though, and it sounded as if the current girlfriend had been pressuring him to divorce his wife and marry her. Wife might have been running scared—as a widow, she'd end up a hell of a lot better off financially than she would have with a divorce settlement. Seth had got the idea Geoff had been backpedaling with the girlfriend, though, and had no intention of divorcing his wife. Girlfriend's grief looked as false as the wife's. She had a low-rent brother with a sheet as long as Seth's arm, too. In fact, Geoff had met the girlfriend when he was defending her brother.

Gratitude wasn't what it used to be, he thought sardonically.

He evaded some of Bailey's questions, but she didn't seem to mind. Talking lowered his stress level, until he thought tonight he could sleep. Sex first would have been good, but even if it were a possibility, he wanted to be more on his game before he tried anything with Bailey.

The oven timer went off and she hopped down

despite his protests to take the pizza out of the oven and slice it for him, even pouring him a second glass of milk.

"Karen sent a couple of pieces of key lime pie, too, if you have room."

"I'll make room. Hey." He decided to use a knife and fork, given that Bailey would be watching him eat. "How'd lunch go?"

"Mostly good." A cloud seemed to pass over her mood. "Things are really tense with Eve."

No comment. He kept eating.

"You know about Karen's quilting business?" She shook her head before he could answer. "You're the one who told me about it. I didn't know she creates her own quilts, too. They're amazing. Eve said they're art, which they are. The thing is, she gave one to me." All her defenses crashed; she looked at him with bewilderment, pleasure and something like shame mixed on her face. "Can I show you?"

"I'd like to see it."

He didn't know enough about quilts to have any expectations. They were bedcoverings. He didn't get the female fascination with them.

Bailey returned, a fat plastic bag with a zip top in her arms, the kind new bedding came in. Keeping well away from his pizza, she unzipped it and drew out something that had him blinking in surprise. The pieces of fabric didn't exactly form a picture, but the colors flowed together and he had the impression of a pond with some water lilies and stitching that formed eddies. Maybe a few flat stones on the edges, possibly a couple of large leaves overhanging the water.

"It's like an impressionist painting," he said, after staring thunderstruck for a minute. "I had no idea she did anything like this."

"No. I've been thinking of her as so…" Bailey seemed to struggle for the right description. "Small-town nice woman. Middle America. You know?"

He nodded.

"And then I find out she has this remarkable creative ability, and I'm thinking, did I know this? I mean, when I was little?"

"Would a six-year-old know something like that about her mother?" he asked. "Except that she might have been fun to do art projects with."

"Probably not." She stroked the quilt as if she found the surface a sensual pleasure. Seth imagined her touching him the same way. But then she looked at him and that bewilderment was still visible. "Do you know what she probably charges for a quilt like this?"

He shook his head.

"Oh, it would have to be, I don't know, a couple of thousand dollars or more. Maybe a lot more. And she *gave* it to me."

"Because you're her daughter," he said gently.

"Eve said—" Bailey swallowed. "She said it's my first heirloom."

He smiled. "She's right."

"This is so new to me. I didn't even know how to thank her. What I said was probably totally inadequate."

"I doubt that. Karen seems to be pretty good at reading people." She'd known how to get to him, he thought ruefully, that was for sure.

"It's funny. I've always loved fabric. I had a foster mother who taught me to sew. I mean, just the rudiments, and then I got moved. But, not that long ago, I was thinking I might get a sewing machine. Maybe it's in the genes or something." She made a face. "Scary thought. Except... I might like to try to learn to make quilts."

He pushed his plate away. "I don't think it's genes, Bailey. You must remember your mom sewing. Maybe making clothes for you. It's there in your head. Her turning a piece of cloth into a pretty dress you loved. You hear a sewing machine whirring or see a fabric store, good connotation."

She stared at him for a long moment, unmoving, unblinking. Then she drew a breath. "Yes. I do think... I can feel myself twirling, and the skirt of my dress forming a bell. It was purple." She plucked, apparently unconsciously, at the quilt she held in her arms. "Velour, I think, or velvet." Her eyes pleaded with him. "It was real, wasn't it?"

He wished he knew what she needed. "Yeah." His voice came out gruff. "I think it was."

"Seth?" This was barely a whisper, but her tone was…different.

Somehow, he'd come to be standing. Because he'd wanted to go to her, hold her, he realized. He managed to say, "Yeah?"

"If you don't want to, you can just say no. But, um, would you kiss me?"

CHAPTER ELEVEN

SEEING THE EXPRESSION on his face, Bailey would have given anything not to have said that. Was he appalled? Embarrassed?

"Forget it," she said quickly. "Dumb impulse."

"No." He came around the breakfast bar, stopping when he was no more than a foot from her. He looked kind. Just what a woman wanted to see when she'd come on to him.

She retreated a step. "Really. I can tell that's the last thing you want to do."

"Bailey, I want to kiss you more than I want to sleep or eat or maybe even breathe." His voice was deep, huskier than usual, and maybe *kind* wasn't the right word to describe the way he was looking at her after all.

This time her "Really?" came out as a squeak.

"Yeah." He lifted a hand and grazed his knuckles over her cheek. "I'm a little conflicted, that's all. You're pretty vulnerable right now. And the idea of scaring you or repelling you… Not so good."

"You don't want me to experiment on you," she

guessed. Which he was smart enough to know was exactly what she'd been asking.

"No, I'm okay with that." His eyes were darker than usual, a brown-black. "I don't want to fail, that's all."

"Oh." She squeezed the quilt, then realized it was in the way. Really smooth. There'd been a time she knew how to seduce a guy. Because it had been all surface. She hadn't felt anything. This was deeper. She wanted not to fail, too. She hoped he couldn't guess how much she wanted that. "Um…" She cast a glance sideways. Kitchen counter. With a couple of steps, she was able to set down the quilt. When she turned, it was to see that he waited where he'd been. A really confident guy she suspected could even be domineering; he was letting her do this her way. *He* was hesitant because he wanted this, too.

That gave her the assurance to go to him and to flatten her hands on his chest, atop the sweatshirt he'd donned after his shower. She liked him in his detective uniform of slacks or chinos and a white shirt with badge and weapon, but she liked him in jeans even better. He was more approachable.

She loved the hard muscles she felt beneath her hands, the beat of his heart, and wished—well, that she knew what he looked like without the sweatshirt.

Her own pulse had speeded enough to make her feel light-headed. *Heights*. For a long moment, he did nothing but look down at her, although his eyes had heated. Finally he lifted his hands slowly, as if he was making a conscious effort not to alarm her, and he framed her face with them. They were big, and strong, and warm. She tilted her head to deepen and savor the contact. His expression changed, hardened in a way, but she didn't feel so much as a flicker of fear.

Finally he bent his head, and at the same moment she rose on tiptoe. Somehow he still kept the contact soft. He rubbed his lips over hers, then nibbled at them. Bailey's eyes closed. In a state of suspended wonder, she quit breathing. The damp tip of his tongue testing the seam of her lips was like an electrical conductor, sending a bolt of heat to her core. She opened her mouth and let him in.

Suddenly the kiss was deep and serious. He cupped the back of her head, his fingers tangled in her hair. His other hand had come to grip one of her hips. He was trying to lift her even as he explored her mouth. He was still holding back, but not by much. When she sucked on his tongue, his body jolted. He lifted his head to stare down at her with molten eyes, before he kissed her jaw, nipped her earlobe, sucked on the sensitive skin on her neck. When he came back to her mouth, she wrapped her arms tight around his neck and plastered her body to his. She was hot, melting, hungry for the very thing she would have sworn she absolutely did not want.

Starting with his hand on her breast. *Her* hands on bare skin.

But that was the moment when a groan vibrated in his chest, and he let go of her hip to rest his hand at her waist, almost as if he was restraining her. "Bailey."

Lost in shocked pleasure at her own response, she took a minute to understand that he was trying to say something. His touch had become gentle instead of urgent. He was backing off.

She whimpered in protest. His muscles tightened, but he said her name again. "Bailey. Honey."

She let her head fall back and really looked at him. His face still had the predatory cast of a man who wanted sex, but determination was there, too. Determination, she realized, *not* to take her to bed.

"Wow," she mumbled.

Seth gave a strained laugh. "Yeah, I'd have said something stronger."

"Like?"

"Holy shit."

That made her laugh a little, which enabled her to ease back and go for light. "The experiment was a success."

"Was it?" His very dark eyes searched hers. "No panic?"

"I...didn't really expect that."

"Then what were you testing for?"

"More like indifference. I've never actually

been swept away." She sounded as amazed as she felt.

For an instant, his fingers bit into her arms before he backed away and rubbed his hands on his thighs. "You know I don't want to call a halt."

Bailey bobbed her head.

"But you need to be sure. This can't be about thinking you owe me."

Outrage cut into the sensual haze. "Owe you?"

"And I don't mind kissing as an experiment. Making love, I guess I'd like to know it's a little more."

"Oh, come on," she scoffed. "You can't tell me you don't take it where you can get it."

His expression went flat. "Take it?"

"You know what I mean." She crossed her arms, feeling defensive. Wanting to retreat, but refusing to let herself.

"Have I had casual sex? Yeah. But I don't do one-night stands with women I don't know, if that's what you were suggesting. And with you, Bailey, sex won't be casual. Not for me." His jaw flexed. "I'd rather it wasn't for you, either."

Dumbfounded, she didn't know what to say.

After a minute, his eyebrows quirked and he took a big step back. "I'm going to bed. Thank you for dinner."

"Oh, but there's pie." Automatic hostess. *Too many years spent waitressing*, she thought in embarrassment.

Amusement flickered in his eyes. "Save it for tomorrow. Good night, Bailey." He surprised her by closing in again to kiss her tenderly and so briefly she could have almost imagined it.

Then she was alone in the kitchen.

"Shit," Seth muttered the next day, as the pages rolled out of his printer.

"What?" Ben asked. "You got something new?"

"Huh? Oh. No. This is a list of all female children, five to seven years old, abducted in the eighteen-year time frame in six states. There are way too many."

Ben grunted. "Of course there are. Why five years old? Why not four? Or eight?"

Seth swiveled in his seat. "It's not impossible Hamby would grab a kid that young, but she'd be a pain to tote alone with him. There's a reason we don't put kids in school until they're minimum of five."

"Okay. That makes sense."

"And eight." He shook his head. "If he loses interest when they start maturing physically, he's gonna want them younger. There are ten-year-olds getting breasts."

Ben grimaced. "Not something I want to think about." A frown tugged at his eyebrows. "May I ask why you're back to hunting down the guy who abducted the Lawson girl twenty-three years ago when we're working a killing that took place thirty-six hours ago?"

He showed his teeth. "Because the asshole probably has a child sex slave right now? And if not, he's hunting for one? That good enough for you?"

"Yeah." Ben sighed. "Those are good enough reasons."

Seth tried to dial it back. "This isn't me thinking with my dick, the way you keep suggesting. It's more than that." Yeah, it was. What he felt for Bailey was way more than that. "I'll put time in on this at home. Identifying possibles from this list could eat up a lot of hours." *And, yes, goddamn it, I am obsessed.* "You ready to go?"

"Yeah. I'm ready."

They planned to talk to the girlfriend's brother, who lived in Lowell, a small town deeper in the foothills of the Cascade Mountains. He hadn't been home when they'd tried to track him down yesterday, and he wasn't answering calls from either of their numbers. He'd been fired from his most recent job three weeks before and the sister insisted he was job hunting but hadn't found the "right" one yet. As in, he hadn't found an idiot willing to overlook an erratic employment history and multiple convictions for crimes relating to a temper, a drinking problem and a propensity for violence. In other words, just the guy you wanted greeting your customers.

Ben wasn't the only cynic, Seth reflected.

He let Ben drive, getting in on the passenger side without comment. The first five minutes passed in silence. Then Ben said suddenly, "Hope is a pretty woman. I can see the appeal."

Seth gritted his teeth.

"Got to say, though, at least on TV the sister is the one who qualifies as a real beauty. And, hey, you've been seeing her. What's she think of all this?"

This time, Seth had the sense his fellow detective was genuinely curious instead of mocking him.

"There's some tension," he admitted.

"I get why she wouldn't like you spending so much time thinking about her sister."

"Eve and I aren't dating. Haven't been for a while."

"Really?" Ben sounded surprised. "Dumped you, did she?"

At this rate, he'd be needing crowns on all his molars.

Ben's mouth curled. "So the tension is between the sisters?"

"Yes." The single, curt word didn't seem like enough. After a minute, he added, "This is a strange new world for Bailey. And she prefers to be called that, by the way. Meanwhile, Eve probably sees her as usurping her place."

"Except she always knew her blonde, blue-eyed sister was out there somewhere," Ben said thoughtfully.

"No, I imagine she thought Hope was dead. Karen and Kirk didn't, or at least they pretended to themselves they didn't, but to Eve, Hope was just a fairy tale."

"Until she arrived to claim her place in the family."

"Yep. Not likely to happen smoothly."

"No." Ben kept his mouth shut for a few minutes, although he looked as if he was thinking hard. "You noticed Darrell and Jordan are stepsiblings, didn't you?" he said abruptly.

"No. Shit, I missed that." Man, he hated to admit it. "Why do they share a last name, then?"

"Her legal name isn't Jordan Swann. It's Dyer. But when her mommy married Darrell's daddy, she started using Swann for her kid, too."

That wasn't uncommon. Still… He mulled over what he'd learned about Jordan and her stepbrother. "I wonder how close they really are?"

"And what kind of close," Ben added. "Darrell was fourteen when his father remarried. So it's not like they grew up together. Even though he's a badass, would he really risk life in prison for her?"

"He's on a path to end up a lifer even if he didn't pull the trigger this time."

Ben shrugged. "True enough."

Seth brooded for the remainder of the drive, shuffling the play cards into a different order in his mind. Maybe they'd looked to Darrell too quickly. They'd assumed he was mad that Moore had insulted his dearly beloved sister by refusing to ditch the wife for her. What if Darrell and Jordan had had a different kind of relationship, and instead he wanted to off the guy who'd taken his place?

Or maybe they should be concentrating all their attention on the women, not assuming either had required a man to pull the trigger.

"We should look more closely at Dulcy Burgess," he said, as the car slowed upon entering the Lowell city limits. She was the woman the wife had been on the phone with when Moore was killed. They knew the call was real, but they had only the two women's word for what was said during the conversation and particularly at the end. How loud the gunshot had sounded, or whether any words might have been exchanged between husband and wife right before Dulcy heard the *bang*.

"I agree." Ben flicked on the turn signal. "Damn, this place is turning into a ghost town."

It was. A once-thriving lumber mill had been the economic heart of Lowell. When it shut down, residents either found jobs elsewhere and commuted, or they moved. Too many vacant storefronts shared the three short blocks with businesses still trying to hang on. Seth noticed a coffee shop he'd really liked that now sported a window blank but for a sign that said For Rent.

Houses got smaller and more ramshackle the farther they drove from the central district. They pulled up in front of a cottage with a moss-eaten roof, sagging porch and one boarded-up window. The cabin where Bailey had stayed looked good compared to this place.

"Nice," Ben remarked before opening his door. Over the roof, he asked, "You want to take lead?"

"Sure." Something about his face and build was intimidating enough to win grudging compliance from men not happy about being questioned. Ben was better with women, who all preened around him. The two of them didn't always divide it up that way, but often.

Seth's head turned as they walked up to the porch. His right hand rested on the butt of his gun. He didn't see anyone watching them, but had an itch between his shoulder blades and could tell Ben felt something similar. Both stepped carefully on the porch, with boards underfoot that had more give than they should. A couple wires stuck out of the wall where a doorbell had once been. Ben eased to one side of the door while Seth knocked.

He kept an eye on the window to his left. A flicker of movement told him someone was home. He nodded slightly at Ben, then knocked again, hard.

The door swung open. Darrell Swann, recognizable from his driver's license photo, glowered at them through the opening. "Jordan figured you'd come looking for me. I suppose you think I shot that rat bastard."

"We're just looking for information," Seth said mildly.

Swann was a big guy even compared to Seth and Ben, who were both in the neighborhood of six feet tall and stayed fit. The DMV had Swann at six foot two and two hundred pounds. Seth was betting he'd weigh in at closer to 230. Mostly beef, a little fat. Tight black T-shirt advertising Harley-Davidson, although the DMV didn't show him having the motorcycle certification. Sandy brown hair brushed his shoulders. The rest of the picture: hazel eyes narrowed to slits and bloodshot, two-day stubble and a stance that looked as if he was ready to swing a fist.

"What if I tell you to F off?"

Nice he'd edited the obscenity. Seth cocked an eyebrow at him. "Now, why would you do that when we might like your answers, thank you and go away?"

Darrell snorted. "Fine. Ask."

"Why don't you step out here onto the porch."
Seth didn't like the fact he couldn't see Darrell's
right arm and hand, or anything he might be holding.

He stared at them for a minute, then backed almost out of sight before stepping out on the porch.
"Might want to watch it," he said without much
interest. "You're likely to fall right through." He
nodded toward a splintered hole a few feet away.

"You rent?"

One massive shoulder jerked. "It's cheap."

"I'm Detective Seth Chandler with the sheriff's
department. This is Detective Ben Kemper. We're
investigating the murder of Geoffrey Moore."

"Don't see what it has to do with me."

Seth appreciated that Ben stood a little to one
side, staying quiet but watchful. "Were you aware
your sister had a relationship with Mr. Moore?"

"Yeah, so?"

"Had you ever met Mr. Moore?"

He sneered. "When would that be? When he
invited me to a dinner party?"

"At your sister's apartment, perhaps?"

"No. I saw him leaving a couple times."

Because he was on his way to see her? Or because he was staking out her place?

"You called him a rat bastard," Seth said. "May
I ask why, if you weren't personally acquainted?"

"He promised to marry Jordan, then got squirrelly. I told her he wouldn't, but she thought he meant it."

"I take it you and your sister have a close relationship?"

"No." Just like that, he was brimming with hostility.

"I'm confused. Weren't you on your way to see her when you saw Mr. Moore leaving her apartment?"

"What does it matter?"

"Your sister has reason to have been angry at Mr. Moore. Did she threaten retaliation in your hearing?"

He let loose an obscenity. "You know she's not my sister, right?"

"I'm aware she's your stepsister."

"Dad never adopted her. She's just this girl that was around."

"And yet you've obviously stayed in touch."

"In touch." His laugh had a vicious undertone. "That's a good one."

Seth was getting the feeling his and Ben's speculation might have some basis in truth.

"Have you had a romantic or sexual relationship with Jordan?" he asked bluntly.

Darrell Swan's eyes burned into his. "You could say that. She's hot."

"Did she dump you when she attracted Mr. Moore's interest?"

That was none of their f-ing business. "Now I'm done." He started for the open doorway.

Seth blocked his way. "May we come in, Mr. Swann?"

"No. You just want to pin that shit on me. I got nothing to do with it. Now get out of my way." He went from semicooperative to unpleasant in a heartbeat by thrusting out a shoulder and slamming into Seth, who stumbled back.

Then, *shit*, his foot broke through a porch board. Darrell plunged toward the doorway and had almost made it inside when Ben grabbed him from behind and slammed him up against the wall of the house instead.

"Not smart, Mr. Swann." Hand planted in the middle of Darrell's back, he reached behind him for his cuffs. "Assaulting a police officer..."

Seth was still wrenching his boot from the hole when Darrell exploded away from the wall. He slammed a fist into Ben's face and lunged across the threshold. Instead of trying to slam the door, he was reaching for something to one side.

Seth's Sig Sauer was in his hands before he made the conscious decision to draw. Out of the corner of his eye, he saw that Ben had drawn his weapon, too.

"Get your hands in sight!" Seth yelled. *"Now."*

Darrell's face, turned in profile to him, was beet red with fury, but he froze. Seth eased forward, the barrel of his Sig never wavering. After a dis-

cernible pause, Darrell lifted first his visible right
hand, then the one that had been out of sight, and
straightened with his back to them.

"Hands behind your back. Do it now."

Seth held his weapon steady while Ben hol-
stered his and snapped on the cuffs. Then Ben
pulled him not so gently backward, out of the
doorway. Seth took the couple steps required to
see the handgun lying on a small table right inside the door. A Smith & Wesson model M & P
Pro, black.

"Well, well," he said. "Would this be forty caliber by any chance, Mr. Swann?"

Not likely to be coincidence that the bullet re-
moved from Mr. Moore during the autopsy was
a .40 caliber.

Mr. Swann chose not to answer.

BAILEY'S PHONE RANG three times that day. First
the Lawsons' number, next the auto body shop
number and finally Eve's. She let all three calls
go to voice mail.

When she heard Seth, she'd gotten up, show-
ered and presented a perky exterior, going so far
as to scramble some eggs for both of them while
he made the toast. She pretended the kiss hadn't
happened. He went along with it. Their minimal
conversation consisted of his questions about
her itinerary for the day—undecided—and a reminder not to answer the door and, when behind

the wheel of the car if she went out, to keep an eye on the rearview mirror. He added a few tips for shaking a pursuer.

She told him to have a good day. Totally Stepford.

As soon as the sound of his engine receded, she sagged against the kitchen counter and decided there was no rule saying she had to do anything at all today if she didn't feel like it. And she didn't.

She thought about going back to bed, but wasn't sleepy. Since she had no intention of answering the door, though, she changed from jeans back into pajama bottoms topped with Seth's sweatshirt, which she was seriously considering stealing. And maybe never washing. She loved his scent.

She didn't feel like cleaning the kitchen, either, at least not yet.

It had to be the most unproductive day she'd spent in years. She watched daytime talk shows, explored his music selection, started a thriller she took from his bookshelf and ate all the junk food she could find in the kitchen.

She tried a couple of times to make herself examine why she was wasting an entire day, but all her effort succeeded in doing was driving her to dish up another bowl of Rocky Road ice cream and take out her laptop to watch an episode of *Game of Thrones*.

At near five o'clock, she had the guilty thought

that the least she could do was cook dinner, even if she wasn't exactly hungry. She found a package of tortillas and defrosted chicken breasts. After exploring the vegetable drawers in his refrigerator and his spice cupboard, she decided she could do fajitas, which wouldn't take long if she marinated the chicken now. This way, she could wait until he walked in the door to start cooking.

When he parked in the driveway and let himself in at almost six, she was shocked at the sight of his face. He looked inexpressibly weary.

"What happened?" she blurted.

His eyes met hers. "Just a day."

"You look as if it was more than that."

"Give me a minute to change," he said, and kept going toward the bedrooms, moving more heavily than usual.

Bailey hesitated, then decided to start cooking. If he wasn't hungry—well, they could refrigerate it for tomorrow.

But when he appeared a few minutes later in well-worn jeans and another sweatshirt, the first thing he said was, "Thank God. I'm starved."

"Fajitas," she told him brightly. "I've already done the slicing and dicing. They won't take long." She added quick rice to the water that was already boiling, then the chicken to the hot oil in the skillet. She jumped when it sizzled at her.

Seth poured himself a glass of milk again and

settled on one of the stools to watch her cook. "What did you do today?"

She raised her eyebrows at him. "You trying to get out of telling me what *you* did today?"

He started with obvious reluctance and was a little scanty with the details, but she got the picture. He'd come within a hairbreadth today of being shot—or having to shoot someone.

"Oh, my God," she breathed.

"Might have been ugly if I'd been alone, but I wasn't." He shrugged.

"You're telling me it wasn't a close call," she said fiercely.

He hesitated, then nodded toward the stove. "You're cooking."

A new kind of fear zinged her like an electric shock, leaving her skin feeling sensitized and her heart racing. She whirled and snatched up the spatula, stirring and flipping the strips of chicken.

When was the last time she'd been scared for someone else?

"I sometimes arrest violent criminals," he said. "That's part of the job. This time, it got close to being out of hand because I damn near crashed through the porch. Shit happens."

Oh, that made her feel better.

She known him a grand total of—she had to count—eight days. Barely over a week. An intense week, but still. What was *wrong* with her?

She didn't say a word, only lifted the now-browned chicken out of the pan, added some oil and, when it was bubbling, dumped in the sliced bell peppers and onions. As they sautéed, she heated tortillas in the microwave.

"Do you want to eat at the table?" she asked without looking at him.

She heard him slide to his feet. "What can I get?"

"Drinks. Sour cream. Silverware. Napkins. These can be messy."

Chicken went back into the skillet along with a little of the marinade. Rice...looked done, so she turned off the burner under it and scraped it into a serving bowl. The spiced chicken and veggies went in another one, the tortillas on a plate. She'd thoroughly learned the contents of his kitchen cupboards today. In fact, she'd given her nosiness free rein except when it came to his home office and bedroom.

Apparently they were both going to drink milk. She didn't often, but oh, well. It was good for bones and all that.

Seth constructed a hefty fajita and slathered sour cream atop it. Bailey, who wasn't all that hungry after her day's overindulgence, made a considerably smaller one.

Not until she was done did she ask, "So you arrested this guy?"

"For assaulting a police officer. The killing is still up in the air. We need to run ballistics tests.

Even if they line up, he says he taught his stepsister to shoot. We found both their fingerprints on his handgun. She's hysterical, says he must have killed Moore out of jealousy. He's gotten smart enough to clam up."

"What do you think?" She was calmer now. Maybe milk had a tranquilizing effect.

"I'm leaning toward him. When we knocked on his door, instead of assuming we were there to ask him about his stepsister, he started angry and ramped it up fast. Was sure we were going to 'pin it on him.' The guy has an ugly temper. That said—" he shrugged "—he's been in trouble with the law plenty of times before and he doesn't like cops. Add in that temper and a streak of paranoia, his less-than-friendly greeting makes sense even if he didn't kill anyone. And the stepsister, she's cold."

He finished the last bite. "Damn, this is good." Without taking a moment to let the first one settle in his stomach, he set about putting together a second, equally enormous fajita wrap.

"Lucky I didn't decide a salad would do us for dinner."

Seth chuckled. He picked up his fork, then looked at her. "Your turn. What did you do today?"

She was a microinch away from lying, but he might find out. Anyway, Bailey felt a weird disinclination to lie to him, of all people. He'd been really straight with her. He deserved the same.

"Nothing," she admitted. She focused on her plate. "I was a sloth."

"Yeah?" His voice was predictably kind. "No invitations you couldn't turn down?"

"They all left messages. I haven't listened to them." She squished a blend of sautéed peppers and onions into a puree with her fork.

"And now you're feeling guilty."

"I should at least have returned calls."

"Bailey, you've been hit by a lot. My guess is you needed to process."

She stared at him. He really did understand her, but how?

"If processing happens subconsciously, I'm good," she said. "Otherwise... I watched *Game of Thrones*—multiple episodes—I ate half a tub of ice cream, made a serious dent in your bag of potato chips, read, napped..."

Seth only grinned. "Of course processing is a subconscious activity. Everything important probably is. We're lucky that's true, given the attention span even smart people have." He chewed, his expression becoming meditative. Swallowed. "Do you have bad dreams, Bailey?"

Something very like apprehension came close to shutting down her breathing. "You mean nightmares. About him."

"Or about being left behind by him. Or even the years in foster care."

She looked down. "Yes."

"Are they bad?"

"Sometimes. Sometimes I don't exactly re-member, but wake up freaked or just feeling op-pressed." She lifted a shoulder. "You must see things that give you nightmares."

"Occasionally. But gruesome isn't the same as reliving something done to you personally."

"No."

"I'm sorry." Those dark eyes were steady on her. "I shouldn't have asked."

"No, it's okay. Remember those years of ther-apy I told you about," she said, almost lightly. "Therapists are big on dreams."

His mouth twitched. "I suppose so." He ap-peared to be considering a third helping, but sighed instead and rubbed a hand on his stomach. "That was really good. Thank you. If you hadn't been here, I'd have gone through some fast-food joint on the way home."

Guilt kicked in again. "Seth, I hope when you really want me gone, you'll say so. I won't be in-sulted. I'm getting... I think I could deal with going to the Lawsons'."

His eyes never left her face while she spoke. "Here's the thing." His voice had a deeper than usual timbre. "That won't be happening. Me want-ing you gone. I really like having you here. Know-ing I have someone to come home to."

Had there been a slight hesitation before he said

"someone"? As if he'd been about to say "you"?
Her heartbeat accelerated.

"Oh," she heard herself say inanely. "Well, um,
that's good, right?"

For a moment, she thought his face looked bleak
before he gave a faint smile. "Sure. It's good."

They stared at each other, her having the alarm-
ing yet also exhilarating realization that she
wanted to make love with this man. Preferably
right now.

He didn't want it to be an experiment. He'd said
sex wouldn't be casual for him. And he'd rather it
wasn't for her, either.

Bailey was quite sure it wouldn't be casual for
her, either. Which made the idea even more fright-
ening. But what if she chickened out and ended
up going back to LA in a few days or a week?
Wouldn't she always wonder?

"What are you thinking?" he asked in the husky
voice that gave her an idea what *he* was thinking.

"That I want you," she whispered.

CHAPTER TWELVE

SETH CLOSED HIS eyes briefly, prayerfully. She wanted him. Thank God. The kiss had made it damn hard for him to continue being a friendly, supportive not-quite friend.

He should have the pride to wonder whether, no matter what he'd said, all she wanted was to experiment, but knew he wouldn't. For one thing—hell, how could it help but be? Did he want her to lie to him?

No.

And if that's all it was, making this good for her might be the difference between her being able to live a full life instead of deciding men, marriage, children were off the table.

His breath huffed out. *Yeah, put a little pressure on, why don't you?*

She was waiting, as nervous as a doe hearing an unexpected noise. Poised to run, but not yet sure she should.

Seth pushed back his chair and held out a hand. "Hey," he said roughly. "Come here."

"Come...there?"

"Yeah." He smiled. "Dare you."

She bit her lip, eyed him narrowly, then seemingly made up her mind and pushed back her own chair. By the time she reached him and laid her small hand in his, he was fully aroused. Not a good way to start. Tonight had to be about her, not his own satisfaction.

"Hey." He tugged her onto his lap, then slid a hand to gently squeeze her nape. He bent to touch his forehead to hers. "Do you know how hard you hit me when you came to headquarters that day?"

She stiffened. "Hope Lawson in the flesh? Are you kidding? I saw your shock."

"I was shocked to have the living embodiment of that drawing appear," he conceded. No way to argue with that. "But I was stunned by Bailey Smith, too. You're beautiful and…" He didn't even know how to explain. "I was sure you'd fit me." What he'd felt was more like the shocked knowledge that he'd found the woman he'd been waiting for without knowing it. The One. Something he'd never believed in. He'd been fighting that certainty ever since because this woman was so damaged—and because he knew that, even if she was attracted to him, too, she had no concept of entering a long-term relationship, never mind settling down in a town fraught with buried memories. He hated to imagine how she'd react if she had the least idea how serious he could be about her.

"Oh." She nuzzled him. "I sort of felt the same. Only I thought, no way."

He chuckled and kneaded her neck beneath the bundle of fine, silky hair, feeling her relaxation. "Let me kiss you, Bailey."

She leaned into him and slipped an arm around his neck just as she pressed her lips to his.

It took more willpower than he'd known he possessed to keep the kiss exploratory, teasing. Coaxing. She'd claimed she wouldn't be afraid, but he didn't believe her. He sucked on her full lower lip and ran his tongue inside it. Her tongue tentatively touched his, and soon they were playing. He didn't pull her tight against him, not yet, but he slid his free hand beneath the sweatshirt to roam her back. Her vertebrae were so delicate, her shoulder blades sharp without the pads of muscle to protect them he had. But he felt shivers of reaction move through her, and he deepened the kiss.

She was the one to press her breasts to his chest. Her little moan made him shudder. He unhooked her bra, but had no access to her breasts with her plastered against him the way she was. That was okay. *Slow*, he reminded himself.

He struggled with the cloth-covered band that captured her hair until she pulled back to deftly slip it out. Her hair cascaded down over his hand. Threading his fingers in it, he said thickly, "I'd swear that's my favorite sweatshirt you're wearing."

"Was. *Was* your sweatshirt."

"Guess that's okay in LA, since they don't have their own football team."

She was saying something when his mouth closed over hers again. About a smell? Wasn't that bad? If his sweatshirt stank, she wouldn't want to wear it, would she? But the concept was beyond him right now. He planned to get her out of the shirt soon.

Maybe now. A groan vibrated in his chest when she found bare skin with her hand, stroking his side and squeezing between their bodies to flatten on his belly. He tugged at the hem of the sweatshirt she wore.

"Can I take this off?"

Bailey lifted her arms. He peeled it off. The pale blue satin bra almost went with it, but in the end caught on her breasts and stayed in place. As if by instinct, for an instant she clutched it protectively in place. Then, gaze locked to his, she shrugged her shoulders and let the bra slip down her arms. Seth took it from her and dropped it on the floor on top of the Seahawks sweatshirt. She tipped her head to one side and watched him studying her.

He had a feeling her boldness was pretend, but he had trouble tearing his gaze from generous breasts tipped with dainty, peaked nipples.

"God, you're beautiful," he said hoarsely.

"Thank you." The color in her cheeks deepened. "Will you take your shirt off, too?"

"Fair's fair." He wrenched it over his head. His erection throbbed at the way her eyes dilated as she looked at him. He clenched his teeth and let her look her fill while he did the same.

Finally, he couldn't stand it. He cupped her breasts, letting the rich swell of flesh settle in his palms, then rotated his hands, loving the way she shivered. She flattened her hands on his chest, then explored his muscles, grazed his nipples and squeezed the thick muscles that ran from his neck to his shoulders. Her lips parted, she appeared fascinated, even wondering, as if this was new to her. Her breath came fast, in time with his heartbeats.

He seized her mouth with his and took some of what he needed, forgetting for an instant what she needed. The kiss went deep and hungry, her fingertips biting into his shoulders, his hands still covering her breasts. She tasted so good, let her head fall back when he finally tore his mouth away and nipped at her jaw, her earlobe, the smooth line of her throat. He fought the desperate need to have her now, to strip her and set her in place right here. Or, God, shove the dishes aside and lay her out on his table.

No condom here.

And she was a woman who'd been repeatedly raped.

The thought hit him hard, made him shudder and ease back. "I love kissing you," he murmured.

"Yes." She didn't let him get away. She took

his mouth with small, biting kisses that were as hungry as he felt, if a little clumsy. She'd implied she had been promiscuous, but he had to wonder what that actually meant. Had she been a real participant, or just let guys stick their tongues down her throat, suck on her breasts and pound into her, slam, bang? *The latter*, he thought with a sharp pang but also something like gratitude. This *was* new to her.

He kissed her back, but let her take the lead.

Finally he said starkly, "I'm dying here," and rose to his feet, gripping her thighs to lift her with him. She gave a squeak and wrapped her legs tightly around his waist, riding him in a way that made the walk through the kitchen and down the hall to the bedroom the sweetest of torture.

He'd been afraid to jar her out of the mood, but she pressed her mouth to his neck, even licking as if she wanted to taste him. He wanted to taste her, too. All of her.

When he reached his bed, he freed one hand to yank the covers back before laying her down. Against the navy blue sheets, her skin was ivory, almost luminous, her hair silver-gold rivers of silk. He looked his fill, his body tightening to the unbearable point. He didn't know if he could wait any longer than it took to peel her jeans off, but he knew he had to. She stared up at him, and as he watched, her dazed, dreamy expression transformed slowly into awareness that he feared would turn into nerves.

One knee on the bed, he bent to suckle her breast. Softly at first, circling each nipple with his tongue, nipping, drawing it into his mouth and using the suction to pull rhythmically. She arched and grabbed at his head, her fingers threaded in his hair. The little sounds that escaped her drove him crazy.

He rubbed his cheek against her belly, then brought all his concentration to bear on unbuttoning and unzipping her jeans, finally peeling them off, taking the panties with them. Her feet had been bare; he'd found himself staring at them while he watched her cook. He loved her feet. Now he took them in his hands, savoring the fine bones and the way her toes curled, and stroked the arches. He wrapped his hands around her ankles, slid them upward over her calves and knees that he couldn't help noticing, with an odd feeling of tenderness, were a little knobby. Her thighs—ah, they were perfection, slender but taut with muscles. He touched her small birthmark. And there was the V of hair, unusual in being as pale as the hair on her head.

Seth fleetingly wondered how a man could be repulsed by the buds of womanly breasts or the appearance of silky, curly pubic hair, then made himself banish thoughts of *him*. The son of a bitch wasn't welcome here.

"Beautiful," he heard himself say again, before he kissed her there.

She reared up. "Seth!"

He stroked his tongue between the folds, the heady scent and spicy taste increasing his agony.

She moaned. He licked again and again, penetrated her with his tongue, his hands gripping and squeezing her butt as he lifted her to him. Her fingers had tightened painfully in his hair, but she wasn't pushing him away. Instead, her hips rose and shifted, following his mouth and tongue. Her small cries shot like arrows to his groin.

He reared to his knees, then slid back off the bed to his feet. His hands shook as he shed his own jeans and boxers. He heard himself cursing when he fumbled with laces, tossed the shoes aside and tore off the socks.

In a fit of optimism, he'd dropped a couple of condoms in a bedside drawer last night. He retrieved one, ripped open the small packet and put it on, only then lifting his head to see that Bailey had gone very still as she stared. In alarm?

Damn it. He closed his eyes and grabbed for the tattered remnants of his self-control. Instead of spreading her legs and driving himself into her the way he craved, he lowered himself to lie beside her and pulled her against him for a long, lavish kiss. With his hands and lips and teeth, he immersed her in pleasure until her body moved mindlessly in response to his every touch.

Only then did he push into her tight, slick sheath, grinding his teeth to keep from thrusting hard and deep.

"Look at me," he said roughly, and she did, lifting astonished eyes to meet his. For a moment he held still, knowing he'd never forget the shocked pleasure he saw on her face.

He gripped one of her thighs, lifting it high, and began to move, his gaze never leaving hers. Deeper, faster, holding on when he didn't think he could, until she suddenly cried out and tightened around him. Only then did Seth close his eyes and let himself go, hoarsely calling her name as ecstasy that was near to pain emptied him out.

BAILEY FELT BONELESS, her body shimmering with the aftershock of something she'd only been able to imagine before. Beneath her ear, Seth's heart beat hard and fast, and his chest rose and fell with his gasps for air.

She'd made men happy before by letting them have her body, so that part shouldn't feel so new. Shiny. But it did. It had to do with him insisting she open her eyes and look at him while he moved inside her. That made her more than a body. He saw *her*. She'd felt raw, knowing she wasn't hiding anything from him. But she couldn't regret that, because he'd let her see what he felt, too. And that was so much.

She heard him say, with a husky timbre, *With you, Bailey, sex won't be casual. Not for me.*

Anxiety stirred, although as amazingly good as she felt, it was slow to work up any momentum. Still, worry crept into her mind that he might want more from her than she knew how to give. She'd said enough, he had to know she'd never really loved anyone. The word *love* came from movies. Caring about friends or people like the Neales, that was one thing. She might feel bad if they were distressed, or go out of her way to help if she could. But for her, there was always a distance. If that person was suddenly gone from her life, she'd be mildly sorry and that was all. She wasn't capable of anything deeper. How could she be? You had to learn when you were young.

Her chest tightened as she remembered the moment when she'd cried on her father.

Maybe I did learn. I just forgot.

The ability might be withered from lack of use but still there. A muscle that could be developed.

"Hey." He lifted his head so he could see her. "You okay?"

Flip words rose to her tongue, but she couldn't say them. "Yes." She cleared her throat. "That was… It was…"

"Extraordinary?" He smoothed her hair from her face, his hand gentle. A smile was in his voice, but beneath it, uncertainty. "Amazing?"

Her cheeks heated. She had to tell him. "It was

both. I've never, um…you know." Who'd imagine
Bailey Smith was too shy to say, *I've never had
an orgasm?* Not her. Live and learn.

His expression changed. "Never?"

She shook her head. "I told you I didn't enjoy
sex."

"Yeah, but—" He sounded stunned. "You don't
need a man to give you an orgasm."

"Just touching yourself doesn't really do it, you
know. I think you have to be able to fantasize. And
what was *I* supposed to fantasize about?"

Seth was quiet for a minute. "I can see that,"
he said thoughtfully.

"So." Suddenly she was scared. She'd spent a
lifetime disguising her vulnerabilities, and here
she was laying them out to be trampled on. Really smart. She needed to change the tone. "Not
meaning to stroke your ego too much, but you
opened new worlds for me. I may look at men
with a slightly different eye now."

"No." He had her flipped onto her back and
reared over her so fast, she hadn't had a hint it
was coming. He looked angry. "We're not interchangeable, Bailey. Is that really what you think?"

She stared up at smoldering eyes and an angular face set in harsh lines. Protecting herself, she'd
hurt him, and he'd given her more in only a few
days than almost anyone else ever had. Slowly,
she shook her head.

"No," she whispered. "It's not. You're the first…"

Breathe. "The only…" Oh, God. What was she admitting to?

His face softened. "That's the way it happens sometimes, whether we're ready for it or not."

Did that mean…*he* hadn't been ready, either? Wasn't sure he wanted whatever was happening between them?

Oh, good. *That* freaked her out, too. The truth was, everything happening to her right now was unfamiliar. She didn't know how to feel about any of it. About any of *them.* Kirk. Karen. *My father and mother.* Eve. Most of all, Seth.

Weight on his elbows, he watched every shifting expression on her face, and she had the disquieting feeling he knew what each and every one meant. Which was especially unsettling considering *she* didn't understand all the conflicting emotions that crowded her chest until it ached.

"You know," he murmured, "practice makes perfect. We should reinforce tonight's lessons, don't you think?" His lips were soft as they skimmed hers. He tickled the corner of her mouth with his tongue, then rubbed a scratchy cheek against hers. The contrast in textures—soft lips, bristly jaw—was unexpectedly erotic.

She lifted her hands, splaying them on his chest and rubbing gently. His big body shuddered, and she reveled in the power he handed her with his open response to her touch.

"I think that's an excellent idea." She found his

small, flat nipples with her fingertips and watched his eyes dilate. "Although you might want to ditch that condom before it gets hard to take off," she teased.

"Pun intended?" One side of his mouth lifted in a very sexy smile. "Unfortunately, you're right. Don't go anywhere, okay?"

She giggled, suddenly feeling buoyantly happy. "I wouldn't think of it."

EVE BARELY TURNED her head to glance at Seth Chandler's house when she drove by it.

It was chance she knew where he lived. He'd certainly never invited her home with him, she thought with a trace of bitterness she knew wasn't justified.

As it happened, she had an appointment first thing this morning at a foster home not far from his house. She'd never had one of her kids in this particular home before. Yesterday, she'd looked at the address and realized with dismay where it was. If he saw her passing his house, he'd decide she was some kind of pathetic stalker.

But an alternate route would take an extra ten minutes of her day, and with her ridiculous caseload she was already running morning to night.

So Hope was staying here with him. Big surprise. Eve had seen the way he looked at Hope and tried to hide how that made her feel. He'd never once looked at her that way. He wouldn't

have fallen madly in love with her even if Hope—
Bailey—had never appeared.

So live with it.

In her more honest moments, she suspected her
pride was hurt more than her heart. She'd liked
him better than he liked her, which wasn't good
for a girl's ego. And then having him topple at first
sight for the adoptive sister she'd already envied
for years... *Of course* that stung.

So she just wouldn't look when she went by
his house.

Only there was movement just as she came
abreast of it, and without her volition, her gaze
flicked to see what it was.

What she saw was the front door opening and
Seth coming out, dressed for work. But he turned
back, as if he'd forgotten something. Eve's gaze
went to her rearview mirror as she continued
down the block.

What Seth had turned back for was one last
kiss. And even after he broke away, Hope stayed
in the open doorway, smiling as she watched him
stride to his SUV in the driveway.

Eve felt as if she'd been kicked in the stomach.
Far enough away she wouldn't be noticed, she
pulled to the side of the road and sat there, gripping the steering wheel until her knuckles ached.
She was aware of nothing but the hateful, hurt-
ful emotions that filled her until she didn't know
how to contain them.

It was a long time before they ebbed enough that her body sagged and her head fell back.

She already felt as if she was losing her parents. They hadn't guessed how their joy and the fact that they couldn't talk about anything but Hope, Hope, Hope had wounded her. But she was going to lose them entirely if she couldn't get past this— or at least learn to fake it better.

Even the thought of having no one again terrified the little girl inside her who knew all too well what that was like.

She'll go back to California. I'll only have to endure her for occasional holidays.

Unless she ended up staying because of Seth. Putting Eve firmly and forever in second place.

Second place was better than not placing at all. Or was it?

Maybe she was the one who should start job hunting, who should move instead of hanging on in her hometown because of that scared little girl who'd been so awed because now *she* had a family and home, like other kids did.

She made a ragged sound that was almost a laugh. She might not be a stalker, but pathetic? Oh, yeah.

"LET'S BRING MS. SWANN in for another talk," Ben said. "Shake her up a little. She might lose some of that composure when she's not on her home turf."

"You know she'll get a lawyer."

"Maybe. She's cold enough she might not think she needs one."

Yeah. Seth could see that. Jordan and Darrell were quite a pair—the one as volatile as TNT, the other as chilly and self-possessed as an iceberg.

Ben shrugged. "If she lawyers up, that's because she's getting nervous."

"She'll be at work by now."

Ben's smile was feral. "All the better."

Seth, too, liked the idea of visiting her place of work, which happened to be an insurance office. Lee Kroeger, her employer, currently had a seat on the city council. Conservative as hell, he'd look askance at a receptionist under investigation for murder of the married man with whom she'd been having an affair.

Seth's mobile phone rang just as he was pushing back from his desk. He took a look—unfamiliar number and area code. He held a finger up to Ben and answered.

"Detective Chandler, this is Sergeant Martin Riser with the Redding Police Department. Northern California," the man elaborated. "I'm calling because I saw a segment on television about Hope Lawson. I understand you're the investigator who launched the search for her."

Seth's skin prickled. "That's correct. What can I do for you?"

"Well, here's the thing. I'm with the Major

Crimes Unit now, but I spent some time with Sexual Assault."

"Did you have an abduction or attempted abduction of a girl who reminds you of Hope?"

"No," the sergeant told him. "Actually, it's the other way around. A few years back, a girl was abandoned in a crummy motel on the outskirts of town. Said her name was Anna. She seemed confused when we asked for a last name. She finally said her 'daddy' was Mr. Hawley, so she went into our system as Anna Hawley. We never found a trace of the father or any clue where she came from. She didn't remember her mother or any other family. No question she'd been sexually molested," he said grimly. "Battered, too. X-rays showed multiple broken bones from past injuries, some that hadn't healed quite right. She was skinny and dirty, too, but a real pretty little girl. Blonde and blue eyed."

"Just beginning to develop physically?"

"Yep. We guessed maybe eleven or twelve. She had no idea how old she was. When I saw the story about Hope, I couldn't help remembering. A lot of similarities. And Hawley and Hamby? Kinda similar names, too."

"Yes. How long ago was it that this girl was abandoned in Redding, Sergeant?"

"I had to look it up. It's been almost four years. Week before Thanksgiving."

Riding a surge of adrenaline, Seth asked, "Is Anna still in a foster home in Redding?"

"Yes, she is. Occurred to me you might like to talk to her."

"I would." Another witness. Damn, if he could have his way, he'd drive straight to the airport. "Will she be willing?"

"I haven't asked her or her foster mom. She was so traumatized then, it wasn't easy getting any sense out of her. I didn't want to set her to worrying if you didn't think it was worth a trip down here."

"It's worth a trip. Will you spell that last name?"

"H-A-W-L-E-Y. Couldn't get a first name out of her then."

"This could be a real break." Seth told him what he'd learned so far about Les Hamby's travels and the effort the FBI was making, too. "I'm thinking your Anna is on this list I've been poring over."

"Finding her family." Riser cleared his throat. "Wouldn't that be something."

"I know I'll never forget the expression on Hope's mother's face when she saw her." He glanced up to see Ben waiting. "Why don't I call you as soon as I have travel plans nailed down?"

"That'll do fine," the sergeant agreed. "I'll look forward to meeting you."

Seth ended the call, feeling dazed.

"A break?" Ben asked.

"A big one. I'm going to see if I can get clearance to fly down to California in the next day or two."

Ben clapped him on the back. "Then what say we try to make an arrest today?"

Seth suspected his own smile was as savage as Ben's had been earlier. "Let's do it."

CHAPTER THIRTEEN

THE TWIN TURBOPROP plane touched down, bounced and with a thump the wheels made contact with the runway again. Seth heard a tiny whimper from beside him. It wasn't a surprise. Bailey had been clutching his hand in a painful grip ever since they took off from San Francisco.

She'd done fine on the Boeing 767 they'd taken from Seattle to San Francisco, although she was quiet during most of the flight. Once she said, "You know, I haven't flown very often."

When he asked, she said she'd flown once to Cabo in Mexico with some friends for a week's vacation and then from LA to Seattle. That was it.

Now as the plane braked and they were thrust forward against their seat belts, she gusted out a breath he guessed she'd been holding for some time. "I'm not sure I like to fly," she confessed.

"Takes getting used to." He wasn't crazy about it, either. He didn't so much mind heights as he disliked being at the mercy of someone else's competence. Then there was the fact that he was too large a man to be comfortable in an economy airline seat.

"We're here."

She made a face. "We still have to get...back."

If he wasn't mistaken, she'd almost said *home*, but corrected herself. He took that as encouragement. "One thing at a time."

After convincing the department to pay for this jaunt, he'd gotten the idea of bringing Bailey. He thought it would be good for her, and that she might be good for Anna Hawley. He'd offered to pay her airfare, but when the Lawsons heard the plan, they insisted on picking up the cost.

"Do you know what it would mean to us if we can help some other family find their daughter?" Karen had said, fiercely enough to startle him.

Seeing her expression, Seth had only been able to nod.

The plane rolled to a stop by the small terminal and he took down their carry-ons so he and Bailey could join the line exiting the plane. Heat slammed them when they stepped out. *Guess we're not in Seattle anymore*, he thought ruefully.

Sergeant Riser had offered to meet them, but Seth had decided to rent a car. He'd reserved a midsize sedan, and cranked the air-conditioning high the minute he got behind the wheel.

"Let's stop by the police station first," he suggested, "then find a hotel and lunch." They'd ended up putting the trip off for two days to arrive on a Saturday when Anna wouldn't have school.

Bailey nodded. "Okay." Her tension was visible—left over from the flight, or in anticipation of meeting a girl who'd bring back her own nightmares? Who knew? She'd noticeably clammed up since hearing about Anna.

Sergeant Riser was middle-aged, tall and lanky with steel-gray hair cut short. He greeted Seth cordially, but his gaze remained riveted on Bailey from first sight.

"Damn," he said in a private moment while she was in the ladies' room. "She looks even more like that drawing in real life than she did on TV."

"I did some gaping the first time I saw her," Seth admitted. And more than a few times since, but for different reasons now. Not that he'd tell anybody else that.

Riser offered suggestions for hotel and restaurants, and gave Seth a map with an X marked on the foster home. "They're expecting you at two. Gives you time for lunch."

Seth held out his hand. "Thank you. You know you're welcome to come with us."

He shook his head. "Don't want to overwhelm Anna. Plus..." He hesitated. "Her memories of me might not be the best." His shrug was awkward. "She got to me. You know how it is sometimes. I've kept in touch with her caseworker to make sure she was all right, but that's all."

"She stuck with you well enough you were able to make the connection when you heard about Hope."

"I'll keep my fingers crossed you learn enough to make it worth the trip down here."

Bailey came out of the restroom, her gaze going straight to him. She never looked away as she crossed the short distance, not until they were saying their goodbyes and she shook the sergeant's hand, too. Seth's heart squeezed every time she looked at him like that. It was as if he was anchoring her.

They checked into a hotel that looked decent—one room, king bed—and found a sandwich shop. He'd already noticed that Bailey didn't eat when she was nervous. It took some nagging to get her to finish half her sandwich. Finally he checked his watch.

"Should be about right if you're ready."

For a fleeting moment, he saw a fragility in her eyes that he knew would stay with him. His admiration for her only increased when she gave a sturdy nod and stood.

"We don't want to be late."

"No," he said gently, and took her hand as they walked out into the heat.

BAILEY GAZED OUT the window at the small white clapboard house with one dormer centered above the front door. The lawn was dried brown; the leaves hung limply from the branches of the single tree in the narrow front yard. The Buick in the driveway had a bumper that sagged on one side and a large spot of rust on the fender. No spring chicken, that car.

Seth was watching her, not the house. He'd kept an eye on her all day and let her crush his hand during the last leg of their flight. Stupid to have nerves jumping in her stomach now.

She straightened and opened her door. "Looks like they're here," she said, sounding stupidly cheerful. *What fun this will be!* her voice suggested.

His gaze cut her way, but all he said was, "Should be. It's two o'clock, on the nose." A minute later, he joined her on the sidewalk, a folder in one hand. She heard the car door locks snick before he gestured her to go ahead of him up the walk.

Bailey surreptitiously pressed a hand to her stomach. God, what if they were no sooner invited in than she had to race for the bathroom to puke? *What do I have to be afraid of?*

But she knew. The prop plane had been a time machine, carrying her back to see herself at fourteen or fifteen. The Neales hadn't taken her in yet. Before them, she'd lived with... Weirdly, she couldn't pull up the names. She could see the faces of the foster parents who had preceded the Neales, the house, her bedroom shared with two other girls, but summoning a name was beyond her.

On the porch, Seth reached past her to knock, then stepped back and rested a hand on Bailey's back. It felt so good, warm and strong. She gave herself permission to accept the unspoken support, even lean a little.

The door opened to reveal a motherly, friendly looking woman with gray-streaked dark hair cut short. She wore Birkenstock sandals, faded jeans and a tie-dyed T-shirt with colors that swirled over her ample bosom. Smiling, she stepped back.

"I'm Betty Wade. You must be Detective Chandler and Hope. I'm so glad you made it." She studied Bailey with shrewd hazel eyes. "I read about you in *People* magazine. To think you might have a connection with Anna!"

Seth scanned the shabby but neat living room in a way that would have looked casual to anyone who didn't know he was a cop. "Anna knows we're coming?"

Her smile dimmed slightly. "Oh, yes. I don't think she's decided how she feels about it."

Bailey totally understood that.

The house felt like someplace she'd been before. Not been, *lived in* before, she corrected herself. People who took in foster kids were rarely well-to-do. Some probably fostered partly for the money, although not all. She thought maybe Betty Wade was one of those who wasn't much interested in the stipend.

"Come on back to the kitchen," the woman said, leading the way past a narrow, steep staircase and a couple of closed doors.

The kitchen was at the back of the house. Beyond a general impression of yellow painted cabinets and aging appliances, Bailey saw only the teenage girl who jumped up from a chair at a table by a sliding door that looked out at a backyard as sun-browned as the front.

Long, blond hair hung in a braid that flopped over her shoulder. Clear blue eyes fixed right on Bailey, guarded but unwillingly fascinated, too, Bailey thought. Her face was thin, her chin arrowing to a point, her forehead high. She was skinny, long-legged and taller already than Bailey. She wore a shirt large enough to disguise her body, and the way she hunched her shoulders made Bailey suspect she might have breasts big enough to make her self-conscious. *God, I remember that age.*

She didn't really look like Bailey, and yet... *I know her*, Bailey thought with sudden clarity. What they had in common was so immense, it made their differences unimportant.

Betty was talking, but the words flew right past Bailey and she didn't think Anna was listening, either. They only stared at each other.

In an instant, her nerves and stomach settled. "Anna," she said softly. "I'm Hope Lawson, although I go by Bailey now. I really wanted to meet you."

"They said..." She cast a nervous glance at

Seth. "Um, that my father might have been yours, too?"

"That's partly what we came to talk to you about. He...made me call him Daddy. But he wasn't really my father, and if he's the same man, he wasn't yours, either."

The hope in this girl's eyes was painful to see. "You mean, I might not be related to him at all?"

Bailey felt the prickle of tears, but she also smiled. "I think the chances are really good you aren't."

"But...we look like we might be sisters."

"That's because he liked blonde, blue-eyed little girls." Or maybe she shouldn't have used the past tense. *Likes.* No, nothing she could say to this girl. She bit her lip. "Can we sit down, Anna?"

Betty took over, pouring everyone glasses of lemonade and offering slices of cake neither Seth nor Bailey felt they could refuse. Bailey introduced Seth to Anna. They chatted for a few minutes, Bailey and Anna assessing each other the whole while. Seth asked if she'd lived with Mrs. Wade long, and she nodded, looking down at the table. "Ever since...you know."

Then she'd been lucky, Bailey couldn't help thinking. At this age, she had already been wearing too-tight clothes and too much makeup. She'd needed the boys to be mesmerized by her, because otherwise she hardly existed. She'd been moved from the two foster homes before the Neales because of that overt sexuality. Nobody knew how to deal with it.

Anna looked like a child still, despite the figure. Maybe, thanks to her foster mother, she didn't feel the need to use her body to garner attention.

Finally Seth showed her the two pictures he'd brought: Hope's only school photo, and then the age-progressed drawing. Betty studied them, too, shaking her head and murmuring her amazement.

"Do you go online?" he asked Anna.

She tore her gaze from the pictures to look up. "I have a Facebook page," she said shyly.

He smiled at her. "Well, I did my best to get these pictures out on Facebook and Twitter and everywhere else I could think of. Eventually, somebody recognized Bailey."

Anna scrutinized the pictures again, then Bailey's face. She nodded.

Bailey said, "We think the man who abducted me might be the same one who took you, even though he called himself Les Hamby when I was with him."

Her expression changed. It was as if she'd just seen a ghost. "Les," she whispered.

"Was that his name?" Seth asked in the gentle voice that Bailey found so soothing.

After a moment, she gave a jerky nod.

"Do you remember anything from before you were with him?"

She was shaking her head frantically before he finished. "No!"

Bailey reached across the table and took her hand. "I didn't, either," she said quietly. "He...hurt me when I did. After a while, you're so afraid of being hurt, you just...don't. Even now, my stomach ties itself in knots when I have even the faintest whiff of a memory."

Anna stared at her with huge, haunted eyes. "But...you know your real parents now," she whispered. "Don't you remember them?"

"Things are starting to come back to me," Bailey admitted. "It's slow. I guess I'm still scared." She took a deep breath. "If we can find your family, I think it might be easier for you. It hasn't been as many years since you've seen them. He took me away from mine twenty-three years ago. That's a long time."

"Did he leave you, like he did me?" she asked timidly.

Bailey managed a sort of smile. "Yes. I kept thinking he'd come back, but he didn't."

"Sometimes I still think I see him," Anna said, a tension in her voice. "A car will go by and I think it's him. Or...or I see someone at the mall."

Seth was watching her unblinkingly. Was he wondering if Les Hamby really was watching Anna?

Sneaking a look at them, Anna continued, "Betty doesn't make me wait for the school bus, because I'm the only kid on this block and I don't like to be alone. You know. In case he does come back for me."

Bailey nodded, tears stinging her eyes. "I do know."

"Did you ever see him again?"

Bailey shook her head. "No. At first, I kept thinking I did, too, but I knew it wasn't really him." She hesitated. Anna had never been willing to provide a description of her "daddy." Sergeant Riser had said she didn't talk at all in the early days, then wouldn't talk about the man at all. But maybe now... "Anna." She squeezed the girl's hand. "Can you tell us what he looked like? So we can be sure it's the same man?"

"I don't really remember that well," she said, voice almost inaudible.

Seth stirred. Bailey shook her head at him.

None of them moved after that. If the room hadn't been so silent, they might not have heard her at all.

"He wasn't that tall. I was almost as tall as him when..." She chewed her bottom lip. She looked up fleetingly, her eyes catching Bailey's with a kind of desperation. "I wanted to grow so much. I thought if I got bigger than him I'd be so strong I could yell 'Don't touch me' and he wouldn't."

"Yes," Bailey whispered, too.

Anna frowned a little. "His hair was brown."

"Was he turning gray?"

"Uh-uh." Her forehead creased. "He had kind of awful teeth."

Bailey's breath caught. Sometimes her stomach would heave when he ground his mouth on hers. Her shudder was involuntary. "And bad breath."

"Yes!"

They stared at each other.

Seth started asking questions, much the same ones he'd asked her not so long ago. What did Les Hawley do to earn money? Did Anna remember any of the towns they'd stayed in? Had he ever been pulled over by the police when she was with him?

She frowned at that. "Once he had to stop because a taillight was out. He was really nervous, but he didn't get a ticket or anything."

"Any other time?"

"I think he got arrested this once. He didn't come back to get me for, like, two days. He was really mad. He yelled about how this— Um, he said a lot of bad words. This other *guy* started the fight. And…something about a drunk tank. I don't know what that is."

"Do you recall where you were when that happened?"

"The town had a funny name. That's why I remember it. It was Truckee. We were only supposed to stop for one night because it was winter and he didn't have chains if it snowed very much, and it did snow while he was in the drunk tank so we turned around and went back the way we came instead of going to Reno the way he wanted. He was mad about that, too."

Listening to the small voice giving a matter-of-fact, almost-dry recitation, Bailey felt something unfamiliar. Rage on someone else's behalf. The idea of him taking out his anger on this slight, vulnerable girl infuriated her in a different way than did her memories of him hurting her when he got mad.

Tangled in the rage was guilt. But she didn't say anything. She only held Anna's hand and listened.

Finally it was time to go. When Seth said so, Anna's head shot up in panic, her eyes fastening on Bailey.

"Will I see you again?"

Bailey hesitated. "I don't know. I hope so." Inspiration struck. "I'll write down my phone number for you, so you can call me. Anytime you want to talk, okay? I mean that. And if Mrs. Wade doesn't mind, I'll take your number so I can call, too."

Anna relaxed slightly. "Okay. I'd like that. Even if we aren't sisters, like I thought."

"We are in a way, though, aren't we?" *More sisters than real ones*, she thought. It was something like the way she identified with Eve. What they had in common was huge.

Saying goodbye was hard. She hugged Anna, who hugged her back. Tears in her eyes, Mrs. Wade hugged her, too. Bailey was blinded with tears as Seth steered her out to the rental car. *I don't cry.*

You mean, you didn't used *to cry.*

New reality. Caring about other people *sucked*, she thought fervently.

Seth started the car, but didn't put it into Drive. He wrapped his arm around her and tugged her toward him. "Come here."

"I'll get snot on you!" she wailed.

He only chuckled. "I didn't think to bring any tissues, so my shirt is as good as anything to soak up your snot."

She tried really hard to keep the weep-fest brief, even though being enclosed in his arms and laying her head against his chest was so comforting. Finally she did wipe her cheeks and nose against his soft cotton shirt before she pulled back. She hated knowing how awful she must look, with her eyes swollen half-shut and her skin probably blotchy. And, yes, big, wet splotches now decorated his shirt, and not all of them were tears.

He smiled through her apologies. "One minute out in the sun and I'll be dry."

Well, that was probably true.

Guilt rose to the top of her cauldron of stormy emotions. "If I'd described him to police and told them what he did to me, he might have been arrested. And then he couldn't have done it again." She closed her eyes. "He couldn't have done it to Anna."

"You could just as well say Anna should have told, so he didn't have a chance to go on and abduct another girl."

She stared at him, shocked at hearing that from him. "But she was—" Seeing his expression, she made a face. "All right, you've made your point. I was scared, too. I know I was. But still."

"There's no *still*." He leaned over to kiss her lightly, then finally released the emergency brake and pulled away from the curb. "I need to talk to Sergeant Riser. How would you feel about taking a nap while I do that? I know you didn't sleep last night."

"You had something to do with that."

He flashed a grin. "Guilty. But I was trying to wear you out so you *could* sleep."

"Totally altruistic."

"That's me." His mouth had a satisfied curl that made her melt.

"You don't want me to hear what you tell him?" she asked.

His eyebrows rose, showing his surprise, and he cast her a quick glance. "What could I tell him that you don't already know? No. I just thought you need to recharge."

Bailey thought about it. "God. We have to fly back to Seattle tomorrow."

"First thing," Seth agreed, sounding cheerful.

"Fine. Drop me off at the hotel."

He caught her hand. "I won't be gone long."

"I'm a big girl. Just in case I can't sleep, I have a book."

He disarmed her utterly by lifting her hand to his mouth and pressing the softest of kisses to her knuckles. "You're something, you know that, Bailey Smith?"

Having him say that so very seriously made a lump rise to her throat. She'd never told him, but she had a 3.95 GPA so far at USC. For the first time in her life, she'd begun to feel some pride in herself. She didn't fully understand what Seth saw in her that made him think something like that, but she couldn't help feeling warmed.

He made the turn into the hotel parking lot and stopped under the portico. "Bailey?"

The different note in his voice had her pausing with the car door half-open. "What?"

"Do you think you ever really did see him after he left you?"

Silenced for a moment, she finally shook her head. "No. It was just…paranoia. I think he drove away and never looked back."

"Okay." He grimaced. "I didn't much like the idea that he hung around for a while."

"Why would he?"

His jaw went taut. "To terrorize you into silence."

She closed her eyes. "There's a thought. Ugh. But no. I really don't think he was there. He'd terrorized me sufficiently already. Anna, too," she said more softly.

"All right, sweetheart." He wrapped his hand around the back of her neck and squeezed. "Sleep. That's an order."

"Yes, sir."

She hugged his last smile to her as she hurried up to their room and let herself in. She didn't know if she really could sleep, but the bed looked tempting.

THERE WERE A couple of obvious possibilities on the list of missing girls who'd be in Anna's age range, but Seth and Riser both knew finding out where she came from might not be that easy. Hamby might have expanded his territory and snatched a girl from Texas or North Dakota or who knew where. Some small police departments still weren't good about adding their crimes to the FBI database. She could conceivably never have been reported missing at all because her parents lived off the grid, or nobody gave a damn— or, most horrifyingly of all, because a parent had sold her.

Riser cursed himself for not considering the possibility back then that she'd been abducted rather than abandoned by a parent.

"She might have been able to go right home," he growled.

Seth understood where he was coming from. He, too, wanted a happy ending for her. He wanted it with a ferocity that shook him. A cop couldn't function if he let himself care this much very often. He knew he'd have cared no matter what, but in this girl, achingly vulnerable, he'd seen a young Bailey. Watching Bailey's face, he'd been able to tell how powerfully she'd identified. How could she help it?

If only she had been restored to her parents when she was as young as fourteen, she'd have been saved from years of isolation. He might have met her sooner. Yeah, he couldn't help thinking, but she wouldn't have been Bailey. She'd have been Hope. Still wounded, but maybe lacking the many layers that gave her such depth and complexity. She wouldn't be self-made. He'd still have been physically attracted to her, he had no doubt of that, but would he have fallen for her the same way? Seth didn't know.

He ended up leaving the search for Anna's family in Riser's hands, although he had every intention of pursuing Les Hamby or Hawley or whatever he wanted to call himself to the ends of the earth. They agreed to keep each other informed.

What Seth couldn't forget was that Hamby had undoubtedly long since replaced Anna. Somewhere out there, another blue-eyed blonde girl was being sexually molested and terrorized. He gritted his teeth. That was the right word for what this monster did to his captives.

Seth might find he'd died or gone to prison for

killing a man in a bar fight sometime since he dumped Anna. Either were possibilities. Part of him hoped neither was true. He wanted the pleasure of seeing him arrested. He wanted to give Bailey and Anna the satisfaction of looking the bastard in the eye as they testified in court. He wanted them to hear the jury foreman declare him guilty as charged, see him shuffle out of the courtroom in shackles.

He let himself into the hotel room quietly, doubting that Bailey had really slept and happy to see that she had. The bedside lamp was on and the same paperback book she'd been reading on the plane lay open beside her. She wasn't very far into the book, confirming his suspicion that she'd been reading a few pages over and over again as an inadequate distraction.

For a minute he stood beside the bed looking down at her. Her lips were parted and her face relaxed in a way he'd rarely seen. Even in sleep, she often looked tense. In the few nights they'd shared a bed, he'd held her half a dozen times as she came out of nightmares. The confident woman she tried to present herself as, wasn't.

I want to make her happy. He thought he could, if she'd give him the chance.

What he felt was too much, too soon, he knew, but it was real nonetheless.

Bailey sighed, stretched and opened her eyes. Then her mouth curved. "You're back."

"I am." He sat on the edge of the bed and bent over her, bracing himself with a hand planted on each side of her. "Are you in a hurry to get up?"

She laid her hand against his jaw. "You want company while you nap?" she teased.

"Something like that." His voice had come out hoarse. He bent lower and kissed her. For a minute it was gentle, because he'd been thinking of her at Anna's age, so vulnerable and alone, but her response was immediate. Her lips parted and the hand on his jaw slid around to his neck to pull him down to her. He tilted his head to take her mouth more thoroughly, stroking her tongue with his, drowning in her taste, her heat.

In no time she fumbled at the buttons on his shirt even as he moved lower and sucked her breast through her thin camisole. Her back arched and she whimpered. Abruptly impatient, he stripped her of the camisole, then took care of the buttons on his cuffs so he could shrug out of his own shirt. Her hands flattened on his chest, where she could feel his heart thundering.

"I love the way you touch me," he managed to say, before he went back to licking and kissing and suckling her breasts until small cries broke from her. He lifted his head and thought she was the most beautiful thing he'd ever seen. Her eyes were closed, her gold lashes fanned on her cheeks. Her earlier tears had washed away her mascara, making her look softer. The arch of her body bared the long, pale line of her throat, the rich swell of her breasts. Her nipples were hard as pebbles, wet from his mouth.

A roar suddenly filled his head. As if a switch had been flipped, he went from wanting her to needing her. *Now.* He'd tried always to be careful with her, but he lost the awareness that he needed to be. Seth yanked back the covers. His hands shook as he pulled down the scrap of blue silk that was all she'd worn besides the camisole. He came down on top of her, thrusting into the cradle of her thighs, too damn close to coming when he hadn't even got his pants or shoes off.

He managed to roll to one side and clumsily work at his belt. Bailey sat up and helped, her slim fingers having a dexterity his lacked right now. "Condom," he growled, and rolled to one side.

Bailey plucked his wallet from his pocket and he rolled back. The wallet sailed over him and hit the floor. She used her teeth to tear open the packet, then said, "Let me," when he tried to take the condom from her.

He groaned at the delicate touch of her fingers on him. She either had no experience putting on a condom or was taking her time. He focused on her intent face, wanting to let her have this much control but not sure he could.

"There," she murmured finally, and he flipped her onto her back and thrust hard into her, unable to stop even though his damn trousers were bunched halfway down. He grabbed one of her thighs to spread her legs wide and drove, over and over, his face buried against her neck. But, thank God, she was moving with him, her fingernails biting into his back, the leg he wasn't gripping enclosing his hips.

She screamed when her climax hit her. His felt like a tsunami was crashing into him, flipping him until he didn't know up from down. When the powerful surge ebbed, his entire weight sank down on top of her.

"I'm crushing you," he mumbled, but she held him tight.

"Don't go."

He did finally manage to heave himself to one side, although he didn't let go of her any more than she did of him. The last thing he knew was the feel of her head resting over his heart, which had damn near beaten its way out of his chest, and he sank into sleep.

CHAPTER FOURTEEN

BAILEY WAS SITTING at the breakfast bar in Seth's kitchen with her laptop, checking email, when she heard his key in the door.

"Seth?"

"Hey." He came straight to the kitchen and gave her what was probably meant to be a quick kiss but ended up being a lingering one. As he straightened, his gaze flicked to her computer.

"My boss *really* wants to know when I'll be back." His emails had been getting more insistent. "I think I'm going to be out of a job if I don't get back pretty soon."

"Can't you find another one?"

She arched her eyebrows. "Because waitresses are interchangeable?"

"You know I didn't mean that."

She wasn't so sure, but understood he just didn't want her to go. "The tips are fabulous at Canosa. Waitstaff tend to stick when they find a gig like that. My boss is flexible enough to let me work around my class schedule. So, yes, I could find another job, but probably not one as good."

His jaw tightened. "Bailey..."

She knew what he wanted to talk about, but wasn't ready. So she hastened into speech.

"The Lawsons want us to come to dinner." She'd gone last night, too, which she could tell hadn't thrilled Seth, but she was in Stimson to get to know her family. She already felt guilty about the day of avoidance followed by the trip to California. "Karen especially hoped you could come, too." She hesitated. "She said Eve suggested it."

His expression didn't change, but she could feel his reluctance even before he muttered, "Damn."

"Hoping you'd come in the door to good smells and a peaceful dinner at home?"

"Something like that." He grimaced. "Guess this is one of those invitations you can't refuse."

"*You* could. I can't."

"Whither thou goest. What time?"

"Um...ten minutes ago?"

"All right." He was obviously resigned.

As they left the house, he scanned the block, but no paparazzi loitered. Bailey wanted to think they'd given up on her.

"Did you make an arrest yet?" she asked when he unlocked his SUV.

"Yeah." His smile was steely, nothing like the ones he reserved for her. "Jordan Dyer aka Swann. I was wrong. It wasn't the brother."

"She was mad because her lover wouldn't leave his wife for her."

Seth shook his head as he slammed his door

and buckled his seat belt. "That's what it comes down to." The engine roared to life. "We found an older kid in the brother's neighborhood who rides his bike a lot and saw her letting herself into his house with a key during the lunch hour the day of the shooting. Darrell's car wasn't there. An elderly neighbor who suffers from insomnia heard a car and looked out the window late that night, saw a woman going in and coming back out a minute later. 'Sneaking in' was how he described it. Says no lights ever went on in the house. He could see her car under the streetlamp, even remembered the first couple letters from the license plate."

Bailey stared at him as he concentrated on backing out of the driveway. "She not only used his gun, she set him up?"

"Oh, yeah. I told you. Cold."

"Is your partner mad at you?"

"He says he understands." The restraint in his voice told her that the other detective hadn't been totally happy to be left to pursue witnesses while Seth flew off to northern California on what must seem like a quixotic quest to him.

Braking at a stop sign on the main street, Seth checked his rearview mirror then looked at her. "There's something else. Riser called."

Her heart skipped a beat. "So soon?"

"Not soon. He got right on it. He's found Anna's family."

She couldn't take her eyes off his face, serious and intent on her. "What? Is it bad news?"

"No. Good. Her parents have divorced since she was abducted, but they both still live in the same town and they're as thrilled as you'd expect them to be."

"Sergeant Riser is sure?"

"Her DNA is in NamUs, but matching her that way would take time."

Bailey already knew about the National Missing and Unidentified Persons System. *Her* DNA was in it, too.

"They went the fingerprint route," Seth continued. "Her name is Gabriella Wilson. Gabby. Her parents live in Tremonton, Utah, which had the advantage for Hamby of being close to the Idaho border."

He looked at the rearview mirror again, made a sound in his throat and started forward. She glanced over her shoulder to see that a car had come up behind them and must have been waiting for him to move.

"Does Anna know?"

"By now she does. You might want to call her this evening."

"I will." The news shook her up even if it was happy. "I hope…"

Seth gave her a minute, then prodded. "You hope what?"

"So many things," she said quietly. "That her

parents are good people. That she has a chance at being a normal teenager when everyone in the world, including the kids she'll go to school with, will know what happened to her. That...that her parents let her stay in touch with Betty Wade, and that they understand she's been Anna for a long time now and can't go back to being their Gabby." She looked down at her hands, clenched into fists on her lap. "That she's not too scared. And that she can remember."

Seth's big hand encompassed both of hers. "That's a lot of wishes."

Her throat felt raw. "What she'll go through isn't easy, you know."

"I do." His tone was somber. "She'll have you to help her, won't she, Bailey?"

"Yes."

He was already braking at the curb in front of the Lawson house. *My home.* And she wasn't ready. *Apparently, not for anything*, she mocked herself. "Thank you for telling me first."

"You couldn't have said what you did in front of your parents. I understand. But they'll be thrilled that finding you means another family is lucky enough to be bringing their missing child home, too."

She thought of the expression on Karen's face when she'd insisted on paying for Bailey's airline ticket, and her heart softened. To her astonishment, she was smiling. "You're right. And you know it's all your doing, don't you?"

He leaned over to kiss her cheek, murmuring, "I gave the first push. You were brave enough to come home."

For a moment, she leaned into him, reveling in his scent, his strength. Finally she sat up. "Shall we go tell them?"

His smile kicked her heart up a gear. "Yeah."

Kirk let them in, and seemed pleased when she gave him a quick hug. It was getting easier. All that practice with Seth.

"Smells good," Seth said, and Bailey laughed.

"You say that no matter what's cooking. You're just happy to have someone else feeding you."

He gave her a slightly wicked grin. "Guilty. And hungry." Becoming veiled, his gaze went past her. "Eve, nice to see you."

Bailey turned, bracing herself, but Eve only smiled, any hostility masked. "I'm glad you could both make it. Mom's gone all out. Wait until you taste her apple pie."

Seth's stomach rumbled, making them all laugh.

The dinner menu was traditional: pot roast, flaky sourdough biscuits and a green salad with a dressing that was apparently Karen's own creation. Bailey's first bite of the pot roast was a revelation. It was so good it seemed to activate some pleasure center in her brain. This could be her favorite meal. She took a second bite, chewed, swallowed—and froze.

Not could be.

This was *my favorite meal. I liked Mom's spaghetti and her chicken with stuffing, but pot roast was the best.*

Concern in his eyes, Seth had quit eating and was watching her. A quick glance told her no one else seemed to have noticed her moment of paralysis.

I remember.

There were two old apple trees in the backyard, a Gravenstein and a Yellow Transparent. Dad had grumbled about them, because the grass didn't grow well beneath their spreading branches and the Yellow Transparent in particular tended to drop apples that squished and did further damage to the lawn. Bailey had stepped on them running barefoot in the yard, and *ick*. It was almost as bad as stepping barefoot on a slug. But Mom canned applesauce, and she said the Transparents were the absolute best for that even though they were too soft to be good eating apples. The Gravensteins were for pies and cobblers. When they were ripe, she'd slice and freeze them. Bailey loved Mom's applesauce and her pies.

On previous visits, she had vaguely noticed the two big trees in the backyard without thinking about them. As if a door had opened in her mind, she heard her voice, girlish and demanding:

Daddy, lift me up! In her heart was complete faith that he would smile, swing her up in his strong arms and settle her carefully on a fat limb, his big hands steadying her until she was balanced. In a dizzying vision, she was looking down at him, staying where he could catch her, making her feel completely safe.

Her heart squeezed. *And then one day I wasn't safe at all.* How he must have suffered, that he hadn't been there when she needed him most.

"I used to climb the apple trees, didn't I? Dad helped me."

Eve had been in the middle of saying something. She stopped midword and everyone stared at Bailey.

"Yes," her father said, his eyes warm and filled with pain at the same time. "The branches are wide and low." He smiled at Eve. "Both of you loved to climb up into those trees, especially the Gravenstein. It has sturdier limbs."

Bailey felt so strange, part of her in the present, part in the past. "This was my favorite meal. Pot roast."

"Yes." Tears brimmed in her mother's eyes even as her smile trembled. "I made it tonight because—" She broke off and pressed her fingers to her mouth as if to stifle a sob.

"Why am I remembering now?"

"Maybe you gave yourself permission," Seth

suggested. Without her noticing, he'd taken her hand under the table in a reassuring grip.

"I'm sorry," she said to Eve. "I interrupted you."

"I don't even know what I was saying." Eve's eyes were shadowed, but her smile was wide. "Maybe going to see that other girl has something to do with you opening yourself to memories."

"Maybe," Bailey murmured.

Seth gave her an assessing glance, then chose that moment to tell them that Anna had been identified and her family found.

Talking about her took them halfway through the meal. Karen and Kirk were as thrilled as Bailey had known they would be. The fact that Bailey was mostly quiet seemed to go unnoticed.

Finally Eve nodded at Bailey and Seth with what appeared to be respect. "She's a lucky girl."

"But probably scared to death right now," Bailey said, recovering her voice.

"With the prospect of a real family instead of a foster home?" Eve countered.

"Anna has been in the same foster home for almost four years, since she was left in Redding. There seemed to be real affection between her and her foster mom. And…she doesn't remember anything from before."

Pain showed on Karen's face. "But…it hasn't been as many years for her."

"Enough," Seth put in. "Anna was only five

when she disappeared, even younger than Bailey was."

Karen's mouth tightened briefly. She hadn't said so, but Bailey could tell she wanted everyone to call her Hope. That insistence was one of Bailey's stumbling blocks.

"It will be a big adjustment," Eve said unexpectedly. "When I came here, I wanted to believe in the promise, but I didn't know how. Having my own bedroom, and such a nice one, felt unreal. And the clothes—" She shook her head. "All I'd had before was clothes that came from donations handed out at school."

Bailey nodded her understanding. In Los Angeles, it was Operation School Bell that provided clothes for kids in impoverished circumstances. She'd been both grateful for them and humiliated. It had been especially hard for a teenager who wanted to look like the other girls who wore jeans that probably cost more than the monthly stipend her foster parents received that was supposed to pay for everything, including food.

"I didn't want to do anything that would get me sent back." Eve's eyes were unfocused. "You know."

Out of the corner of her eye, Bailey saw how appalled Karen looked. She might have heard this before and understood, but wanted to believe in a rosy tale of the pretty little ragamuffin who became a princess once she crossed their doorstep.

Eve gave herself a shake and her dark eyes regained focus. "You're right, Bailey. It won't be easy for Anna. I hope her family isn't so deeply religious that they have trouble dealing with the fact she was sexually molested."

"I had the same thought," Bailey admitted. "I promised to stay in touch with her. In fact, I'm going to call her tonight, after Seth and I are back at his house."

Eve nodded. "Good. Having you to talk to will be invaluable. Here you are, going through some of the same experience except as an adult."

Bailey sometimes forgot that Eve was not only a former foster child herself, but a caseworker who supervised children in both their own homes and foster homes under court order. She could do more than empathize; she *knew* what those children were going through.

"I won't forget her," Bailey said. Realizing nobody was eating, she slipped her hand from Seth's and reached for her biscuit. A bite, and she hummed in pleasure. After swallowing, she smiled at Karen. "This is the absolute best dinner I've ever eaten."

Looking flustered, Karen smiled back. "Thank you. Oh, my. I hate to think what both you girls went through."

"Then let's not think about it anymore tonight,"

Seth suggested. "The present is looking pretty good to me."

Bailey felt his gaze. She didn't meet it, but she did reach beneath the tablecloth and lay her hand on his thigh, just for a moment.

Eve asked whether Bailey was thinking about grad school once she had her BA, and told her about the master's degree program in social work at the University of Washington. "It's kind of a natural field for people with our background to go into." She wrinkled her nose. "Although the pay mostly sucks."

"Law enforcement, too," Seth agreed.

"I have thought about social work," Bailey said. "But also becoming a therapist. The last one I had helped me so much. I'm not sure I'm together enough to be qualified, but then I've read that psychiatrists mostly go through psychoanalysis themselves, and they're doctors. Maybe if a therapist is too, well, normal, she'd be impatient with clients that weren't."

Eve laughed. "You have a point. Even when I *do* understand what they're going through, some of the kids I deal with make me really impatient."

"I get exasperated with myself," Bailey heard herself confess. "I'm so good at, I don't know, blocking out anything I don't want to deal with." *Like what I'm going to do about these feelings for Seth*, who once again was watching her with his eyes slightly narrowed. *Because he knows what I'm thinking.* Of course he did.

"Maybe," Eve remarked, "to survive you had to practice denial. Make yourself live in the moment."

All Bailey could think was, *Yes.* "That sounds so obvious," she said after a minute. "I'm sure you're right."

Her adoptive sister's expression was both friendly and understanding. Which of course made Bailey suspicious, but maybe that said more about her than it did about Eve.

The apple pie à la mode was every bit as good as promised. By that time, Bailey was too full to have more than a small slice, but Seth happily consumed enough to make up for part of her share. She shuddered at the thought of how hard it was going to be to go back to the gym once she was home.

And then there was her empty apartment.

Won't think about that right now.

She caught herself about to roll her eyes. Geez. Denial in action.

When Karen and Eve rose to start clearing the table, Bailey joined them. Karen shook her head at Seth, who started to push back from the table, too. "You keep Kirk company. My kitchen isn't big enough for four of us."

They'd already begun loading the dishwasher before serving the pie, so cleaning up didn't

take long. Bailey wanted to go home and call
Anna, but—

Fear swamped her. *Not home*. She couldn't believe she'd thought that. Home away from home,
sure.

The panic quelled, she thought, *It's time*.

"Would you mind if I go look at my bedroom?"
she asked Karen, at a moment when Eve had gone
back to the dining room for something.

Her mother's eyes widened. "Of course you
can! I kept it just the way it was in hopes it would
bring back good memories for you."

That still sounded creepy to Bailey, but she
smiled as if maintaining a household shrine to a
missing child for twenty-three years was the kind
of thing everybody did.

"Can I go alone? Just for a few minutes?"

Karen's face fell, but then she gave a gentle, luminous smile. "Nobody will notice if you
sneak away right now. I'll finish here. Shoo." She
flapped her hands.

Bailey stepped quietly from the kitchen into the
hall, then hurried down it. Part of her wanted Seth
with her, but the other part knew she couldn't afford to become so dependent on him, not when
she'd be returning to her regularly programmed
life in a matter of days. A life that didn't include
him.

But maybe later, after I graduate...

Oh, why was she even thinking about this? Seth hadn't exactly gone down on bended knee.

Like I'd drop out of school even if he did. She had the confused thought that asking her to give up finishing her degree wasn't something he'd ever do, not when he talked about admiring her for being self-made.

She shook off thoughts of him when she came to that closed bedroom door. Just looking at it made her heart race. Her hand trembled when she reached for the doorknob, but she didn't let herself hesitate. She *knew* nothing bad had happened here. The disconcerting part was that she'd remembered this bedroom when everything else was gone, even the people who had loved her.

She turned on the light, stepped inside, and went completely still. *Oh, my dolls.* Some were porcelain, and she'd understood she couldn't play with them, but she loved them anyway, and she had plenty of others that weren't breakable. Two long, white-painted shelves ran the length of one wall, and were crowded with dolls. On the top shelf were the porcelain, collectible ones—babies, princesses, fairy-tale characters, and one that looked just like her, with silver-blond hair and bright blue eyes.

Below—some of those were more ragged. All their eyes seemed to be on her, standing just inside the door staring. *Her* eyes filled with tears. This felt more like a dam breaking than a door opening. Snippets, all jumbled together—there and then not there as more poured out, tumbling over each other.

The bed—oh yes, it was exactly as she recalled it. She could lie on her back and stare up at the white lace canopy. A hot pink boa hung from one bedpost. She saw herself tossing it around her neck. She'd loved to dress up and model for her parents or perform cheerleader routines or concerts. Oh, heavens—*Jem and the Holograms*. She'd wanted *her* hair dyed pink, too, and Mommy said maybe for Halloween, only that Halloween never came because...

Don't think about that.

And Rainbow Brite. She'd loved that cartoon, and the doll...yes, there she was. She flinched, because she'd had another Rainbow Brite doll later. No wonder she'd clung so to that doll.

A bookcase was still filled with stories she'd loved. The white-painted trunk with gold trim at the foot of the bed had held her dress-up clothes and accessories. Would they still be in it? As if in a dream, she moved forward, lifting the lid and—yes. On top were the yards of white tulle that could be a wedding veil or a ballerina skirt or anything she could imagine. Bailey fell to her knees, lifting it out, finding the paper grass hula skirt and cheerleader pom-poms and grown-up-size high heels she'd teetered around in. *I was such a girlie girl*, she thought in amazement.

There was a tiara, now shedding its sparkles, and a wand with a fountain of ribbons shimmering from the tip. Pink ballerina shoes and other bits of cloth and grown-up clothes that could be anything at all her imagination had been able to conjure. Tears blurred Bailey's vision as she plopped down to sit cross-legged, the dress-up clothes heaped around her. From here, she could just see the stuffed animals on the bed, covered with a comforter sporting golden-haired princesses posed with unicorns in front of castles.

It was all so absurdly—*perfect*. The little girl's dream bedroom. *I was spoiled rotten*, she couldn't help thinking. Although the room hadn't been anywhere near this neat when she lived in it. Sometimes it was ankle-deep in toys and dirty clothes, until Mommy made her put everything away. Mommy had got especially mad when she found dirty dishes in here.

"You're lucky you don't have an ant colony in your carpet," she would scold.

Openly crying now, Bailey heard a soft noise behind her and swiveled on her butt to see who had followed her.

Karen—*Mommy*—was already crying at the sight of her. "Oh, honey. I'm so sorry. So sorry. I will never forgive myself." And then she fell to the floor, too, and wrapped her arms around Bailey, who wept against her shoulder. "Never, never, never," she whispered.

At last the sense of what she was saying penetrated, and Bailey pulled back to stare at her mother. "Why?"

"Why?" Karen blinked at her.

They even cried alike, Bailey couldn't help thinking.

"What is it you can't forgive yourself *for*?" she asked. She used a child's skirt that looked washable to wipe her face, then offered it to her mother.

"Oh, this is too nice..." Half laughing, she blew her nose on it, then crumpled the fabric in her hand. "If I hadn't been late that day—"

"He'd have found another opportunity," Bailey said flatly.

"But if he just happened to see you..."

"You know the chances are good he'd been stalking me, waiting for his chance."

"He might have grabbed you because you were alone."

Instinct had Bailey shaking her head. "No. From what Seth has found out, he liked blonde, blue-eyed girls of a certain age. What are the odds he stumbled on his prime prey when she was briefly unprotected? He might have been watching me for days, Mom. If he hadn't gotten me that day, he could have sneaked through the gate into the backyard when I was out there alone, or grabbed me when I was riding my bike." A pink bike, of course. She remembered it vividly. She'd been allowed to ride up and down the street if she watched *very carefully* for traffic and always wore her helmet.

"I should have been there."

"You couldn't always be. It's impossible. It was not your fault. It was his." Her voice went flat and hard. "He's evil."

She lifted her gaze past her mother to see that Seth filled the doorway. The compassion and grief on his face made her heart swell. He never looked at her with pity. That, she couldn't have stood.

Suddenly Karen gripped her hand. "You called me Mom." New tears filled her eyes. "You do remember."

Lips trembling, Bailey nodded. And finally she tore her gaze from Seth's and, this time, took her mother in *her* arms.

CHAPTER FIFTEEN

BAILEY SCROLLED THROUGH the upper level psych classes offered at the University of Washington. *Just to see*, she told herself.

Implicit and Unconscious Cognition. Gee, maybe she'd learn something about denial.

Stress and Coping sounded up her alley, too. There were plenty of other classes that appealed to her, too: Social and Moral Development, Human Factors, Judgment and Decision Making.

She had all the basics out of the way already, including Abnormal Psych, Learning and Memory, classes in statistics and research methodology even though she knew she wouldn't pursue research.

She allowed herself a wistful moment before closing the website. She was already registered for her fall classes, and looking forward to them. Even if she wanted to transfer, it was too late for fall quarter. The UW was competitive enough not to have spots sitting open waiting for the student who decided at the end of August that, gee, she might like to change schools.

I couldn't afford out-of-state tuition anyway, she

reminded herself—then had the startled thought that she'd probably qualify for in-state, now that she had parents who lived in Washington.

It didn't matter, she told herself firmly. She was committed. She could consider applying for grad school up here, if that's the direction she intended to go. She might like to be closer to her parents. Having her nearby would make them happy, and she was beginning to think she'd like to really get to know them.

Something to think about, she told herself briskly. Seth—well, no matter how tenderly he'd made love to her last night, she was afraid to believe anything could come of it.

Time to start dinner. She'd had lunch again with her father, then called her boss at Canosa, who had reluctantly agreed to give her five more days.

She'd been drifting, but now she had a deadline. Should have bought her airline ticket, she realized. *After dinner.*

Tonight's meal would be a ginger-beef stir-fry over brown rice. Perfect because she could slice everything, then wait until Seth arrived to actually start cooking. Dinners that took an hour and a half or more to cook weren't so good, given a cop's irregular hours. She mulled over ones that could be reheated easily. She made a fabulous minestrone soup, if she did say so herself, and reheating that would never be a problem.

Suddenly chilled, she thought, *I'll be here only*

a few more nights. To make it back to work in five days, she should leave in four days. Or less, depending on when she could fly cheapest. Probably she'd have dinner at least a couple more times at her parents'. She didn't need to plan a whole lot of menus to accommodate Seth.

She was reading a text on her phone when Seth got home.

The sight of him hit her hard, as it always did. Maybe more tonight, because of that deadline. He was just so solid. Big enough to make her feel dainty, even though she wasn't really. *Handsome* wasn't the right word for him, but his face was so male. Angular, hard, and yet capable of the tenderness she'd seen on his face last night.

She even liked his everyday garb of slacks and white shirt. Ridiculously, his badge and gun made her feel safe. She didn't know why, since what he did also scared her more than a little. He'd been so casual about having to pull his weapon on a guy going for his own gun. Maybe women who were, well, in a long-term relationship with a cop became inured to the anxiety, or just more philosophical in a "what will be, will be" way.

On an exhalation that left her emptied out, she knew that what was most powerful was the way he looked at her, as if nothing and no one else existed. There was such intensity there, as if he was reading her every fear and hope.

And, okay, *that* was scary, too.

"Good day?" he asked, kissing her lightly.

"Um…it was okay." She lifted the phone. "I could get my last year of school totally paid for if I wanted to sell my story to a tabloid."

"What?" Frowning, he took the phone from her. Head bent, he read the text. "Sleazy bastards."

"It's a lot of money."

He cocked an eyebrow. "You're thinking of taking it?"

Bailey made a face. "Not a chance. For that kind of bucks, they'd want their money's worth. Details, details, details. And sex sells, right?"

"Brutalizing a child isn't sex," he said grimly. "It's a crime."

That warmed her. She accepted the phone back from him and deleted the text.

"You might need to change your phone number," he suggested.

"If I hear from any other reporters, I will." She let go of the worry. "I'll start cooking."

A smile wiped the momentary bleak expression from his face. "I've been looking forward to this all day."

She opened her mouth but closed it before she could say something stupid. Like, *How else can I repay you for what you did for me?* That would only piss him off. And it wasn't even true. She was bored. What else was she supposed to do? And she liked to cook. She didn't get a chance to do that much of it at home. Either she was tired and wanted something quick, or she was taking advantage of the free meal at the restaurant on her working nights.

Seth disappeared, returning once he'd changed into jeans and sweatshirt. Bailey turned down his offer to help, then related some of the things Kirk had told her about her childhood and what the years after the abduction had been like.

"A lot of marriages fail under that kind of stress," Seth commented.

She stirred the rice then restored the lid. "I actually asked if he ever blamed Mom. I mean, she blames herself. You heard her, didn't you?"

"Yeah." His brown eyes were wary. "I lurked outside the bedroom after Karen went in."

"Nosy."

"I wouldn't be much good at my job if I wasn't."

She wrinkled her nose at him. "I suppose that's true." As she scraped the sliced and marinated flank steak into the wok, where the oil already sizzled, Bailey continued. "Anyway, Dad—um, Kirk—said no. Never, not for one minute." She pondered that for a moment. "He's a really nice man."

"Yeah," Seth said gently. "I think he is."

"I keep thinking about Anna today." Her parents would already be in Redding, the first meeting over—or still happening. Probably they were having dinner at Betty's. "It'll be weird for her, having a sister and brother to get to know, too."

"Her mother didn't remarry, though."

She had no doubt he was curious to find out where she was going with this, but he gave her space to get there on her own. *Do I have a direction in mind?* Almost at random, she said, "I wonder if their divorce has anything to do with her abduction."

"I had the same thought and checked on the timing. They separated not much over a year later. Doesn't mean either blamed the other. Emotions are heightened, though."

"I was looking at class offerings today online, and saw one called Stress and Coping." *And why did I tell him that? Or...was that where she'd been going?* What if he asked whether that was a class she'd be taking? How to say, um, it's not available at USC? She continued hastily, "Stress is a chicken-and-egg thing. Marital problems, or parent-teenager conflict, cause stress, but also can arise in the first place because other stresses are present."

"Can't argue with that." A glint of amusement in his eyes made her realize she'd sounded like a professor pontificating in front of the class. "You might want to check that rice," he added.

Bailey whipped the lid off the pan and saw that he was right. The water was gone and the rice was already sticking to the bottom. Even so, she rolled her eyes. "Backseat driver."

Now he grinned. "Happy to offer advice when you need it."

"Next time, *you* can cook. But for tomorrow night I was wondering if you'd mind if I invited Mom and Dad here for dinner. It seems only fair."

"You know I don't mind."

"I feel like I should take a turn. I mean, it may be my only chance, unless they fly down to visit me." She was careful not to look at him. Part of her wanted him to say something—and part of her didn't. She was too mixed-up to give him any kind of answer to whatever he asked of her.

Seth didn't say a word. *Thank goodness*, she told herself.

"Then I will," she said brightly. "If I aim for six o'clock, do you think you can make it home?"

His "I'll do my best" was terse.

"I thought about inviting Eve, too, but..." She hesitated, examining her discomfiture. "Did you ever have her over? I mean, when you were dating?"

"No." Terse had become curt.

"It would be sort of awkward, wouldn't it? Maybe I'll take her out to lunch one of these days instead," Bailey decided. She turned off and unplugged the wok. "I think we're ready to eat."

Without being asked, Seth poured milk and carried the glasses to the table she'd set earlier, then went back to carry one of the serving bowls.

Bailey made a production of dishing up. "Back

to Anna," she said. "It's good her mom and dad both went to get her, even though they're divorced."

He grunted. "Hope they're in agreement on custody."

"Oh, Lord! I didn't even think of that."

His eyes met hers for the first time in a few minutes. "Do you know whether they're taking her home right away?"

"They're giving the handover some time, thank goodness. I don't know if Sergeant Riser talked to them, or they're just using common sense, but the plan is for them to stay at least a couple of nights in Redding. Visit, but leave her at the foster home tonight, maybe have her stay with them tomorrow night, but still let her go back and say goodbye to Mrs. Wade. Anna said they promised not to hurry her if she needs more time than that. She's freaked with a little excitement percolating under there. I kind of wish I could meet them, even though that's silly when I barely know *her*."

"You feel protective."

"I can't help it." She went quiet for a minute, aware of his gaze lingering on her face. "I was thinking today," she surprised herself by saying.

"About?"

"What I want to do after I graduate. It would be logical to get a master's degree and go into social work, like Eve did, but I think I'd like to become a clinical psychologist. It'll mean getting a PhD, but…" She shrugged.

The respect in his eyes was a big ego booster. "I thought you might go that route. You obviously had a good role model along the way."

"I did. Her name was Selena Rodriguez. She really helped me pull it together. We still exchange Christmas cards, and she calls once in a while. She claims to be proud of me."

Seth smiled. "With good reason."

"You keep saying things like that," she said in perplexity, "but I haven't been all that mature about connecting with the Lawsons."

"You were scared. When you're scared, you become flippant. You pretend you don't care. I could see you trying to do that, but realizing that would hurt their feelings. You lowered your guard more than you were comfortable doing, Bailey. That took courage."

She looked at him helplessly. "I don't feel brave. I feel like putting a pillow over my head and making it all go away."

"Even me?"

Instinct urged her to deflect him. Maybe say a sultry *You can share my pillow anytime*. Be flip. But he thought she had courage. Being courageous meant being honest.

She took a deep breath. "Sometimes."

And saw hurt before he shuttered his expression.

"I'm sorry," she said softly. "This has been…intense." She gestured toward him and then herself.

"You deny it, but it's not like I'm a nice woman a friend introduced you to. I'm Hope. I'm your miracle. And I'm Eve's sister."

His jaw tight, he listened but didn't respond.

"And me, my whole life has been turned sideways and upside down. You're the man who did this amazing thing when you dedicated yourself to finding me. You've been my rock through it all. You've taught me to enjoy sex." Her cheeks had heated. In this context, *enjoy* was so bland. So inadequate to describe the storm of passion, the sweetness, the sense of closeness, all new to her. "So sue me. I live all day for you to come home and look at me the way you do, and talk to me, and take me to bed." She gripped the fork as if it were a weapon and glared at him, however totally unfair that was. "And that scares me. Can you blame me if I sometimes wish I was back in my little cocoon?"

"What do you want me to say, Bailey?" For possibly the first time, he showed her what might be his cop face, completely closed off. He reached for a serving bowl and took a second helping.

"Nothing," she snapped. "I'm being honest. That's all."

For a moment, he went utterly still. His eyes were intense in a still-expressionless face. "Bailey. You know I don't want you to go, don't you?"

She wanted to cry. How was she supposed to know that? He'd never said anything. But now that he had— "And you know that I have to, don't you?" Her voice wavered, but she stared right at him, chin held defiantly high.

"I do. But there are other possibilities, you know. We could keep seeing each other. Talk on the phone." He hesitated, expression wary. "I could look for a job down there."

Suddenly she couldn't breathe. He was offering to change his entire life for *her*? What if he did, and then realized he'd made a mistake? Maybe worse, what if he made that kind of sacrifice and all she did was end up hurting him? She'd never believed she'd so much as enjoy kissing a man, having sex with him. The jump from that to imagining herself trusting someone enough to go home to him every day, doing something like getting married...? And, oh God, would he want children?

Completely panicked, she shook her head and kept shaking it. The rest of her was shaking, too. "I'm not... I can't..."

"Okay." Expressionless, he set down the bowl and picked up his fork. "Good dinner. Thank you."

Subject closed.

HE'D BLOWN IT, big-time. Seth winced, listening to Bailey rattling around in the kitchen. In theory, she was brewing coffee and loading the dishwasher. He wondered if she'd come back. And whether, if she did, he shouldn't make his excuses and retreat to his office, or turn on the television. If he wasn't mistaken, a Mariners game was on.

He sighed. Should he raise the subject again? Push a little, try to find out whether she'd reacted only out of fear, or whether she just didn't feel that much for him?

Instinct told him that, unless she said something, he had to back off for now. She'd started by issuing a warning: *I'm going and you can't stop me, so don't even try.* Then he tried anyway, and that sent her into full retreat. Giving up—that wasn't in him, but patience was going to be hard to come by this time.

Despite his determination, he was left wounded enough he almost hoped she'd head for the guest room tonight rather than assume they'd cavort in bed like always. He gritted his teeth hard enough to crack a molar. *I'm being an idiot.* If he was serious about her, what he needed to do was use every minute left to them to tempt her. Make sure she understood that he would never hurt her. Lower his pride enough to make sure she knew how he felt—assuming what he'd already said wasn't enough.

If he was serious. What a crock. Of course he was. Had been since he'd galloped straight past the lust at first sight and got to know the complex, fearful, brave, smart woman she was. Hadn't he just offered to quit his job and move to LA—concrete and smog?

He sensed her presence before he turned his head and saw her approaching the table, a cup of coffee in each hand. Her eyes held trepidation, which shook him. Was she *afraid* of him?

Pretending not to notice, he said, "Thanks."

"You're welcome." She set down his cup and carried her own to the other side of the table. To the place that had, in a matter of days, become *hers*. "I didn't even ask how your day was."

He'd take as encouragement the fact that she actually looked as if she cared.

"I talked to Drew Stuart."

She nodded. It wasn't as if she'd have forgotten FBI Special Agent Andrew Stuart. Hamby was on the FBI radar big-time now, given his predatory nature and frequent crisscrossing of state lines. Seth had never had occasion to work with the FBI before, although he'd heard enough stories to be wary. There hadn't been any need. Stuart had been gentle with Bailey and seemingly open with Seth during their continuing phone calls. He wanted Hamby, too, and had more resources than Seth did.

"Under the name Anna gave us, he was picked up for drunk driving in eastern Washington." He paused, still feeling the intensity of the hunt. "Only eight months ago. No child with him. He spent the night in the Grant County jail, set up a payment schedule for the fine and hasn't been seen or heard from since."

"He went back to pick her up wherever he'd stashed her," Bailey said flatly.

"Probably." He gusted a sigh. "He might be between."

Her troubled blue eyes met his. "Do you think he made another name change after that?"

"I think he probably just hightailed it out of the state," he said in a hard voice.

"But...he must have seen articles about me. Even though he's changed his name once, what if he does again?"

"Why would he? And, remember, it's not that easy to do. He can't afford good quality fakes."

She nodded. Those eyes dominated a face that had become pale. "He may not come back to Washington for a long time."

"I think you're right. Doesn't matter, though. We have a BOLO out. Stuart has been talking to agencies in a six-state region. Hamby's name— *both* names—are flagged. He's in deep shit if the state patrol anywhere pulls him over."

"You really think you'll catch him." Her hands wrapped her cup of coffee more as if she was warming them than as if she had any intention of taking a sip.

"Probably not me personally," he conceded, wishing like hell he'd have the chance, "but I have every intention of keeping the pressure on. Next time he gets behind the wheel drunk, plants a fist in someone's face or has a taillight out, his name should light up in neon colors when an officer runs his license."

Bailey gazed down into her coffee. "If only I'd—"

"I thought we'd laid your guilt to rest."

"It's…hard."

"I know, honey," he said huskily. "I know it is."

She lifted one shoulder before looking up. He knew even before she opened her mouth that she didn't want to talk about Hamby anymore. And surely not about them.

"You're really okay with me having Karen and Kirk here for dinner tomorrow?"

His eyebrows quirked. "Is it so hard to say 'Mom and Dad'?"

The expression in her eyes damn near broke his heart. He'd just had to open his big mouth.

"I'm trying."

Seth nodded. "Yes, I'm glad to have them here for dinner. They're good people, and they're your parents." He laid some emphasis on the last, not surprised by the hint of nerves he saw on her face before she pulled up a smile.

"Mom's such a good cook, I feel challenged. Gotta produce my best." Rambling on, she suggested and discarded half a dozen menus.

When he said he thought everything she'd cooked had been as good as her mother's meals, Bailey made a face at him. "You're like a perpetually hungry teenage boy who inhales whatever somebody puts in front of him." She frowned. "What do you *do* with all those calories?"

He patted his stomach. "Metabolize 'em." With a grimace, he added, "Usually I run, lift weights at the gym, get up in the mountains with a pack. Belt felt a little tight this morning."

"Oh, God, it's going to be grim when I get back to the gym. It's been *weeks*. Plus, usually I'm on my feet and hefting trays of food at the restaurant. An eight-hour shift is a workout, believe me."

He didn't like the reminder of how soon she'd be gone, but did his best to hide his reaction. "I do. I've always wondered how waitresses keep smiling."

"Tips," she informed him. "The sunnier the smile, the higher the tips."

"Bet yours are sky-high," he said, voice a note lower than usual.

"If that's a compliment, I thank you, sir." The bright smile she offered just before she jumped to her feet was the kind she'd offer diners at Canosa, he guessed. Did any of them ever suspect it was as fake as a counterfeit hundred-dollar bill? The spots of color on her cheeks, though, that was something different. "I need to finish cleaning the kitchen," she said over her shoulder.

Right before she fled, leaving him to brood about his next move. Less inept than the last, he hoped.

THEY HADN'T EXACTLY had a fight, but Bailey knew she'd hurt Seth. Of course he'd shut down. She was lucky he'd been willing to talk to her after, that he could still say, *I know, honey,* in that tender voice.

Just thinking again about his offer to move, for her, made her start to hyperventilate. He said he admired her courage, but she didn't feel brave. In fact, she'd never felt more like a coward. Couldn't he see that? And if he did, why would he want her?

Sex—he could do that with other women.

Yes, but what she and Seth did wasn't just sex, meaningless and lacking real emotion. It was making love. And that knowledge explained the panic that had her heart beating at the speed of a hummingbird's wings.

Because now she had a new fear. Had Seth accepted her no as final? What kind of fool was she to hope that, well, he hadn't? That he'd give her time to figure out how much of what she felt now was real? And even if it was—did she really think she had even a glimmer of an idea how to love a man and accept his love? How to have a normal life?

Would he still want her in his bed tonight?

He was in the living room watching a baseball game. She stood just out of sight for a long time, hugging herself and feeling lonely in a way she didn't when she was really alone. As she was used to being.

Finally she nerved herself to peek around the corner. Seth didn't look as if he was enjoying himself. His expression was withdrawn, preoccupied. Some kind of action erupted in the game that had a player leaping into the air in an attempt to catch a ball that cleared his glove by inches. He smashed into a barrier and crashed to the artificial turf. Although Seth's gaze was trained on the TV, he showed no reaction to the action. He didn't care— or he didn't see it at all.

Bailey closed her eyes for a minute, took a deep breath and strolled into the living room, nonchalant. "Hi," she said.

His head turned and his gaze snapped to hers. He didn't say anything.

She nodded at the TV. "Who's winning?"

"Ah..." He glanced back at the game, telling her she'd been right. He'd been oblivious to the action.

"I'm bored," she said softly. She sauntered closer, giving her hips a little extra swing.

His eyes darkened.

Bailey took a chance and plopped herself down on his lap. To her relief, his arm came around her. His mouth tilted. "Want to go out dancing?"

"I haven't actually been dancing in years," she confessed. "Since my wild phase."

He gave a crooked smile. "I've been a couple of times in the last few years." He paused a beat. "Reluctantly."

"I've always thought I'd like to learn to ballroom dance, though." She snuggled in, lifting a hand to his hard jaw. "I might take a class."

"Don't you need a partner?" He could have been strangling.

"Um." Bailey loved the rasp of his evening stubble against her palm, which had never felt more sensitive. "A partner is good." She sounded sultry.

"If this is an attempted seduction, it's working." Seth tilted his head enough to kiss her palm, then flick his tongue out. At her shiver, a dark gleam showed in his eye.

"Well, there's the boredom factor," she said lightly.

His hand slid up to cup her breast, gently shaping and reshaping it. "We ought to be able to take care of that."

"Please," she whispered, and kissed his throat.

A groan rumbled out of him and he groped to one side to lower the leg support on the recliner. "Bed."

"I don't know. I was kind of thinking this chair had possibilities."

Seth froze.

"Do you have a condom in your wallet? Or do I need to go fetch?"

Jaw tight, he ground out, "I have one."

Bailey batted her eyes. "So you can be spontaneous?"

"Something like that. Damn." With no warning, he yanked her shirt over her head and sent first it, then her bra flying. A fraction of a second later, his mouth closed over her breast, hot, wet and urgent.

Bailey arched her back, moaned and tangled her fingers in his dark hair, holding herself up, and him close.

Every tug of his mouth sent a spasm through her. He switched to her other breast and she wriggled on his lap, wanting—

Eyes heated, he lifted his head and gripped her around the waist. "Straddle me."

That was what she wanted. Once her knees were locked to each side of his hips, he claimed her mouth in a kiss that was all-out. The recliner rocked as their bodies rocked, intensifying the sensation. She rode the hard ridge beneath her, wanting him naked but also discovering the zipper and denim fly felt really good.

It was Seth who wrenched his mouth away and looked at her with eyes so heated, they singed her skin. "Enough!" he growled before tearing his shirt off, then zeroing in on the button at her waist and her zipper. "Bailey," he said desperately. "Up."

Mind fogged, she tried rising on her knees before realizing that, no, her jeans weren't coming off unless she stood up. She slid off his lap, him grimacing, and they both peeled the denim and panties down. She ached. Every touch of his hands laid a trail of fire in its path. She looked down to see that she still wore fuzzy socks, but didn't care.

She scrambled back onto him even as he said, "Wait. Let me—"

She helped. He lifted his hips enough to grab his wallet, take out the condom and pull the jeans down enough to free his erection. The wallet thumped to the floor and he tore open the wrapper.

"Let me," Bailey whispered.

"I don't know if I can. *God.*" It sounded like a prayer, but he handed her the condom and watched as she slowly, delicately, covered him. And then with a strangled sound, he lifted her into place and lowered her until he was pushing inside her, going deep, so deep.

Each hard thrust rocked the chair. They looked into each other's eyes as they moved. Bailey couldn't even blink. She was so turned on it didn't take a minute before she began to spasm, a keening sound escaping. Seth grabbed her hips, lifted and pressed her down, once, twice, his back arching so he could go deeper than seemed humanly possible. And just as she felt the throbbing inside, he flung back his head, his eyes closing at last, his grimace in the throes of pleasure fiercely male.

It was a very long time before they moved at all. And when they did, he cut off the TV with a stab on the remote, still ignorant of the score. Clothes were left where they were.

CHAPTER SIXTEEN

"So." BAILEY DIPPED a tortilla chip in salsa, studying her "sister," who faced her across the table in the restaurant booth. "Do you still hate me so much you kick your puppy every time I cross your mind?"

Eve's dark, sculpted eyebrows rose. "I don't have a puppy."

"Someone else's puppy, then." Bailey popped the chip in her mouth. The salsa had enough bite to be surprisingly good.

Suddenly Eve laughed. Really cracked up. "No. Not that much, anyway."

Her own mouth curved. "Just a little?"

Eve grabbed her napkin and dabbed below her eyes. What was left of her smile didn't reach her eyes. "Okay. Maybe a little."

"Because I'm blonde and blue eyed? Because I have such a sweetly sentimental name? Because you didn't get a canopy bed and I did?" Bailey never looked away from her even as she dipped some more salsa. "Or because of Seth?"

Eve gazed coolly back. "*E*, all of the above?"

Bailey nodded. "Just so you know, I'm leaving

tomorrow. Don't tell Mom and Dad. I'm making dinner for them tonight. I thought we could have a nice evening before I rip the bandage off."

"Really? You have to go back already?"

"I could have stayed a couple more days." Bailey surprised herself with her honesty. With the fact that she wanted to tell someone the truth, and had chosen this maybe sister. She shrugged. "But I thought I'd just get it over with. You know?"

Bitter chocolate eyes warmed with what she thought might be sympathy. "I hate goodbyes, too," Eve said. She made a face. "Once you know…"

When she hesitated, Bailey finished for her. "How often they're permanent."

"Maybe that's it." Eve turned her head and smiled, and Bailey realized the waiter was bringing their entrées. A vegetarian burrito for Eve, a quesadilla for Bailey. Both looked and smelled wonderful.

"This was a good suggestion," she said after he'd left them alone again. "We have fabulous Mexican food in LA, but I wouldn't have expected it up here."

"Are you kidding?" Eve said. "Every crop in the state is harvested with migrant labor. Plenty of people like the area and stay. Skagit County just north of us is heavily Hispanic. Some of the elementary schools are half-day Spanish. We have active immigration issues, too."

"Really."

"You didn't ask, but, yes, my mother was Latina. She was actually from Costa Rica."

"Thus the gorgeous hair."

Eve stared at her incredulously. "You think *my* hair is beautiful, when *yours* is gilt?"

Bailey set down her fork. "I guess that answers my original question, doesn't it?"

"What are you talking about?"

"What you really mean is my hair is the color of Mom's. Right?"

Eve closed her eyes and visibly fought some dark emotion. When she opened them again, she looked regretful. "I guess I do. And you're right, I am jealous. But it's not your fault. I'm just…" She trailed off, seemingly groping for words.

Bailey sighed. "I'm sorry. I shouldn't have called you on it. I don't blame you for feeling jealous. Just living with that bedroom right across the hall from yours is reason enough. I know they meant well, but seeing that perfect little girl's bedroom, frozen in time, must have been worse than sharing Mom and Dad with a little princess of a sister would have been."

"Yes." The word was choked. "It was. Mom would go in there to dust or vacuum, and I'd hear her crying. I know they care about me. I know I'm lucky, but I always wondered what would happen if you came home. Would they still want me?"

"You know better than that."

"Yeah." She half laughed. "Of course I do. They're nice people. They wouldn't reject one child in favor of another. I do know that. Here." She touched her temple.

Bailey nodded. "I understand."

"So. You will be back, won't you?"

"Yes. I couldn't do that to them, even if I didn't want family."

Eve's dark eyes were almost as knowing as Seth's. "*Do* you want family?"

The "yes" was wrenched out of her. The "no" came more slowly. "I keep panicking," she finally admitted.

"With Seth, too? Or is long-term not an issue?"

Bailey frowned. "Do you really want to talk about Seth?"

"I actually don't mind." She offered a twisted smile. "To my surprise."

"You mean that."

"I do. I was really hurt I didn't keep his interest, but it was partly pride." She hesitated, then made a face. "Being brutally honest here, some of my tangled feelings had to do with the fact that he jumped right on your story and became completely fixated on finding you. Bringing Hope Home." Her tone made it a headline. "And, not so coincidentally, that was when he lost interest in me."

"Because his interest turned instead to the missing, golden-haired, perfect daughter who, all unknowing, had been your rival for years and years."

Eve's pretty face went through some more contortions. "Got it in one," she finally admitted. "That doesn't say anything very nice about me, I know—"

Bailey snorted. "Oh, come on. How could you *not* feel that way?"

Another incredulous stare was followed by a short, sharp laugh. "You know what? I think I could get to like you."

Bailey let herself laugh, too. "I…actually kind of hope so." She rolled her eyes. "Do you know how hard it is to avoid using the word *hope*?"

"Are you kidding?" This chuckle was more relaxed. "I'm a past master. I even dug out a thesaurus. I never hoped for something, I *wished* for it. *Wish* was one of my favorite words. *Want* is good, too. I used to *wish* we were British so I could have a *fancy* for something."

Bailey shook her head. "Obviously, I need to explore the alternatives."

"You do that, because Mom is *not* going to accept that your name is Bailey."

"I got that."

They ate in silence for a few minutes. Then Eve said, "Only one more year to your degree."

Stabbed by pain at the reminder that she would be back in her old life by tomorrow night, Bailey agreed. Because they had to talk about something, she told Eve some of what she'd been thinking.

"I always knew I wanted to be a social worker—"

"Because one rescued you along the way?"

Their eyes met. Eve nodded slowly. "Guess neither of us are hard to figure out."

"Nope."

"You know the graduate program in psychology at the UW is highly regarded, don't you?"

"I did notice, but..." Her mouth twisted. "Whether I come here will depend on a lot of factors."

"Like Seth."

"Maybe," she admitted. "But also I have to be accepted. I'll need to look at other programs, probably apply at several. And, ugh, I suppose the GRE is in my near future."

"Ya think?" Eve said cheerfully. "You might want to brush up on that math."

"More ugh. Although I kind of liked stats, even though I don't want to do research."

They were off, trading stories of favorite classes, educational debacles, past jobs. Eve even shared a few war stories from her current job as a caseworker with the Department of Social and Health Services.

Eve insisted on paying for both of them. "*I'm* working full-time."

In the parking lot, they reached Bailey's car first. She unlocked, then faced Eve. "Thanks for lunch. I guess this is goodbye until, I don't know yet, Thanksgiving or Christmas maybe."

"You have my phone number. You could call."

Bailey grinned. "If talking to me won't make you want to kick a puppy."

Eve laughed again, then leaned in for a quick, hard hug. Her dark eyes shimmered when she stepped back. "Take care," she said, and hurried away.

Bailey blinked and discovered her own eyes burned. So, okay, it wouldn't be so bad to have an almost sister.

HER ANNOUNCEMENT OVER coffee that evening went less well.

She tried not to look at Seth, but couldn't help noticing how very still he had gone. Both her parents stared at her in shock.

"But...tomorrow?" her mother faltered.

"My boss at the restaurant gave me a deadline, and I really don't want to lose the job." It wasn't exactly a lie, because she hadn't told them *when* the deadline was.

"But—"

Kirk's hand covered his wife's, and she quit talking. He said calmly, "We'd have liked you to stay longer, Bailey, but we understand. There's something we've been meaning to tell you. We put away money all these years to pay for college for you, in the belief you'd have the chance. We can make this last year a little easier for you, let you concentrate on your studies and not work the hours I suspect you do. The rest can go toward graduate school, if that's what you decide to do."

She opened her mouth, but couldn't say a word. Oh, damn. Tears streamed down her cheeks, and she snatched up her napkin to mop them up. Seth had said they might do something like this, but she hadn't taken him seriously. Now—

"I can't believe— Oh." They both watched her kindly, her father smiling. Seth, she didn't know. She still couldn't look at him.

I should have told him first.

But her parents had already been here when he walked in the door.

She could have called him.

Should have called him. Of course he was hurt. *Did I do it on purpose? Did I want to hurt him?* Oh, God. Maybe.

Think about it later, she ordered herself.

Right now... She sucked in a few breaths and managed to mostly stop crying.

She gazed at the two people looking back at her so hopefully. *No, no—choose a different word.* Her mind took a byway. *Wishfully? Dreamily? Fancifully?* Of course, none of them worked.

"I can't believe you really saved money when I'd been gone so long. Are you sure you aren't trying to give me your retirement income?"

Her father shook his head. "We really did, Bailey. It was a way of..." He hesitated.

"Showing faith," her mother said. "Giving our belief substance."

After that, there was no way she could refuse their help, even though she'd learned to take great pride in accomplishing everything on her own.

Seth stood up and began clearing the table. Bailey let him, listening as her parents detailed what they intended to do for her.

Finally she circled the table to hug them each in turn. And, damn it, she was crying again. So was her mother.

Sitting back down, Bailey wiped her cheeks again and firmly blew her nose. Then she looked at her parents. "I could probably change my flight, but—" How to say this?

She didn't have to. Her father only nodded. "You need to go." His voice was impossibly gentle. His smile was sad. "Regroup. Get ready to start classes."

Bailey nodded and kept nodding until she forced herself to stop. *Yes*. She needed to separate herself from all these people and find out whether these feelings were real or situational.

Did Seth understand, too?

He might have, if she hadn't just blindsided him.

And I did that because I was afraid I couldn't leave him, she thought, stunned by what she knew was the truth. She'd needed to drive him away before he asked her again to stay, or to commit to something that still frightened her. Because she might have succumbed despite this desperate need to have room to breathe and think.

The knowledge felt right.

Seth quietly refilled all their coffee cups, then retired to the kitchen. Bailey told her parents about having lunch with Eve. "We have a lot in common," she said.

"We know," her mother murmured. "Some of it, I wish neither of you had had to go through."

"I wish we hadn't, either, but it's part of what makes us who we are. And maybe will allow both of us to help kids who've gone through some of the same stuff, the way Eve already is."

Karen had been looking weepy again; now she smiled tremulously. "We're so proud of both of you."

"Thank you." Bailey managed an answering smile. "But don't say any more, or I'll be sobbing again."

The dreaded moment came when she walked them out and had to say goodbye. Through her tears, she hardly saw their car back into the street and drive away.

Still blinded by this completely unfamiliar grief—another new emotion to pin up on the bulletin board of her life—she stumbled back into the house. And, oh, God, she now had to face Seth.

BEING PISSED WAS all that held the pain at bay.

Seth could not freaking *believe* she had booked a flight for tomorrow without telling him. So that was it. Thanks, and goodbye.

And, goddamn it, but he hurt.

He rinsed off plates and filled the dishwasher, then began washing pans because it gave him something to do while he waited for her. Or would she even pause to talk to him on her way to pack?

He heard a soft footfall behind him. Setting the last pan in the dish drainer, Seth reached for a hand towel and turned slowly to find Bailey hovering in the doorway. Her face was blotchy, her eyes puffy, the way she held herself achingly uncertain. He contrasted the Bailey who faced him now with the brittle, defiant woman he'd first met, the one who didn't want to feel anything.

"I'm sorry," she said. "I should have told you first."

His jaw flexed. "Why didn't you?"

"I only made the reservation this afternoon. And…and my parents got here before you."

"But you must have already made up your mind to leave tomorrow."

Her eyes widened at his implacable tone. "No, I—" She swallowed. "My thinking was…vague until I studied flights."

"Uh-huh."

"What does a day or two matter?" she cried.

"You're eager to get the hell away from here,

aren't you?" Staying mad seemed to be his only defense against the need to beg.

"No!" Her throat moved. "Oh, in a way, but not like you're suggesting."

"You mean, this isn't your way of saying, 'Hey, thanks for everything, but you've served your purpose, so I'm on my way'?" Seth asked with deliberate cruelty.

She bristled. "That's hateful."

"Or maybe honest."

"No!"

He leaned a hip against the counter and crossed his arms. "Then what's this about, Bailey? The Lawsons are giving you enough money you don't have to work this year if you don't want."

"I can't just call my boss and say sorry, I'm not coming back. I have to work out some notice, give him time to replace me."

"He's apparently replaced you these couple weeks."

"He juggles staff. Some of the people are working way more hours than usual to make up for my absence."

Seth shook his head, as much at himself as her. "Why are we talking about your job? It's not really the issue here, is it? And, just for a minute, do you think you could be straight with me?"

Bailey stared at him unblinkingly. Then she crossed her arms, too, except the way her shoulders rounded, it looked as if she was trying to hug herself, or maybe make herself smaller.

"I told Eve today, I hate goodbyes. Dragging this one out won't make either of us feel any better."

Seth tensed, and pain crawled up his neck. "Why am I arguing? You've made up your mind. Go pack, Bailey. You won't have time in the morning." Deliberately, he turned his back, then stared at the refrigerator, wondering what he was supposed to do next.

"You don't understand," a small, broken voice said behind him.

He let his head drop forward and pinched the bridge of his nose hard, feeling the cartilage creak. It took him a minute to get his facial muscles under control so that he could turn to look at her again.

"What don't I understand?" he asked, his tone almost neutral.

"I'm not used to living with anyone. I'm not used to having anyone look at me the way Karen does, with this desperate, all-consuming hunger for something I don't know how to give. I'm not used to anyone treating me… I don't know, tenderly. Giving me vast amounts of money. I'm really not used to wanting a man, or trusting him, or—" She finally had to suck in air. The look in her eyes was as desperate as the one he, too, had seen in Karen's. "I need to get away. I have to evaluate. Figure out what's real. What I… I miss." She bit her lip. "And what I don't."

The last, soft words fell like a hammer blow. Her meaning was unmistakable. She might miss him—and she might not.

And there wasn't a damn thing he could do about it either way. He'd thought he hurt before, but it was nothing compared to this crushing pain. A part of him knew she was right to make no commitments until she'd gained some distance and perspective. She was emotionally damaged. The two of them hadn't known each other very long. What he felt was too much, too fast. And just because he thought it was real and lasting didn't mean she shared his certainty. But she wasn't even leaving a door open. Giving him any hope.

He huffed out a breath at the irony of his thought. Nope, she wasn't leaving him any hope at all.

"Then get on with it," he said brusquely. "You can let me know once you've made up your mind which category I fall into."

She looked stricken, but after a minute she turned and left the room. He didn't move a muscle until he heard a bedroom door close. Then he braced both hands on the countertop, bent his head and felt his face contort.

HER HEAD HEAVY from lack of sleep, Bailey tentatively opened the guest room door. She'd heard

Seth moving around earlier. If she was lucky, he'd have left for work. It would be so much easier if he was gone, if there were no more goodbyes to be said. Leaving on harsh words was hugely preferable to wrenching herself from his arms, seeing emotions in his eyes she didn't know whether to trust. But a painful constriction in her chest made that a lie. God help her, she wanted to see him one more time. Feel his arms tight around her.

And such a stupid craving made her a glutton for punishment.

Only quiet greeted her, but she smelled coffee. Bailey used the bathroom quickly, thought about showering, but couldn't stand the suspense. Her hair was doing weird things and one cheek had a crease, but did it matter what she looked like?

She had the absurd memory of a magazine article asking when you should let a guy see you without makeup for the first time. Who cared, when this guy had already seen her terrified, stunned and sobbing?

Moving on silent feet, she followed the smell of coffee to the kitchen, then came to a sudden stop when she saw the man sitting at the breakfast bar. Waiting.

"I thought you'd be gone," she whispered.

A flash of pain came and went, after which he raised his eyebrows. "Hid in your room until you thought I left?"

"No. I just woke up. I didn't sleep very well."

It was obvious he hadn't, either. Exhaustion carved deep lines in his face, aging him. His gaze met hers, expression bleak. "I couldn't take off without saying goodbye, Bailey. And apologizing for last night. I was a jackass. You need to do what feels right to you."

Oh, crap. She was going to cry again. All those years with *him* she didn't cry, and now she was a watering pot. "I'm scared. I'm running away. Okay? You were wrong about me. I am a coward."

"No." Despite his tiredness, he rose fluidly from the stool and came to her, his hands closing gently on her upper arms. "No, Bailey. You're not. Don't ever say that, or even think it. You survived hell and walked out on the other side with your head high."

"I'm not—"

"You are." Very carefully, he pulled her close.

With something like a lunge, she wrapped her arms around his waist and pressed her cheek to his chest. The feeling of his arms enclosing her filled her with a painful tumult because it was so good, and this was the last time he would hold her unless— She blanked her mind to the "unless."

"Another thing you need to know," he murmured, nuzzling her temple and ear. "Finding Hope, that was really something. But for me, finding Bailey was a life changer."

Oh, God. She bobbed her head to say, *I understand.* Her sinuses burned.

"And, Bailey? I'll miss you. And I'll be waiting. You got that?"

Another nod.

His "Good" was rough, hardly articulated. With one finger, he tilted her chin up, and then he kissed her. Hard, hungry and brief.

Next thing she knew, the front door was closing and she was alone in the kitchen. An animal cry of pain burst from her.

SHE MADE IT through that day, feeling robotic. Two-hour drive south to SeaTac, mostly on I-5. She focused on what she had to do *now*, on the next minute. Flow with the traffic, change lanes when she absolutely had to. Watch tensely for road signs, then signs leading her to the airport, and finally for rental car return. Check her bag, hoist the giant tote that held her laptop and some of the purchases she'd made here in Washington, clutch her quilt in the other arm. Security. Plod to a far gate, sit on an uncomfortable chair pretending to read until her row number was called. And then grip the seat arms, knuckles white, because she couldn't hold Seth's hand.

The flight passed in a blur. In a window seat, she didn't so much as glance out. Sleep beckoned, but she couldn't catch it. Instead she read the same few pages over and over, and endured.

There wasn't much of a wait for the airport shuttle, thank heavens. She blinked when she stepped outside into a dry, hot day, the sky a smog-tinted blue. Southern California. Instead of a sense of homecoming, the scene felt alien.

She was dropped outside her small apartment building. Inside the shabby lobby, she gazed at the mailboxes and thought about checking for mail but didn't care. Tomorrow. Maybe tomorrow.

Expecting some comfort when she stepped into her apartment, Bailey instead had the strange feeling she'd walked into someone else's. It was her pink bedroom all over again. Another life, barely remembered.

Tomorrow, she told herself again. By tomorrow, this would feel like home again. It had to, because it was.

The apartment was also stiflingly hot. To hell with her utility bill—now a woman of independent means, she could afford air-conditioning. She adjusted the thermostat to a shockingly low level before scrounging in her cupboards for something edible, settling on a can of soup. Groceries could wait until tomorrow, too.

At last she stripped and fell into bed, pulling only the sheet over herself. Mercifully, oblivion came fast.

SETH REMAINED AS close to numb as he could make himself until late afternoon, when Ben walked back from the coffeemaker, cup in hand, and paused by Seth's desk.

"When's Bailey heading back to start school?" he asked casually.

Pain stabbed, so intense Seth lifted a hand to rub his breastbone in an attempt to ease it. "She's gone."

"Gone? Already?"

"What's that mean?" Seth asked tightly. "She has a job, too. It was time."

Ben regarded him in silence for a minute, then nodded and continued past to his own desk.

Seth went back to staring at his computer monitor without seeing it. He'd accomplished jack shit today. Should have just stayed home, except... He couldn't.

God, he was dreading the unavoidable moment when he had to walk in his front door to the absence of Bailey. He knew already that he'd be getting something to eat on the way, if he could work up any appetite. If he were a drinking man, he'd have gone to a bar, but waking up tomorrow feeling like crap because he'd gotten plastered tonight wouldn't bring her back, or make the house any less empty tomorrow night, or the next night. It wouldn't make her miss him.

He couldn't say his depression eased in the week that followed. He checked his phone incessantly, hoping he'd missed a call from her, but there wasn't one. The way they'd left things, Seth didn't feel as if he could call her. She'd openly expressed her need to give herself distance and space. She might feel as if his calling was meant to put pressure on her.

She might even be right.

He encountered Eve after a twelve-year-old boy collapsed during PE at the middle school, and upon examination at the hospital was found to have hideous bruises and broken ribs, one of which had punctured his lung. Even after regaining consciousness, he refused to name his assailant. X-rays indicated a long pattern of abuse, though, and Seth did some serious leaning on the mother and stepfather as well as the father, who had the boy two weekends a month.

"James asks me almost every time I see him if he can't live with me," the father said, his voice heavy with guilt. "I keep saying no because I travel so much for my job. I thought he was doing okay with his mother. If he'd told me—" He began to sob.

The stepfather claimed to have been on a hunting trip the week before the kid collapsed. Mom supported his assertion, but Seth felt sure she was lying. He'd long since quit wondering how a mother could support an abusive son of a bitch of a man even when he endangered her children.

When he encountered Eve at the hospital, they sat down in one of the small rooms set aside for doctors to talk privately to family members. She asked if he was close to making an arrest.

He shook his head. "I need to find some witnesses who can place the stepfather home that week. I've been doing a door-to-door, but I'm getting the feeling the neighbors are afraid of him, too."

"The father has already put in for a transfer to a job that won't demand so much travel. I'd ask for an assessment of him as a secure placement for James, but I can't do that until you're sure he wasn't the abuser."

"I can't tell you that with a hundred percent certainty yet," he said.

She sighed. "I have a receiving home lined up once he's released."

"I'll do my best to get answers."

She gave him a small, twisted smile. "That's good enough for me. Your best is exceptional, Seth."

"Thank you," he said, surprised.

She picked up her briefcase but didn't stand. "Have you heard from Bailey?"

He shook his head.

"Me, either. She called Mom and Dad, though. Said she worked for a few days, but couldn't deal with being recognized. She might look for an office job or something, maybe on campus, but hasn't decided. They said she sounded good, but... too upbeat. They worry she isn't really happy."

He hoped like hell Bailey wasn't really happy, then castigated himself for wanting that. She of all people was owed some happiness.

When he didn't say anything, Eve gave a small nod, acknowledging whatever she saw on his face. "Let me know," she said, and left him sitting there in the small room, unsure whether she'd been referring to answers about the boy—or Bailey.

After a moment, he rubbed a hand over his face, allowed himself one groan, and heaved himself to his feet. One of the stepfather's supposed hunting buddies had been dodging him, which suggested he didn't want to outright lie. Time to corner him.

CHAPTER SEVENTEEN

CALLING SETH THE first time was really hard. Bailey was afraid she'd break down, just hearing his voice. No, it wasn't only that—she was afraid of so much. She was afraid he'd be angry because so much time had passed. It had been a whole month since they'd said goodbye, since she'd felt his arms around her.

And, she knew better, but still feared that, given so much time, he'd discovered he didn't miss her, that whatever he'd felt had evaporated.

No, believing in anything good was still hard for her.

She had denied herself permission to call him until the month had passed because she needed to know she could do this on her own. That she wouldn't be turning to him for the wrong reasons. And maybe she'd wanted to be immersed in classes so she *couldn't* run back to Seth.

She had needed this month to think, and to absorb what she'd learned about herself, about her newfound family and about Seth. To an extent, it had worked.

She'd realized he and her father didn't have

much in common on the surface, but what they shared was the remarkable ability to be tender without ever looking at her with pity. Her memories of her early years were still few and fleeting, as they probably were for most people, but in the ones that included her father, she had always felt both loved and safe. The word *safe* might not have occurred to her then, but it was a powerful one for the Bailey who had learned so painfully how it felt *not* to be safe.

She thought a lot about the physical part of her relationship with Seth, since that was new, too. It hadn't abated. When she pictured him, she felt a deep, aching knot that only he could loosen.

But, always, she came back to the reassurance and belief in her he offered. So, in the end, she closed her eyes and pictured his face as he told her how strong she was. And then her thumb pressed Send, and a moment later his phone was ringing.

She'd forgotten the resonance of his deep voice.

"Bailey?"

"Yes, it's me." Great start. "Um, I wanted to say hi."

"I'm glad you called. I've been thinking about you."

"Really?" Oh, pathetic. What did she want—him to tell her how miserable he was without her? *Yes?*

"Your mother called a few days ago. Said you're liking your classes."

"School is really good." Prompted by questions from him, she told him about some of her current classes, including Intro to Clinical Psychology and Children's Learning and Cognitive Development. A little shyly, she admitted to being in the honors program, which meant taking a senior honors seminar spring semester and writing a thesis. "Oh, and I'm taking Pilates. I've got to do something to make up for my lazy lifestyle now that I'm not slinging heavy trays."

He laughed, as she'd intended, but then said quietly, "No ballroom dance?"

A lump formed in her throat. "You kind of do need a partner."

"Really? To take the class?"

"No, but...without the right partner, it wouldn't be much fun."

The silence throbbed with everything she wanted to say but couldn't—wasn't ready to say— as well as with whatever *he* wasn't saying.

"Did you see the article in *People* about me?" she asked. She'd finally chosen them for an exclusive. Freelancers still trailed her sometimes, but she'd learned to ignore them. Mostly, interest was waning.

"I did. They did a reasonably sensitive job of it."

"I thought so," she agreed. She still hadn't got over the weirdness of seeing her own face on the cover of a magazine displayed at seemingly every checkout in every grocery store in the country, or of flipping it open to see more photos of her, quotes from her.

"People treating you any differently than they did before this all blew up?" he asked.

"Yes."

The new self-consciousness had dimmed her pleasure in returning to school. She'd known almost immediately she couldn't stay on working at Canosa. Her boss, a brusque man uninterested in the private lives of his employees, was just about the only person who didn't gape, or ask intrusive questions, or whisper with others when they thought she was out of earshot.

"People ask all the time if I'm Hope Lawson. I don't think I could have kept on as waitstaff at Canosa or anywhere else. If not for the help from Karen—" she stopped herself "—Mom and Dad, I'd have had to find an office job where I didn't interact with the public."

"What about at the university?"

"There, too. I'm a five-second celebrity." She tried for the light touch, but doubted he bought it. "I mean, I can tell the other students all read the articles about me. I think most of them went online to pull up the press conference, too. But it's getting better. Except for Pilates, I'm in upper level classes, and everybody is feeling some stress because it's our last year. Most of them are a lot younger than me, too, you know. Sometimes I feel ancient compared to them."

He chuckled. "In other words, at their age, they're self-centered enough to have lost interest in you pretty quick in favor of themselves."

Bailey laughed. "I'm afraid so. And around campus...well, I've gotten pretty good with the disguises. I haven't dyed my hair brown yet, but sunglasses, baseball cap, baggy USC Trojans T-shirt, and I pass incognito."

His amusement pleased her. He commented that he'd heard she talked to Eve a few days ago.

"Mom told you?"

"Actually, Eve did. We're working a case together. Kid that was brutally beaten. I made the arrest, she put him initially in a receiving home, then placed him with his father."

"Then...it wasn't the father who hurt him?"

He talked about the investigation, and how he'd finally got lucky—although it sounded to her as if it would be more accurate to say his persistence had paid off—when one of the stepfather's buddies had admitted that the guy had left for two days in the middle of the hunting trip that had been his alibi. Once that friend had broken the wall of silence, the others had come forward, too.

"The stepfather talked to his wife every evening. The others wondered about that a little, but he was a controlling SOB, and it fit his pattern. He was mad about something she said one night and he told them he had to make a quick trip home to take care of something."

Assaulted by memories, she murmured, "His stepson."

There was a momentary silence. "Hell," Seth said. "What was I thinking? You don't need to hear about anything like this."

"Yes. Yes, I do. It's…it's part of your life." And if she was to let him in, she needed to know he wouldn't close the door on what he did on the job. "Plus, you achieved justice for this boy. I want to hear about that. There was a time I didn't even know it was possible."

"Damn, Bailey."

"What?"

"You break my heart."

"You've said that before," she said stoutly. "But you must hear stuff almost every day as heartbreaking."

"With anyone but you, I can maintain some distance."

Some of her tension subsided, leaving a warm glow in its place. Of course he was waiting, just as he promised. He was a man who meant what he said. She had a sudden image of herself clambering up a tree, not afraid in the least that a branch would break and she would crash to the ground, because there Seth was, standing below, prepared to catch her.

Past a constriction in her throat, she said,

"Thank you. For saying that, I mean. I kept thinking…" She had to stop.

"What? That I was so mad at you I'd decided, to hell with her?"

She clutched the phone tight. "Something like that."

"No, Bailey." His voice hit a lower timbre. "I was never mad. I was afraid I was losing you. But I understand why you had to go."

"Thank you," she whispered again.

"There's nothing to thank me for."

She composed herself. "Will you tell me the rest? I mean, about the boy?"

After a pause, he said, "There's nothing that will surprise you. Once his story was blown, the boy's mother confessed to what really happened. She'd told the bastard that the kid had pleaded with her to leave him. During that phone call, she made the mistake of saying, 'Maybe I should. Unless you start treating us better.' So he felt obligated to go home and beat the crap out of the boy and say, 'Keep your goddamn mouth shut or it'll keep happening.' So she did."

Bailey didn't ask how the mother could have been so frightened of her husband, she had chosen obedience over her child's safety. *Because I know.* Except it had been different for her. She'd been terrified into silence, too, but there hadn't been anyone she felt the need to protect. If she'd had a little sister, would she have done anything differently? Bailey hoped so.

And I was a child, not an adult.

"Have you found out anything more about Hamby?" It was all she could do not to say *him*. Probably Seth would have known who she was talking about, but maybe not.

"Nothing new," he said, in a voice that told her he knew everything she felt.

"Are you still looking?"

"I will *never* quit looking. I promise you that, Bailey."

Comforted, she could breathe again. "Okay."

He asked if she'd talked to Anna, and she was able to smile.

"She's doing great. A lot is coming back to her. She still calls Betty every few days, but she said her mom is okay with that. Her parents have put her in counseling, too, which is good."

She and Seth talked for a few minutes more, about everything and nothing. At the end, he said, "I like hearing from you. Call me anytime, Bailey."

"I will. I promise," she added, and he was gone.

She knew now; she wanted to go to him, or at least ask him to wait for her. She was beginning to believe he would. But she had no practice at all in believing in people, so she convinced herself she had to give it longer.

Calling him next time would be easier. He'd said, "Anytime, Bailey," and she thought he meant it.

She believed.

SETH WAS WALKING out of a pawnshop where he'd been checking for some expensive jewelry stolen during a recent break-in when his phone rang.

His pulse quickened at the number displayed, as it did every time FBI Special Agent Drew Stuart called him.

"Chandler here."

"We've got him," Stuart said, voice rich with satisfaction. "The kid he had with him, too." Here the pleasure was mixed with the darker knowledge of what this girl had endured and what she still had to face.

Ceasing to see his surroundings, Seth leaned against the fender of his car. "How? Where?"

"Suburb of Phoenix. Far as we know, he was just passing through. But he got in a fender bender, his fault, and the other driver was pissed when Hamby tried to take off. It was a woman, believe it or not. She managed to block his car in until the police arrived. And that's where we got really lucky."

"The officer remembered the BOLO."

"He did. Saw the pretty little blonde, blue-eyed girl in the car. Sounds like he had Hamby in cuffs in the back of his unit quick enough to make his head spin."

"The woman who prevented him getting away deserves a medal."

"I agree."

"Now what?" Seth asked.

"I'm guessing the first and best trial will take place in your county. That's assuming Hope can identify him. Then we've got Gabriella Wilson. Utah will want a shot at him. And we'll have a slam dunk once we identify the latest girl."

Exultation and rage rose in a flash flood that slammed through Seth. "Damn," he said. "Do you know what a long shot it was when I decided to try to find out what happened to Hope?"

"I do. But she's not the first cold case you've closed. You're good. The Bureau could use you. That's an official invitation from higher up, by the way."

Seth gave a half laugh. "Right now, I'm happy where I'm at."

"You change your mind, you'll get an enthusiastic recommendation from me."

"Thanks." He hesitated. "Have you called Bailey? Hope?"

"No, I thought you'd want to do that."

"Thank you."

They talked some more about the steps required to bring Hamby back to Washington state. After they were done, Seth got into his car, then sat there. Bailey might be in a class right now…but he didn't want to wait to give her the news. She was entitled.

She answered right away. "Seth! You called me."

It was a first, although they'd now talked half a dozen times since she left for California. So far, he'd left her in the driver's seat, contrary to his nature though that was. But this was different. He couldn't decide whether she sounded pleased or only surprised.

He went for blunt. "I just heard from Stuart. Hamby is in custody."

The silence went on so long, Seth began to worry. He'd have given a lot to be able to deliver this news in person, to see her face. To be available to hold her.

"I never really believed…" she said, softly enough he had to strain to hear her.

"That we'd get him?"

"Yes." She was quiet again for a minute. "He's like…this monster that might be real but sometimes I'm not so sure."

"He's real," Seth said grimly. "He had a girl with him."

"Oh, God." Her swallow was audible. "So many."

"But he's done, Bailey. If all goes well, he'll be facing so many consecutive sentences, the closest thing he'll get to a vacation will be the trip between one state's correctional institute and the next."

He had to tell her they were hoping she'd be able to identify him, which he could tell shook her, but she calmed down when he reminded her they'd have other shots at him—Anna, too, would have a chance to pick him out of a lineup, and once they identified the girl he'd had with him, they would have him cold.

"But he should serve time for taking me, too."

"Yes, he should."

"The only thing is, it's been an awful lot of years."

"I know it has. He may have changed enough you won't recognize him. No one will blame you if you can't. You know that, don't you?"

"I want to look him in the eye and send him to prison," she said with such ferocity, Seth relaxed.

There was his gutsy girl, determined never to let herself be a victim again.

Too bad it was still an open question whether she'd ever be able to trust anyone again, either. He was beginning to think she wanted to, but still wasn't sure herself that she could.

Yeah, but she was calling him more often, talking more openly.

"I'll let you know when we need you," Seth told her. "It'll be a while. Weeks if not months." He mulled that over. "Unless they decide to have you go to Arizona. That's a possibility. If it comes to that, you won't do it alone. I'll be there with you."

"Okay." She sounded almost meek now. Stunned, probably. "Thank you, Seth."

Two hours later, she called him back. "I don't know why I never thought of this, but... I still have a couple of things that he left with me in that motel. I don't know why I kept them, but—I had so little. What if they have his fingerprints on them?"

This time, he'd been walking into headquarters. He stopped dead in the middle of the parking lot. "Why didn't I think to ask you?"

She giggled, a happy sound that told him she was reveling at her power over the monster who'd continued to live in her closet. "Because there was no reason to think I'd *want* to keep anything associated with him?"

"What do you have?"

"A doll. A motel owner gave it to me. I think she almost called child protective services, but he convinced her we didn't have much with us because his mother had had a heart attack and we'd left home suddenly to get to her. I had to plead with him to let me keep Rainbow Brite. It's funny, because even though I didn't remember, I had the same doll before. It's still there, in my bedroom at the Lawsons'. The body is cloth, but her head is plastic." She paused. "And there was this one book I really loved, *The Borrowers*, about these little people who live like mice in secret parts of a country manor. They've both been in a box I hauled along with me through all the foster homes. I'm sure he touched both. I remember rescuing the book this one time after he'd dropped it in the trash."

A mix of pride and triumph had Seth grinning. "Don't get them out, if you haven't already."

"No, I'm at school. I just got to remembering."

"Good. I'll arrange for someone from LAPD or the LA branch of the FBI to come and pick them up."

"Chain of custody," she said wisely, then giggled again. "I like murder mysteries."

When Seth called, Stuart was as pleased as Seth had been, and promised to have someone do the errand. "If his fingerprints are really on either the doll or the book, it won't matter if she can't pick him out of a lineup. Jurors will understand why she might not recognize this guy eighteen years later, especially given that she was only eleven the last time she saw him."

Seth would prefer that he didn't see Bailey the next time only because she was flying up here to identify Hamby, or he was joining her for a trip to Arizona. For one thing, either way, it probably wouldn't be soon. For another—damn. The longer she was away from him, the greater grew his fear that she'd go back to thinking *alone* was right for her.

He swore out loud. The worst thing he could

do was put pressure on her—but his patience had about reached it's limit.

HER PARENTS OFFERED to fly to California for Thanksgiving, if she couldn't come to Stimson. "Eve says she'll come, too," Karen said. "We'd really like you to be part of our holidays from now on, Hope."

"I'll come home," she heard herself promise. She hadn't known she'd 100 percent made up her mind, but evidently she had.

After that, she pondered whether it would be horribly awkward if she asked that Seth be invited for Thanksgiving dinner. Only—he probably went to his mother's, or her and his sister's family to his house.

And then there was Eve.

After she'd said goodbye to her mother, Bailey sat cross-legged on her twin bed and ran a hand over the quilt, the most amazing gift anyone had ever given her. Her first heirloom. So far, she kept it folded at the foot of her bed where she could admire it and touch it. At night, she laid it carefully over a rocking chair. She really should buy a new bed so she could use it and get the whole effect, too; the space would be tight, but she could fit in a full-size bed. On her way to the campus, she went right past the mattress store where she'd bought this one, but she always kept going because—well, just because.

Maybe for the same reason she hadn't registered for ballroom dance. Without a partner, she didn't really *need* a larger bed.

Tonight, as she stroked her quilt, pain gripped her and squeezed hard. No, not pain—hope. *My least favorite word.* And yet...

Seth had a bigger bed. And he was the partner she wanted.

Bailey drew a shuddering breath. Thanksgiving was too far away. She needed to see him. The phone calls weren't anywhere near enough.

THE MINUTE SETH heard how softly the pawnshop owner was speaking he'd known the information was going to be good.

"If you could get here quicker, I'd try to stall the little punk," he said. "But he got antsy when I made an excuse to go to the back room. What should I do?"

Seth had been waiting for a break on this investigation. The stolen jewelry he'd been keeping his eye out for hadn't appeared locally. He'd begun to think the thief was smart enough to go as far as Seattle to pawn it. Instead, it sounded as if all he'd done was wait long enough to convince himself nobody would be looking for the stolen items anymore.

Seth had had dealings with this particular pawnbroker before. He genuinely kept an eye out for stolen merchandise, and contacted law enforcement if and when it appeared. His description of the particular pieces he'd seen sounded like what Seth had been looking for.

"Drag it out as long as you can," he instructed, "but don't try to hold him. Ask to see ID, and, if you can, get a license plate number if he leaves. I'm on my way."

He arrived to find the kid gone, but was able to positively identify the couple of pieces the pawnbroker had accepted. When asked for ID, the boy began to twitch and claimed to have left his wallet home, but it didn't take Seth two minutes to match a name to the license plate number.

The vehicle belonged to the home owner whose jewelry had been stolen, and the kid, as described by the pawnbroker, matched Seth's memory of the sulky teenager lurking in the background when he'd been at the house taking a report.

Shaking his head, he took the two pieces of jewelry. The son's fingerprint on either piece wouldn't do them much good, as he might have had reason to pick up his mother's jewelry at some point or other. Too bad for him the pawnbroker had been held up enough times, he now had a hidden camera. Seth looked forward to confronting the little prick, but was sorry for the parents.

He detoured to buy a deli sandwich and took it back to headquarters. The parents would be at work, the kid in school. He'd do some research on other cases in the meantime.

He was stuck on a never-ending hold with an insurance company when he was buzzed for an internal call. With some relief, he ditched the hold and answered.

"Someone here to see you," the desk sergeant said laconically. "Says she has information for you."

"On my way down."

He couldn't see anyone beyond the counter until he'd reached the divider. There he froze.

A woman stood with her back to him. Moonlight pale hair, five foot five or six, great ass, long legs.

Déjà vu.

His heart leaped into overdrive. "Bailey?" he said hoarsely.

She turned, her expression momentarily so vulnerable the sight pierced his chest like a scalpel. She had her bottom lip caught between her teeth and anxiety darkened her eyes.

Then she smiled, but it was the one she saved for show, to hide what she really felt. "Hey. I know this might be a bad time for you, but—"

Released from his paralysis, he wasn't even aware of moving until he'd already pushed through the waist-high door and his hands closed over Bailey's upper arms. He searched her face with a hunger she wouldn't be able to mistake. "You're here," he said, not so intelligently.

Her smile faded to something a lot shyer. "I don't know why, but I wanted to surprise you."

"This surprise, I like," he said huskily. God, he wanted to kiss her, but two deputies were walking in, the desk sergeant watched them and half a dozen people sat waiting only a few feet away. "Are your parents expecting you?"

Eyes never leaving his face, she gave her head a quick shake. "No, I didn't tell them I was coming, either."

Suddenly, he laughed out loud, swooped her up and swung her in a circle. "Damn. You're here."

She was laughing, too, her cheeks pink. When he set her down, Seth was vaguely aware everyone else around them was smiling.

"I know you have to work," she began.

"No, I don't have anything going that can't wait. Don't move," he ordered her. "I'll be right back." He bounded upstairs, shut down his computer, grabbed his cell phone and was back in the waiting room in two minutes or less.

The smile that dawned on Bailey's face at the sight of him had Seth feeling buoyant, hopeful. She was here. Not just in Stimson, but here in front of him. She'd come to see him before her parents.

No, he thought, what she'd done was replay their first meeting. Was there a message in that? Or had she just wanted to see his expression when he hadn't expected her?

He hustled her out, realized with disfavor that she had a car, and said, "See you at the house?"

"I think I can still find it," she teased.

The drive wasn't long, which was fortunate, since he barely took his gaze from the rearview mirror. The silver compact sedan stuck right behind his bumper and pulled into his driveway beside his SUV.

"You're staying with me, right?" he asked, over the roof of her rental.

A hint of nerves showed in her eyes. "If you want me to."

"That's safe to say. Pop your trunk."

He grabbed her small suitcase, gave her a minute to grab the hefty bag he knew held her laptop along with the usual contents of a woman's purse, and led the way to his front door. He was so damn aroused, he wasn't sure he could make it. And it wasn't as if he could fall on her like an animal the minute they got inside.

Except maybe he could, because he'd no sooner closed the front door behind them than she dropped her bag with an audible thunk and flung herself at him. Letting go of her suitcase, he caught her but staggered back a step. The suitcase fell, too, then toppled over, but as long as it didn't trip them, he didn't give a damn about it.

"Oh, Seth."

"God. Bailey," he said thickly, and sought her

mouth. Not hard to find, since she had risen on tiptoe and met him with equal fervor.

This kiss was almost frantic—desperate, passionate, awkward. Their noses bumped, their teeth clanked, their tongues warred, but he couldn't seem to summon an iota of control. Bailey was in his arms, plastered against him, and nothing else mattered.

Until he felt the dampness against his cheek, and on a pang of fear, pulled back. "You're crying."

"What?" Her eyes opened. "I'm not—" She took one hand from his shoulder to touch her cheek. "Oh, no. I am. I don't even know why!"

He led a weeping Bailey to the sofa, sat down and pulled her onto his lap, enclosed in his arms. She grabbed his shirt and crumpled it in one fisted hand, as if she was afraid to let go. Then she laid her head in the crook between his shoulder and neck, and took deep, careful breaths.

"I don't know why," she whispered again in apparent bewilderment.

"You came to me. God. I've been so afraid—"

She lifted her head to stare at him. "*You've* been afraid?"

"That you wouldn't miss me. You said—" He couldn't finish.

Tears still dampened her cheeks, but awareness filled her eyes. "That I'd find out what I missed..."

"And what you didn't."

"I'm sorry I said that. I think I always knew I'd miss you most of all." Her grip on him hadn't loosened any. "Oh, Seth. I missed you by the time I got to the airport."

He tried to smile but knew it was askew. "And you had to fly without me. I hope you didn't grab your seatmate's hand."

This giggle was watery. "No, but I may have done some damage to the armrest."

He touched his forehead to hers. "I missed you, Bailey. Every minute."

"I'm here." She laid her head against his shoulder again, going boneless as if letting herself melt into him. The only remaining tension was that small fist.

He had to ask. "For how long?"

"I leave Tuesday morning, really early. If I hurry, I can get to my three o'clock class."

Seth's eyes closed. He breathed her in. Four days. Four nights. Not nearly long enough.

"That's a start," he said huskily.

For a long time, all he did was hold her, happy as long as he didn't let himself think ahead. He was still aroused, but making love wasn't the assurance he needed most from her. He soaked in what he could, and waited for her to be ready to tell him why she'd come.

Finally she rubbed her cheek against him and straightened again to look gravely into his eyes. "I came to find out whether you want to…to try to make this work, like you said. I mean, I have to go back. So, we wouldn't see that much of each other until I graduate—"

The ability to breathe restored, he squeezed her hard. "Did you think I'd say no? Bailey, whatever hit me the minute I saw you turned into the real thing damn near as fast. I've been hanging on by my fingernails since you left. You have no idea how much I wanted to fly to LA and knock on your door. If I hadn't been sure that would back-fire, I'd have been there. But I really thought you needed to come to me, not the other way around."

"Like a bird whose broken wing you healed, after which you held out your hands and let her fly free."

An odd note in her voice made him cautious. "Something like that," he said, "except I didn't heal you. In fact, I'm still not sure if I did you any favor. Your parents, yes." His mouth quirked. "I still get home-baked cookies once a week, but now they're offered with a radiant smile instead of grief and hope."

Bailey was silent for longer than he liked. "That's…part of what I didn't know." Her eyes briefly focused on his. "I mean, when I left. There were good moments. The first time Kirk hugged me, and I knew he was my dad. When I actually remembered. That was one." She gave a funny lit-tle shrug. "But a whole lot of the time I wished I'd never come. These strangers who claimed to love me. The press." Another grimace. "Eve. Without you, I think I'd have turned tail. But you see, *that* freaked me out, too, because after *he* dumped me, I never let myself really, truly depend on anyone else again. I knew, bone deep, that allowing someone else power over you is not safe."

Her face held pain that he sensed went just as deep. Her voice almost shook at the end with the force of her conviction. He'd known how she felt, as much as someone could who'd never experienced the horror she had—someone who hadn't been held captive for years, molested and hurt and brainwashed and then abandoned when she was at her most vulnerable.

When he could make himself speak, he said, "That's why you ran away. Because you didn't feel safe."

"No," she corrected him, "because I *did*. And… how could I trust that?"

Seth nodded. Crap. Was he close to crying?

"At first I wondered why you didn't call, why you waited until I did. But then I realized you really did understand. You weren't…tricking me into thinking I was free to make my own decision, when actually you intended to keep the pressure on."

"You took so long to call—" He cleared his throat. "I was so damn afraid you'd put me out of your mind. Why would you want me? Cop in a backward county with nothing to offer someone as smart and beautiful and determined as you."

She gaped at him. "You're kidding, right? I'm the one with the history. I mean, little girl forced to have sex with her 'daddy'? Later, slutty because that's all I knew?"

Suddenly angry, he gave her a shake. "What you had with that scumbag wasn't sex. You were assaulted. How many times do I have to say that? And don't use the word *slutty*. What you did was come out fighting. You took control. It was *your* choice. You were proving *you* held the power, something you didn't have for all those years with Hamby. Given your horrific experience, what you did was brave. There is *nothing* about you that I'd change for my sake. It's only for your own—" His voice cracked.

Eyes shimmering, she blinked hard a couple of times. "Thank you," she whispered. "Oh, Seth." She lifted herself to press a clumsy kiss on his mouth, one he returned with fervor, trying to tell her without words everything he felt.

But then he had to say it, too. "I love you, Bailey. Maybe you don't want to hear that yet, but—"

"I do." She sounded choked up. "I do. I never thought—"

"Anyone would love you?"

"That anyone could. And now...now I have to readjust everything I used to believe."

He cupped her jaw, stroking his thumb over her lips. "Can you?"

"I'm here, aren't I?" she said simply.

"For four days."

"And at Thanksgiving. And Christmas. I have a long break then. And…and you could come and visit me, you know."

"I can. If you want me to, I'll start applying for jobs down there."

Now her gaze held astonishment, even wonder. "You really meant that."

"Damn straight." Since she'd left, he had tried river rafting, hiking, a scramble up one of the smaller peaks in the Cascades. Bailey had filled his thoughts whatever he was doing.

"Oh, my God." The second "Oh, my God" was so soft he hardly heard it. "I can't believe it." Then, despite the fresh tears clinging to her lashes, a smile appeared, gathered force, until he saw on her face what he'd already seen on her mother's: radiance. "No, that's not true," she said more strongly. "Because I do believe it."

He laughed in joy even as the most profound relief he'd ever felt weakened him to the point he wasn't sure he could have stood up. "Shall I give my notice tomorrow?"

"No." The glow was gentle now, loving. "This feels like home, you know. I don't want to stay in LA. We don't even have seven months to go. I'll apply to UW for graduate school. I can commute from here. If I don't get in and have to go somewhere else…" Here she hesitated.

"That's when I'll give my notice," he said huskily. "I can get a job anywhere."

"Oh, Seth." Her smile wobbled. "The day I came to find you was the best day of my life."

"Sort of like jumping out of an airplane without knowing whether your chute would open?"

Happiness rang in her laugh. "Exactly." With a suddenness that took him by surprise, she swiveled to straddle him. Now her lips were temptingly close. She slid both hands up his chest and to the back of his neck. "If I tell you that now I know the difference, can we make love?"

"Yeah." He covered her breasts with his hands, gently rubbing. "Now we can."

And, just before he kissed her, she said those three words for the first time since she was six years old.

I love you.

* * * * *

Be sure to check out the next
TWO DAUGHTERS book,
IN HOPE'S SHADOW,
coming in October 2015
from Janice Kay Johnson
and Harlequin Superromance!

LARGER-PRINT BOOKS!

GET 2 FREE LARGER-PRINT NOVELS PLUS

2 FREE GIFTS!

H™ HARLEQUIN®

Romance

From the Heart, For the Heart

HRLP15

LARGER-PRINT BOOKS!

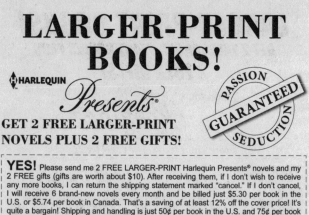

HARLEQUIN

Presents®

GET 2 FREE LARGER-PRINT NOVELS PLUS 2 FREE GIFTS!

PASSION
GUARANTEED
SEDUCTION

YES! Please send me 2 FREE LARGER-PRINT Harlequin Presents® novels and my 2 FREE gifts (gifts are worth about $10). After receiving them, if I don't wish to receive any more books, I can return the shipping statement marked "cancel." If I don't cancel, I will receive 6 brand-new novels every month and be billed just $5.30 per book in the U.S. or $5.74 per book in Canada. That's a saving of at least 12% off the cover price! It's quite a bargain! Shipping and handling is just 50¢ per book in the U.S. and 75¢ per book in Canada.* I understand that accepting the 2 free books and gifts places me under no obligation to buy anything. I can always return a shipment and cancel at any time. Even if I never buy another book, the two free books and gifts are mine to keep forever.

176/376 HDN GHVY

Name	(PLEASE PRINT)	
Address		Apt. #
City	State/Prov.	Zip/Postal Code

Signature (if under 18, a parent or guardian must sign)

Mail to the Reader Service:
IN U.S.A.: P.O. Box 1867, Buffalo, NY 14240-1867
IN CANADA: P.O. Box 609, Fort Erie, Ontario L2A 5X3

**Are you a subscriber to Harlequin Presents® books
and want to receive the larger-print edition?
Call 1-800-873-8635 today or visit us at www.ReaderService.com.**

* Terms and prices subject to change without notice. Prices do not include applicable taxes. Sales tax applicable in N.Y. Canadian residents will be charged applicable taxes. Offer not valid in Quebec. This offer is limited to one order per household. Not valid for current subscribers to Harlequin Presents Larger-Print books. All orders subject to credit approval. Credit or debit balances in a customer's account(s) may be offset by any other outstanding balance owed by or to the customer. Please allow 4 to 6 weeks for delivery. Offer available while quantities last.

Your Privacy—The Reader Service is committed to protecting your privacy. Our Privacy Policy is available online at www.ReaderService.com or upon request from the Reader Service.

We make a portion of our mailing list available to reputable third parties that offer products we believe may interest you. If you prefer that we not exchange your name with third parties, or if you wish to clarify or modify your communication preferences, please visit us at www.ReaderService.com/consumerschoice or write to us at Reader Service Preference Service, P.O. Box 9062, Buffalo, NY 14240-9062. Include your complete name and address.

HPLP15